# The Front Wing

## A Harold and Bella
## Paranormal Mystery

# Novels by Mike Befeler

Unstuff Your Stuff

Death of a Scam Artist

The Mystery of the Dinner Playhouse

The Back Wing

Court Trouble

Paradise Court

The Tesla Legacy

The V V Agency

Murder on the Switzerland Trail

*Paul Jacobson Geezer-lit Mystery Series*

Retirement Homes Are Murder

Living with Your Kids Is Murder

Senior Moments Are Murder

Cruising in Your Eighties Is Murder

Care Homes Are Murder

Nursing Homes Are Murder

# The Front Wing

A Harold and Bella
Paranormal Mystery

## Mike Befeler

Encircle Publications, LLC
Farmington, Maine, U.S.A.

Published by: Encircle Publications, LLC
PO Box 187
Farmington, ME 04938

Visit: http://encirclepub.com

Printed in U.S.A.

# CHAPTER ONE 🦇

Harold McCaffrey smacked his forehead at the realization—he had resided in the Mountain Splendor Retirement Home in Golden, Colorado, for exactly three months. How his life had changed. When he first arrived, he viewed this as a death sentence after having lost his wife, Jennifer. Moving into a retirement home represented the slippery slope to oblivion. He had pictured himself sinking into an easy chair and never emerging again.

But he had been surprised. Really surprised. Once ensconced in his room on the fourth floor of the retirement home's Back Wing, he immediately witnessed a number of strange occurrences. He hardly ever saw residents of the Back Wing during the day. These were night people.

And the name. The Back Wing. It had a certain ring to it, especially when he first encountered a bat flying around the hallway, bashing into the walls and light fixtures. Little did he know at the time that this was only one small incongruity out of many unusual circumstances.

For years Harold's major excitement had been playing golf. When his wife succumbed to cancer, he hung up his clubs. Then he became forgetful, which led to his son, Nelson, insisting that he move into a place where meals and housekeeping would be provided. Thus the sale of his house and the forced march off to this facility.

Harold chuckled to himself. He had ended up in a room between Bella Alred and Viola Renquist. Two most eccentric people. He tried to avoid Viola as much as possible. Between her dementia and attempts to nibble on his throat, he could do without her, but it was completely different with Bella. Harold had never expected another woman to catch his eye, but Bella had done so. And she also shared

1

this mutual feeling. Warmth spread through his chest at the thought of Bella. What a wi… woman.

Harold's mundane life had been turned on its ear in the last three months. So many new experiences. Rather than being bored out of his gourd, he had been kept hopping and had even become an amateur sleuth. Imagine that. Nothing in his first seventy-nine years had prepared him for this new existence.

A frown crossed his face. The facility also had a Front Wing. Yuck. The people in the Front Wing were normal but snooty. He had tried to reach out to them but had made only one friend in the Front Wing. Ned Fister — a guy who defied the Front Wing stereotype. They enjoyed each other's company for meals. Ned amused himself by being the volunteer gardener at the retirement home.

Compared to the snobs of the Front Wing, the most interesting but friendly residents of the Back Wing appealed to him. For example, he no longer felt the same when listening to a howl at a full moon nor wondered when he heard reports that blood had gone missing from the nearby blood bank.

His thoughts were interrupted by the jangle of his phone. He picked it up to hear the retirement home director, Peter Lemieux, on the line.

"Harold, I have a favor to ask."

"Just as long as it doesn't involve looking for missing women."

"No, that problem is behind us. This is quite simple. We're having an open house this afternoon for people interested in becoming residents of Mountain Splendor."

"I thought we were full up."

Peter clicked his tongue. "We are, and although that's a nice problem to have, we scheduled this event a month ago when we had a number of vacancies. We can't cancel now. I'm expecting thirty to forty visitors. These will include potential residents and family members."

Harold imagined the chaos that would ensue. "And given the mob scene, you want some crowd control and for me to guard the food so no residents try to steal it?"

"No. I don't think that will be a problem today. I wonder if you might be able to help with an administrative task."

Harold realized his organizational skills could be put to good use this afternoon. "I get it. You'll need to build a waiting list."

Harold could practically feel a smile through the phone line. "You have this way of hitting the nail on the head. That's exactly where I could use your assistance. Andrea was going to be the person to staff the table for people signing the waiting list, but Stacy called in sick so Andrea will need to stay at the reception desk. Would you be willing to pitch in?"

"And you don't have any volunteers from the Front Wing?"

Peter cleared his throat. "I've asked around, but I couldn't convince them to give up their scheduled bridge or poker games this afternoon. I know you've always been willing to assist so thought I'd give you a call."

"Let me check my busy social calendar." Harold paused and looked up at the ceiling. He knew things would be busy after dinner, but during the day the Back Wing was as quiet as a crypt. "Nope, nothing scheduled. You can sign me up. You want me to bring along anyone else from the Back Wing?"

Peter gulped. "As much as I like the residents of the Back Wing, I think it might be a little early to expose prospective Front Wing residents to the... ah... different lifestyle of the Back Wing."

Harold chuckled. "I know what you mean. So I take it you're not recruiting new members for the Back Wing at this time."

"No. Right now we've only invited normal people who would rather live in the Front Wing."

"Yeah, dull."

Peter harrumphed. "Some people like a nice calm retirement home. Not everyone wants to experience what you seem to enjoy."

"That's me — living on the wild side."

"Actually that's true. You're the only conventional person who has ever chosen to live in the Back Wing. Thanks for agreeing to help with the open house."

"My pleasure. When and where do you want me to show up?"

"Two p.m. in the dining room."

"Anything I need to bring?"

"Your pleasant smile and handshake."

"As a retired insurance salesman, I can handle that."

Harold signed off and sat for a moment contemplating his world of three months. He'd be happy to contribute to keeping Mountain Splendor financially solvent. He wanted this place to last, at least as long as he did. After the previous director almost drove the place into the ground, Peter had successfully turned it around, retained some residents who threatened to leave and improved the services. Harold would do his small part to help.

Another thought struck him. His grandson, Jason, would be coming to visit next weekend. This gave him a shot of adrenalin. He enjoyed doing things with his grandson, and Jason had become very popular with the residents of the Back Wing. He'd have to plan some activities for Jason with the Back Wing contingent.

Jason who used to read all those crazy teenage vampire books and watch the silly vampire movies. After visiting last summer, Jason had given these up, finding them too boring. No, after living in the Back Wing for a week, Jason had decided that Harold's fellow residents were much more interesting than any character in a book or movie. And both Harold and Jason had learned a simple lesson — *never believe the myth that vampires don't age; they get older, move into retirement homes, lose their teeth and gum people on the throat.*

# CHAPTER TWO 🦇

Harold sat on the couch in his living room, planning what he'd do for the rest of the day. He'd go to lunch in fifteen minutes, then the open house, followed by a walk. He enjoyed getting out every day to stretch his legs and to take in the scenery. He had his walking poles that also gave his arms a good workout as well as his lower body. At his age, he needed to keep his limbs moving. That would take him until dinner. After dinner, the fun would begin when the Back Wing came alive, and he'd get to see his new friends, particularly Bella. Bella. He couldn't wait to see her.

It was almost as if she read his mind, because as he stared at the picture of Bear Lake he had recently hung, Bella stepped through the wall.

Harold flinched as his heart rate increased twofold. "I'll never get used to you doing that, Bella."

She came over and gave him a hug. "I figured you were here all alone and would like some company."

"You know I enjoy seeing you, but I'm afraid you'll give me a heart attack one of these times when you enter that way."

"Then I'd need to resort to mouth-to-mouth resuscitation."

"They don't recommend that any longer for CPR. Only pushing on the chest. Although, I would accept any mouth-to-mouth resuscitation from you."

"Aren't you becoming the forward one?" She planted a kiss on his lips.

He returned the kiss, until Bella finally pulled away. "Don't start anything. I know you'll be going to lunch soon."

"Me? You're the one who started it."

5

"True. Woman's prerogative."

Harold feigned a furtive look over his shoulder. "Are you checking to make sure I don't have any other girlfriend hiding here?"

"No one else would dare."

Harold laughed. "Good thing. One witchy girlfriend is all I can handle. Not that I can handle you, anyway."

She wiggled her right index finger at him. "And remember that."

"Oh, I will. I don't want you casting a spell and turning me into a frozen statue for the rest of my life."

Bella adjusted her black skirt and sat next to him on the couch. "What are your plans for this evening?"

"I thought I'd cruise the Front Wing to pick up hot chicks."

Bella rolled her eyes. "Right. What else?"

"Nothing planned."

"How'd you like to join me to watch a movie in my room? I ordered *Bell, Book and Candle* from Netflix. And I do enjoy Jimmy Stewart."

"To say nothing of Kim Novak."

Bella swatted him. "I can ogle the men all I want, but you're not supposed to ogle the women."

Harold waggled his eyebrows at Bella. "Other than you, of course."

At that moment there was a loud pounding on the door.

"What now?" Harold stood and moseyed to the entryway. He turned the doorknob, where he kept his key on a stretch band, and Viola Renquist burst into the room, wearing a purple robe, her hair looking like she had been standing under a descending helicopter.

"What are you doing in our meeting room?" Viola shouted.

"You've forgotten again, Viola," Bella called out from the couch.

"Forgotten what?"

"Harold has been living here for three months."

"Tarnation. Is that why this old guy is blocking my way?" Viola pushed past Harold and plopped down on the couch next to Bella. "You seen my choppers?"

Bella pointed. "Um, there's something caught in your hair."

Viola reached up and removed the false fangs from her tangled coiffure and popped them in her mouth. "That's better." She pointed at Harold. "Is the old guy here providing lunch for me? Has a good long neck. Kind of scrawny, but might give me a full meal."

Bella gave a resigned sigh. "Viola, your false fangs won't do the job any more. Bailey and you get takeout from next door."

"Takeout?"

"Yes. The two of you stock up from the blood bank. You probably have a supply in your refrigerator."

"Why didn't you say so?"

Harold watched the performance and eventually came over and dropped into his easy chair. He wouldn't temp fate by sitting next to Viola on the couch.

"What are you doing up so early?" Bella asked.

"I had a bad dream that I was out in a forest and became thirsty. I searched and searched until I found a glass full of dark liquid. I thought I had been saved until I took a sip. Yuck. Someone had substituted prune juice for blood. I woke up with a cotton mouth. Then I heard a male voice in our meeting room, so I came to check out the intruder."

"I hate to remind you, Viola, but at your age, you do need to have some prune juice from time to time."

"Piddle. Am I getting that old?"

"Yes."

Viola regarded her wrinkled and liver-spotted hand. "Who the heck put a spell on my skin?"

"No one. And try to remember next time you knock on this door. Harold isn't an intruder. He lives here now."

Viola jumped up and stomped over to inspect Harold's throat. "I'll be danged. That's one throat I would have enjoyed in my earlier years."

"You stay away from him," Bella said. "He's mine."

"I didn't think you liked blood."

"I don't. But Harold has other redeeming qualities."

"Besides providing blood?" Viola peered at Harold. "I don't see it. He only looks like a blood container to me."

Harold stood. "Okay. If you two are going to keep talking about me as if I can't hear you, I'm going to lunch."

"Don't go away mad," Bella said.

"I'm not mad, only hungry."

"You're excused," Viola said. "Then we'll have our meeting room to ourselves. Take your time. Eat a good nourishing meal. Don't rush back. But if you find any hunky throats send them in."

"Viola, you wouldn't know what to do with a hunky throat anymore."

"Oh, yeah. Try me."

Harold stepped toward the door and reached for the handle. "You ladies can continue your conversation. I'm outta here."

"Don't forget the movie tonight," Bella said.

Harold turned and smiled. "Wouldn't miss it for the world. Lock up when you leave." He grabbed his key and departed.

# CHAPTER THREE 🦇

At lunch, Harold looked for Ned Fister, but his gardener buddy wasn't there. Must have become too involved with the begonias to come in to eat. Since none of the other Front Wingers ever deemed to invite him to their table, Harold had his turkey sandwich, potato salad, ice tea and cookies by himself at a table in the corner. He closed his eyes for a moment as he chewed, hearing the background hum of conversations, occasional laughter, the clatter of utensils and the footfalls of the wait staff moving around the room. He sniffed the ever-present aroma of coffee. After he opened his eyes and took another bite of sandwich, he scanned the crowd of primarily women who waved their hands in their small groups of three or four to a table. No great loss.

He completed his meal by consuming two chocolate chip cookies, licked his lips, and dropped his napkin on the table, before leaving the dining room to take a short stroll outside. He spotted Ned Fister hard at work with a spade in hand. "If you don't get a move on, you'll miss lunch."

Ned checked his watch and nodded to Harold. "Dang. Time got away from me. You want to join me for a bite?"

"I finished eating, but I'll meet you for dinner."

Ned stood. "Good. Do you want to include your girlfriend?"

"She doesn't eat in the dining room. I'll see her after dinner."

"Hot date?"

"We're going to watch a movie in her apartment."

"I should come meet some of those Back Wing women. I can't stand all the snobs in the Front Wing."

"You're welcome any time, although you have to keep an open

mind."

Ned chuckled. "I may take you up on that one of these days, but right now I need to replenish my bodily fluids."

They parted and Harold headed out the driveway to walk around the neighborhood. He exchanged greetings with a woman walking a schnauzer and watched a mom herd two preschoolers into an SUV. The typical afternoon scene in suburbia.

Back at Mountain Splendor, he stopped by the shuffleboard court and watched two Front Wingers play for half an hour. One of them groused that the other had cheated by stepping over the line when sending a puck down the court. Her opponent told her to mind her own business. Before they started whapping each other over the head with their poles, Harold retreated inside to help with the open house.

In the cleared-out dining room, Peter Lemieux directed Harold to a table covered with a white tablecloth. On the top rested a clipboard with sheets of lined paper and a Montblanc pen.

"High class writing instrument," Harold said.

"Nothing but the best for our prospective residents. One thing — make sure no one walks off with it."

"You expecting some sticky-fingered visitors?"

Peter grinned. "You can't be too careful."

Harold took a seat on a folding chair behind the table and saluted. "I'll guard the pen with my life. What's the plan with the waiting list?"

"After the group is assembled, I'll say a few words and tell people to stop by your table to sign up, first come, first serve."

"I'll have to monitor all the pushing and shoving."

Peter gave an exaggerated eye roll. "There also will be refreshments. Some will want to eat first before they sign up. We'll see how it goes. You never know at these events. Sometimes there's lots of interest, and other times few sign up."

"You're an excellent salesman, Peter. I expect I'll have a good crowd to deal with."

People began to filter into the dining room, and Harold watched from his vantage point. One family arrived consisting of an elderly woman accompanied by a middle-aged couple and two teenagers.

He spotted one older married couple and a number of people who showed up by themselves.

Peter strolled to the front of the room, picked up a microphone and tapped it. The sound echoed through the room. He placed the microphone several inches from his mouth. "Welcome to Mountain Splendor."

The conversations in the room ground to a halt.

"I'm Peter Lemieux, the director of Mountain Splendor, and it's my pleasure to serve as host to all of you today. We have refreshments including some freshly baked cookies, and I can take any of you on a tour after our program. Let me give you a brief history of our establishment." He launched into a two-minute summary.

Harold appreciated the short, informative speech. The previous director had been too full of himself, and his speeches went on way too long. Peter knew the right balance.

"Now I'd like to open it up for questions," Peter said.

A woman in a bright red hat shouted out, "How good is the food here?"

"You can sample for yourself." Peter pointed toward tables on one side of the room. "In addition to the cookies I mentioned, we have salmon, quiche and a wide variety of freshly baked pastries for you this afternoon. Please help yourself after I've answered all the questions. Next."

"Can we take a doggy bag home with the leftovers?" a woman who looked like a bag lady asked.

Peter gritted his teeth. "You can ask one of the wait staff to box up a few of the leftovers if you want. I see another hand over there." He pointed to a man in a tweed jacket and bow tie.

"How much have you increased the fees over the last two years?"

"Good question. Two years ago, our monthly room rate went up three percent. Earlier this summer the rates were announced to go up another five percent. When I took over, I rolled those back, so, in effect, the rates have remained the same for the last year. I'm expecting that we can maintain this for another year or more."

A murmur ran through the crowd, and chins bobbed up and down.

Another hand waved and Peter pointed to a man in a dark blue blazer.

"Do you have a storage area for residents to keep items that don't fit in their apartments?"

"That we do. We realize people may need to downsize from houses or larger condos when they move here. You can keep furniture and other belongings that you may want to save."

After a number of other questions, which Peter deftly handled, the audience ran dry. "Now I would like to invite those of you who are interested in Mountain Splendor to let us know that you'd like to join us. We are currently full, but will start a waiting list today for those who want to become residents in the future." Peter pointed toward Harold. "Stop by the table manned by Mr. McCaffrey and you can add your name to the waiting list and also fill out the complete application form to leave with Mr. McCaffrey. For those of you interested in joining me on the tour of our facility, meet me at the door to the dining room in thirty minutes. Enjoy the refreshments and thank you for joining us today."

A buzz ran through the crowd, and a bow wave of people surged toward Harold.

As he had feared, several people started pushing each other.

Harold cleared his throat. "Form a single line, and everyone will have a chance."

A slight woman wearing tennis shoes stood at the head of the line. She obviously was fast and had worn the right kind of foot gear to reach the front of the line. Harold watched as she filled out her name, address and phone number. Harold could read upside down, a trick he had learned when selling insurance policies. First person on the waiting list, Henrietta Yates.

"Thanks you, Ms. Yates. Fill out the application form and leave that on the table. Next."

The man who had questioned price increases moved toward the table. He tweaked his bow tie and bent over to sign. Name of Frederick Jorgenson.

There was some more shoving in line, and one woman called out. "Watch it. Everyone will have a turn." Harold caught a glimpse of a woman with silver hair in a slinky skirt swat at a man who wore a dark blue blazer.

The next man in line announced, "I'm a retired dentist. If you have any teeth problems, I can set them straight." He chuckled and grabbed the pen.

Harold rolled his eyes. That's all they needed. A guy who told dumb jokes. The signature was illegible, but the printed name indicated Edgar Fontaine.

The woman who had shouted stepped forward. "I do hope you have a theater group here. I had many successful roles on the screen and stage."

"I'm sure you'll have a chance to pursue your interests." Harold looked at the name. Celia Barns.

Celia picked up an application form, turned and glared at the man behind her, the guy who had asked about the storage area. Then she brushed past him. He dusted off his blazer and picked up the pen. "I hope there aren't too many women like that here." He looked intently at the list and wrote very precisely a name that Harold could easily read. Duncan Haverson.

"Good penmanship," Harold said.

"I was an engineer. Precision is important to me." After getting an application form, he disappeared into the crowd to be replaced by a woman named Phoebe Mellencourt. Phoebe, the woman in the red hat who'd asked the question about food, was one of those overly bubbly women who informed Harold that she had been an executive secretary to some very important businessmen.

The line had thinned out and only one person remained. Compared to Phoebe, this woman had pursed lips that looked like they had never formed a smile. She quickly filled out her information and departed. Harold looked at the last line. Gertrude Ash.

No one else came to his table, but Harold waited twenty minutes until the room had emptied. He picked up the clipboard and the stack of applications and approached Peter Lemieux. "Seven prospective residents for you."

"That's good. If we have any open rooms, we'll be able to fill them quickly."

"Those people seemed pretty eager to get in here. A tribute to what you've accomplished over the last several months."

Peter gave a shy smile. "I have a good staff supporting me. Could you do one last favor? Take the waiting list down to Andrea at the

13

front desk and ask her to run a copy, file the original and leave the copy on my desk. You can also leave the application forms with her."

"Will do."

"Now I need to lead a tour."

Harold watched as Peter joined the group of prospective residents near the door. All seven who had signed the waiting list stood there. After a few words with them, Peter led them away.

Harold gathered all the paperwork and took the stairs down to the lobby rather than bothering with the slow elevator. He saw a woman wearing a flowered dress, slumped over and sleeping in a chair next to the receptionist's desk. He handed Andrea the clipboard and applications and gave her Peter's instructions before taking the pokey elevator up to his room to retrieve his walking poles for another outing.

An hour walk served to keep his joints mobile and to give him a chance to admire the scenery on this nice Indian Summer afternoon. Some trees sparkled golden in the sunlight, and others displayed their bare branches. He paused to watch a flock of geese fly east. Not migrating but heading for a pond somewhere.

He patted his stomach. His walks helped to prevent him from looking like some of the overstuffed specimens residing in the Front Wing.

*****

When Harold returned to Mountain Splendor, he found an ambulance, fire engine, police car and unmarked car blocking the driveway. He entered the lobby to see Peter Lemieux speaking with Detective Deavers, who Harold had worked with during the summer.

"What's all the commotion?"

Peter wrung his hands. "Alice Jones was found dead in the lobby after the open house."

"I don't know her," Harold said.

"She's only been in the Front Wing for two months."

Harold turned to Deavers. "If you're here, this may not be an accident."

Deavers nodded to Harold. "That's correct. We're treating this as a suspicious death."

Harold tapped his cheek. "Was Alice Jones by any chance wearing a flowered dress?"

"Why would you ask that?"

"I saw a woman sitting in a chair near Andrea when I dropped off the waiting list and application forms. I thought she was sleeping."

Deavers arched an eyebrow. "That was Alice Jones. After you saw her, she slumped to the floor where the receptionist discovered her and called 9-1-1."

# CHAPTER FOUR 🦇

Harold took the elevator with the red door up to the fourth floor of the Back Wing, pondering what Detective Deavers had said. A suspicious death here at Mountain Splendor. The detective had declined to elaborate on why this wasn't believed to be a heart attack or stroke, the normal cause of death around here. Obviously, something led him to a different conclusion.

The memory of being involved in the investigation of two missing women when he first arrived at Mountain Splendor, pulsed through Harold's brain. He hoped this wasn't a portent of new problems. No, he was sure this was an isolated event and not a new crime wave to ruffle the peace and quiet of the retirement home.

When he exited the elevator, he scanned the hallway. No one in sight. Still too early for his neighbors to be causing any commotion. How ironic for him, a morning person, to be in the Back Wing.

After a shower, Harold dressed and had a little time before dinner. He decided he didn't want to turn on the television. That would only lead to depressing news of international turmoil, Denver-area homicides and acts of God wreaking havoc somewhere around the globe. Too bad there wasn't a good news channel. But people seemed attracted to disasters.

He reached for his book on the history of witchcraft, which Bella had lent him, to resume reading for a few minutes, when his doorbell rang.

With a resigned sigh, Harold lifted himself out of his easy chair, padded to the door and opened it to find the wiry frame and pinched face of Tomas Greeley. "Come in. Come in."

"Thanks, Harold. I thought I'd stop by and find out when your grandson, Jason, would be visiting again."

"You two sure became good buddies when he was here during the summer. As it so happens, he'll be spending the coming weekend with me."

Tomas punched his right fist into his left hand. "Oh, boy. That will be great. Maybe he can toss the Frisbee for me."

"He'll want to do that, as long as you both remember to stay well away from the windows."

"Yeah, we learned our lesson."

"In the meantime, I could throw the Frisbee for you. It's too close to dinner now but maybe tomorrow."

"That's okay. I'll wait for Jason. You don't have that much oomph."

Harold flexed his arm as if modeling a strong man advertisement. "I beg your pardon. I could fling a Frisbee pretty far in my day."

Tomas grinned. "Yeah, but your day has come and gone, old man. I want some real exercise."

"Okay. You can wait for Jason. He can uphold the family honor. I'm surprised to see you so early today, Tomas."

Tomas scratched behind his ear. "I woke up from my nap early. I think I had a flea. I might have to resort to one of those flea collars."

"When we had a dog some years ago, it didn't have any fleas. Combination of the dry climate and altitude, I think."

Tomas scratched again. "Maybe I imagined it. Whatcha doing tonight?"

Harold peered at Tomas. "Hmm. Interesting, You're the second person to ask me that question today."

Tomas shrugged. "Just checking up on you."

"And why'd you want to do that?"

"Wouldn't want you to miss your surprise party. Oops." He put his hand over his mouth. "I shouldn't have said that."

"What are you up to? Now that you've spilled the beans, you might as well tell me the whole story."

"Bella's going to kill me."

"No, but she might put a spell on you to suffer from sore paws or mange."

"Yuck." He scratched his ear again.

"Okay, back to this surprise party. What gives?"

Tomas gulped. "Bella arranged for all of us to give you a surprise party to celebrate you being here three months. I was supposed to check to make sure you'd be going to dinner at the regular time so we could set up while you're schmoozing with the Front Wing yahoos."

"I'll be going to dinner at the usual time and then coming back to my room. You can pass the word along."

"That's good. Please pretend like you're surprised. Don't tell anyone I blew it. Bella will be so disappointed if you act like you knew about the party."

"Okay. I'll fake it." Warmth pulsed through Harold's body. His new friends were doing this for him. "I hope there will be cake."

"Bella has all kinds of goodies lined up—Jell-O shots, cake, cookies and punch. I hope Warty doesn't mess with the punch."

The only member of the Back Wing who Harold really disliked. Warty and his misfiring magic caused problems. And Warty had this thing for Bella that wasn't reciprocated. She had her way of dismissing him, but he was persistent. "Maybe you could tell him the party starts at midnight."

"Good idea. That would be the safest solution for everyone. Say, did you see all the commotion in front of the building earlier?"

"You mean the police car, fire engine and ambulance?"

"Yeah. When I got back from the dog park, the place looked like a practice area for the SWAT team."

"A woman from the Front Wing died."

Tomas shrugged. "No loss. None of them are very friendly."

"There are a few who are okay. I didn't know this woman, Alice Jones. But it may have been more than a heart attack. Detective Deavers arrived to investigate. I'm sure we'll hear more from Peter Lemieux over the next few days."

"That means we'll soon have a new resident to take her place."

"The place is full, but I went to an open house this afternoon. There's a waiting list so the person at the top will be able to move in soon." Harold thought back to the people who had stood in line. First on the list, the short, skinny woman, Henrietta Yates, would have a new home. He wondered how long it would be before she moved in. To her credit, she didn't act snobby. Might be a good addition to the Front Wing. "You mentioned going to a dog park."

"Yeah. I discovered this great place. Even ran into an attractive old lady with an even more attractive Dalmatian. We've only progressed to the sniffing stage. I like both of them."

"Must be hard for you to decide between the dog owner and the dog."

"Hey, watch your language. There are no dog owners, only dog guardians."

"I stand corrected."

Tomas stood on one foot and then the other.

Harold regarded his clean carpet. "You better go walk yourself before you have an accident."

"Good idea." Tomas raced out of the room and slammed the door.

Harold listened as the receding footfalls changed into a patter. He parted the curtain and looked outside. The last rays of sunshine lit the maple tree on the front lawn. He had to admit this was a well-landscaped facility. Much of it due to Ned Fister's volunteer gardening.

A mutt shot out of the lobby and headed into the shrubbery across the driveway. Harold shook his head. Who said you couldn't teach an old dog new tricks?

# CHAPTER FIVE 🦇

At 5:30 Harold grabbed the key on the stretchy cord from the inside handle of his door, locked up and headed to dinner. He didn't know why he bothered to lock the door. Bella would come through the wall and let everyone in for the surprise party anyway. He could imagine all the setup and confusion. There would be cleanup afterwards as well. Still, they were doing it for him. He'd play along as if he hadn't been alerted.

As he approached the elevator, he noticed a leather Chesterfield sofa with rolled arms the same height as the back. He never knew when new furniture would sprout up and what it would look like.

Harold whistled. "Good work, Alexandra. You've gone upscale today."

The couch transformed into a small, stout woman wearing a leather skirt. "Hey, Harold. I'm glad you like my latest attempt. I've been experimenting today and have all kinds of scrumptious options available. I need to make a final decision on what I'll look like tonight. Would you help me select the best one?"

Harold regarded his watch. "Sure, I have plenty of time before they run out of food downstairs. Hit me with your best shot."

"Okay. Let's start with the basic style. Tell me if you like number one or number two. Here's number one." An English rolled-arm sofa appeared.

Harold ran his hand over the compact and recessed arms. "Nice plush seat cushions and fully upholstered."

"Oh, my," Alexandra giggled. "I'm ticklish."

Harold pulled his hand away. "Sorry. I'll be more careful."

"That's all right. Here's number two for you to consider." The couch transformed into a Lawson-style sofa.

Harold stroked his chin. "Hmm. I'm a traditionalist. I like the all-American look of number two. It combines comfort with a casual appearance."

"Good choice, Harold. Next we need to consider pattern. Pay close attention. Here's number one." She transformed into a flower pattern. "Or number two." This time a solid color.

"You're making it tough for me with all these options. I guess I'll go with number one. I like a little variety."

"That's why you and Bella get along so well together. There's nothing whatsoever plain about her."

The thought of Bella made Harold smile. "You can say that again." He couldn't wait to see her after dinner at this party she had arranged.

"Next, the matter of color. Here's number one." The sofa turned pink.

Harold immediately shook his head.

"And number two." Gray and white appeared.

Harold imagined he was in the optometrist's office having an eye exam. "Definitely number two. I couldn't have a pink sofa in my apartment."

"I know. Not manly enough for you."

"Any other decisions I have to make?"

"One last one. The type of fabric. I want you to touch the two choices, and I promise not to giggle. Here's number one."

Harold carefully touched the arm, not wanting to take the risk of venturing into the main part of the couch. "That's smooth."

"And number two."

Harold tapped a course fabric. "I'll go with number one."

"You are smooth aren't you, Harold?"

He shrugged.

"We're set. I'm going with this." Alexandra reappeared wearing a gray and white dress.

"You've sure taught me a lot about couch styles and fabric over the last three months," Harold said.

"That's right. Tonight is your par... um... you've been here three months, haven't you?"

Another Back Wing resident almost spilling the beans. "Yeah, some of the best three months of my life." Harold regarded Alexandra as she ran her hand through her tousled hair. "Were you ever married?"

"Yeah." A faraway look appeared in her eyes. "Many years ago when I was young and beautiful, I met a wild, adventurous man. It was love at first transformation. He changed into bobcats, jaguars, panthers, tigers and lions and nuzzled against my fabric." She shivered. "The effect that man had on me. He romanced me, and I succumbed to his charms. Following a glorious two-month courtship, we were married. I remember the wedding bells as we left the church. Rather than rice, his friends threw cat kibble at us. After a three-week safari honeymoon, we returned to life in the suburbs." She sighed loudly. "The marriage only lasted a year."

"What happened?"

"As much as I loved him, he got on my nerves. I couldn't stand the hair on my fabric. And I developed an allergy to cat hair. We divorced over irreconcilable differences. The only saving grace, he never scratched me. So here I am in the Back Wing. I have the freedom to try all kinds of different looks without sneezing."

"Maybe you'll find someone again."

Alexandra winked at him. "If you ever get tired of Bella, there will be a soft place for you to sit."

Harold gulped. "Bella has me fully occupied right now."

"I know. I'm kidding. Say, did you see all the turmoil in the lobby this afternoon?"

"You mean the woman who died?"

"Yeah. I was down there practicing a neoclassical French-style settee. She was in a chair next to me. Half an hour into my practice run, she slumped to the floor. Before I could transform back to human shape to help her, the receptionist, Andrea, came running over."

"Did you notice anything before the woman died?"

"She mumbled that her room was being used for a tour stop for prospective residents. She was a nervous sort. When a crowd of people came by she spilled her purse, and several people helped her pick up pill bottles that fell all over the floor. It was pretty chaotic for a while, and I couldn't see clearly with everyone milling around."

"Her name was Alice Jones. Had you seen her before?"

"Didn't know her name, but I saw her in the lobby once before when I was trying out a Cabriole sofa. She sat on me and rummaged through her purse. She had bottles and bottles of pills. Talked to herself about her weak heart and began guzzling pills. I couldn't believe it. She swallowed them without any water. How can anyone do that?"

"I couldn't, but my wife used to."

"That's right, you were married before, too."

Harold sighed. "A long and happy marriage."

"Versus my short and erratic one. Now you have Bella."

Harold considered the wonder of being attracted to a woman again, much less a witch. "All comes with living in the Back Wing."

"Got to get going. I'll see you after dinner. Oops." Alexandra scampered down the hallway and disappeared.

Harold pushed the down button for the elevator. This would be his last meal before he would have to act surprised for the party Bella had organized. With this crowd, there were bound to be a number of surprises in store for him.

# CHAPTER SIX

Harold scanned the dining room and spotted his friend, Ned Fister, sitting at a table for two in the corner. He moseyed over and plunked down in the open chair. "I see you saved me the best seat in the house."

"That's right. From here we can watch all the old biddies without having to listen to them blabbing."

"Oh, don't be such a cynic."

Ned shrugged. "Only being realistic. I enjoy your conversation but can't say I want to hear the latest hat fashions or local gossip regarding who's sneaking a nip from the congregational wine."

"But you enjoy discussing gardening."

Ned's eyes sparkled. "Yeah, but that's important stuff, not the inane babble from these other people."

"In that case, tell me the latest in the world of dirt clods, roots and leaves."

Ned flexed his arm. "You'll never believe this, but I vanquished a whole hoard of aphids today."

"That reminds me of the story my mom read to me when I was a kid—'The Brave Little Tailor' who killed seven in one blow. Seven flies."

"I remember that story. Much the same. I waved my magic trowel and the enemy met their doom. Someone has to protect the garden from vicious intruders." Ned raised his fist in the air. "Let's hear it for flower power."

"Don't get too carried away."

"I have to celebrate my small victories. Death to the daisy destroyers."

This made Harold think of the dead woman in the lobby this afternoon. He considered bringing up the subject with Ned, but the sound of a knife striking a glass, interrupted all the conversations in the room.

Peter Lemieux stood and spoke into a handheld microphone. "I want your attention, please."

"You giving out birthday cake and ice cream tonight?" a voice shouted from a table across the room.

"Next Tuesday is our monthly birthday celebration. We'll have birthday cake and ice cream then."

"All you can eat?"

Peter grinned. "You bet. But make sure you don't overdose on sugar."

"Sugar is what keeps me alive."

"And we in the administration at Mountain Splendor want all of you to stay alive. But I have a sad announcement to make. One of our residents, Alice Jones, passed away this afternoon. Some of you may have seen the various emergency vehicles in the driveway. Since I've had numerous questions, I thought it would be best to make an announcement when many of you are here so you understand exactly what happened. You may have noticed that we had a number of visitors in this room earlier this afternoon. We held an open house for prospective residents. Right after the open house, Alice died in the lobby."

"I hope it wasn't something she ate at the open house," a voice shouted.

"No. She didn't attend the open house. The authorities are investigating and will determine the cause of her death. I want to introduce Detective Deavers from the Golden Police Department. He asked to say a few words to you."

Peter handed the microphone to Deavers, who ran his other hand through his hair. "Thank you, Mr. Lemieux. It's unfortunate when a suspicious death takes place—"

"Suspicious like in murder?" someone called out.

Deavers held his free hand up. "I'll explain. We don't know yet if the death was due to natural or some other cause. When there is uncertainty, we label it a suspicious death. The official police investigation is under way, and the coroner's office will be conducting an autopsy to make a ruling on the cause of death. In the meantime, I'd like to ask for your cooperation. I'm only one person, but with all of you in this room, you might have seen something or noticed some suspicious behavior."

"Yeah, Madeline cheated at bridge today," came a retort. "That was pretty suspicious."

Deavers gritted his teeth. "I can't comment on your card games, but if you saw Alice Jones or noticed anything unusual in the lobby area at approximately three this afternoon, please contact me. I'll leave a stack of business cards with Mr. Lemieux, so take one on your way out and give me a call if you think of something that would aid our investigation. Thank you."

He sat as a murmur ran through the crowd.

Ned leaned toward Harold. "That should give the old bats a new conversation topic."

Harold thought of the one old bat he knew in the Back Wing. Pamela Quint wouldn't mind being called a bat but would hate to have the "old" added to it. With the subject he wanted to address having been broached by the announcement, he decided to pursue it. "Ned, did you know Alice Jones?"

"Oh, yeah. I even sat at a table with her once. I nicknamed her Alice P. P. Jones, for pill popper. That woman had a purse full of medicine and told everybody all the junk she was taking for her heart ailments. She had more pills than you'd find at a pharmacists' convention."

"Was her heart condition that bad?"

"Hard to tell. I never knew how much was real or imagined. She might have been a hypochondriac. Her doctor could have given her placebos to shut her up. She certainly relished taking pills."

"Maybe her heart condition killed her."

"I don't know. In spite of all her yammering that she was on death's door, she seemed to be a pretty robust old broad."

Interesting. Had she died of natural causes, or as the detective said, might there have been some human-induced problem?

Harold's thoughts were interrupted by Peter Lemieux tapping him on the shoulder. "May I have a word with you in private?"

"Sure." Harold stood, and they moved away from the tables.

"What's on your mind?"

"After the open house and dealing with the unfortunate death, I went to my office. I couldn't find the copy of the waiting list you took to Andrea."

"I left it with her, and she said she'd make a copy for you. Didn't you ask her?"

"I looked for her, but she was on break at the time."

"She very dependable. Maybe she hasn't had a chance to do it yet."

Peter clapped Harold on the back. "You're probably right. I'll check later."

"I've heard from several people that Alice Jones took a lot of medication for her heart. Do you know how serious her heart condition was?"

"Don't know. I heard her mention a weak heart but never saw any obvious symptoms."

A woman at a nearby table waved and called out, "Oh, Mr. Lemieux, might we have a word with you?"

Peter rolled his eyes. "Uh-oh. The members of the bridge foursome have some complaint. I better go find out what's the problem this time."

Harold watched Peter join the four ladies and returned to have dessert with Ned.

"The big muckety-muck have some secret message for you?"

"I helped out with the open house today. He was trying to find the waiting list that I compiled."

"Waiting list? Are all the rooms taken?"

"Apparently. But someone on the list of replacements will get Alice's apartment."

They finished their apple pie. Ned said he wanted to make one final pass through the lilac bushes, and Harold headed down to the lobby. He found Andrea behind the reception counter.

"Peter Lemieux said he couldn't find the waiting list copy. Did you put it on his desk?"

"That's funny. I filed the original, and put a copy on his desk. Let me go check."

She disappeared and in five minutes returned, scratching her head. "Are you sure he didn't pick it up? It isn't on his desk."

# CHAPTER SEVEN 🦇

Pondering what had happened to the copy of the waiting list, Harold punched the button by the elevator with the red door and waited for it to appear. The original existed so Andrea could make another copy for Peter Lemieux.

After the usual interminable delay, the door opened and Harold stepped in. He checked the schedule for the next day, attached to the interior wall, and noted the poker group would be meeting in the afternoon. He and Jason had participated in a game when Jason stayed here during the summer. Jason was a good poker player and had shown the old fogies what a kid could do. Although Harold used to play poker once in a while himself, he had no desire to join the Front Wingers unless Jason was here. He'd probably take a long walk the next afternoon anyway. He completed the ride to the fourth floor without stops at any of the other floors.

Once out of the elevator, he found Bailey Jorgenson blocking his way. She had flaming red hair and too much rouge on her cheeks. She reminded him of a valkyrie ready to determine who lived or died in battle.

She squinted at him. "Is that you, Harold?"

"Yes, Bailey."

"I couldn't be sure with my macular degeneration. You look like a fuzzy blob with ghostly shadows."

"You say the most flattering things."

Bailey burped. "Excuse me." She pounded on her chest and burped again. "That's better. I think there was a bit too much salsa in my last meal. I have to be more careful. Spicy blood disagrees with me."

"That happens to me if I eat curry."

"I need to enlist your assistance, Harold."

"What do you have in mind?"

Bailey rubbed her hands together like a child ready for the ice cream man. "It's time to go for takeout again. I thought you'd give me a hand. You've always been so helpful. What do you say?"

"When is your expedition planned?"

"Friday night."

Harold tapped his cheek. "I'm not sure. Jason will be here. It's probably not the most appropriate activity for including him."

"He's welcome to join us. The more hands the merrier. That way we won't overload any one person and risk dropping important nourishment. Can't let that good red stuff go to waste."

Harold tried to sneak past her, but she moved like a good offensive lineman guarding the quarterback. He was able to catch a glimpse of people dashing through the corridor. Sure enough, someone went into his room. He would play along.

"How do you expect to get into the blood bank? You have the key to the door?"

Bailey pulled a cord out from her ample bosom and displayed the key. "Yep. Keep it close to my heart."

"I hope they don't change the lock on you."

"So far they haven't been suspicious of our raids. That's why we don't take too much at one time."

Harold wondered if some administrator would eventually notice a discrepancy, but Bailey had previously assured him that there was some allowance in the inventory numbers for dropped or damaged containers of blood.

Bailey moved toward him, grabbed his arms, and put her face near his throat. "I can't see too clearly, but is that a spot on your neck?" Then she sneezed.

"Your allergy to skin acting up?" Harold asked.

She backed away. "Yeah. I should know better than to get too close to a throat. Here I was once a connoisseur of throats, and now I can't even get near one."

"I know what you mean. I used to love shrimp, but I can't eat it any more. Talk about stomach problems—shrimp gives me cramps."

"Getting old is a pain in the heiny. I never had these problems when

I was younger. I could stay up all night, guzzle any flavor of blood and never sneeze when approaching a choice throat."

"We all have to make some concessions as we get older. Comes with the territory." Harold tried to step around her again, but she moved to block his way. She obviously had been assigned to detain him. He wondered how much longer the delaying tactics would continue.

"I woke up early today and saw an ambulance in the driveway," Bailey said. "Any idea what happened?"

"There was a death."

Bailey did a double take. "No kidding. The meat wagon here for a pickup. I hope no one from the Back Wing."

"A woman from the Front Wing named Alice Jones was sitting in the lobby, and she slumped to the floor. A detective came to investigate since the authorities aren't sure if it was a medical condition, accident or something more suspicious."

"Whew." Bailey wiped her forehead. "We can spare one of those Front Wingers, but we have to protect our own kind."

"That sounds like a statement someone from the Front Wing would make."

Bailey hung her head. "You're right. I should be more tolerant. Sometimes I forget that without you... uh... so-called normal people, I wouldn't have a source for dinner. It's like with mountain lions. No deer, no meal."

"That's right. No us, no takeout." He tried to fake to the left and move right, but Bailey met his move. For her size she had the agility of a point guard. Maybe she had played basketball. He peered past her and saw Warty duck into his room. Harold looked forward to seeing the other Back Wing residents at the party, but Warty's appearance always meant trouble. The guy couldn't control his magic.

"Have you seen Bella today?" Bailey asked.

Harold wondered again when the stalling tactics would cease. "Yeah, I chatted with her this afternoon."

"That Bella. Quite the looker." Bailey planted an elbow in Harold's ribs, causing him to gasp.

"That she is. She showed up in my room, and Viola also joined us."

"Viola will also be on our takeout expedition, that is, if she remembers. I'll have to remind her Friday afternoon. Her memory isn't getting any better. You seem to have all your marbles, Harold."

"Yeah, with all the entertainment in the Back Wing, I have to keep my wits. So far no mental glitches."

"Me neither."

Harold regarded his watch. Bailey had detained him five minutes. He heard music coming from somewhere down the hallway. It sounded like the theme song from the television show *The Munsters*. Maybe the party was ready to start. He peered around Bailey again and saw Pamela Quint smack into the corridor wall. She rebounded, straightened herself and headed toward Harold's room.

"If you don't mind, I best be getting to my apartment," Harold said. "I need to use the bathroom, and I don't want to have an accident."

"You having problems like Tomas?"

"No. But I have to get going, so to speak."

Bailey looked back over her shoulder and nodded. "Sure. I don't know why you're keeping me here. Have at it."

# CHAPTER EIGHT

Harold took a step toward his room, then turned toward the stairwell, having decided to have a little fun at Bailey's expense. "On second thought, I think I'll head downstairs and go for a walk. It's such a pleasant evening. You want to join me?"

Bailey grabbed Harold's shoulders and spun him back toward his room. "No. You better go use the bathroom first. As you said, we don't want any accidents. Move it."

Harold shrugged out of her grasp. "The urge has passed. I'm okay. I think a nice stroll outside for several hours will do me a world of good. I need to enjoy the outdoors before winter sets in."

A look of panic crossed Bailey's face. "You can't do that. You—you." She looked down at Harold's feet. "You should put your walking shoes on first. That's it. I'll accompany you to your room."

Harold decided he had tweaked her enough. "Good idea. I'll go to my apartment and change my shoes and get my walking poles."

Bailey let out a loud burst of air as if purging her lungs of noxious fumes.

Harold whistled his off key rendition of *Be Happy, Don't Worry* and strolled toward his room. He paused at his door and listened, hearing someone shushing the others. He noticed Bailey standing right behind him. She wouldn't let him escape. Taking a deep breath he opened the door and stepped inside.

At first he was met with darkness, and then the lights flashed on.

"Surprise!" came the chorus. Toy horns sounded, and people whooped and hollered.

Harold put his hand to his chest and feigned the most surprised expression he could muster. "You almost gave me a heart attack."

"You need to keep that heart pumping good red blood," Bailey called from behind him.

Bella sashayed forward in a slinky black gown and planted a kiss on his lips. "Happy three months at Mountain Splendor."

Everyone applauded.

Harold put his arm around Bella's waist and took a moment to regard his apartment. Balloons festooned the walls, and a card table stood in the middle of his living room with all kinds of snacks including a cake with chocolate frosting. Two punchbowls rested on the counter of his kitchenette. One held a yellow concoction with ice cubes and lemon slices floating on the surface. The other one bubbled and gave off a green mist. He would stay away from that bowl.

Bella led him toward the table and picked up a knife and tapped it against a metal bowl of mixed nuts. "I want your attention, please."

Everyone stopped talking, and all eyes turned toward Bella.

She set the knife back down on the table. "We're gathered here today to recognize a special event. Harold has been a member of the Back Wing for exactly three months."

A round of cheers rang through the room.

"In addition to having his friendship for that period of time, I want to note that he is the first person without special powers to survive for such a period of time in the Back Wing."

Hoots and whistling ensued.

Bella held up her hand. "Now, Harold, would you like to say a few words."

Harold cleared his throat. "I'm trying to get over the shock of finding all of you in my room."

Pamela Quint shouted out, "What did he say?"

"Turn up your hearing aids," Bailey said.

Pamela tweaked her ears. "What?"

"Turn up your hearing aids."

"I just did. Why are you shouting?"

Knowing that he had not given away his knowledge of the surprise party, Harold continued. "Now this statement about special powers. I may not be able to change into a couch." He held his hand out toward Alexandra who wiggled her fingers at him. "Or walk through walls." He gave Bella a squeeze around the waist. "I'm not much at howling at the moon or slurping takeout from next door, but I'm pretty good at eating cake. So let's get on with the food. Thank you."

Tomas thrust a noisemaker in the air and twirled it to make a whirring sound.

Bella picked up the knife again and sliced the cake.

Off to the side, Pamela Quint transformed into a bat and flew around the room. After one successful circumnavigation, something flew to the rug. Harold reached over and picked it up. "Look out, Pamela, you dropped one of your hearing aids.

The bat bashed into the wall, popping a balloon, careened into another balloon and dropped to the floor.

Pamela sat there rubbing her arm. "I think I dented my wing."

Harold handed her the hearing aid. "Put this back in, and you should be able to navigate better with full sonar."

She stuck the device back in her ear. "That's better. I think I'll have some cake."

Kendall Nicoletti limped over with his walker. "I hear your grandson will be visiting again."

"This weekend," Harold said.

"Good. It will be almost a full moon. He can come howl with me."

Harold regarded Kendall, amazed again at the incongruity between his bald head reflecting the light from the living room chandelier and his hairy wrists peeking out from the cuff of his long-sleeved shirt. "He'd enjoy that. I'll mention it to him when he arrives."

Harold ate a piece of cake, savoring the cream filling and rich chocolate frosting. Next, he helped himself to a green cube of Jell-O knowing better than to eat the red ones. Then he went over to get a cup of punch.

"Stick with the yellow punch," Bella said. "The other is Warty's mix. You don't want to risk trying it."

Harold peered inside the green bubbling brew. "There appear to be things swimming inside it."

Bella leaned over. "Yep. Tadpoles. As I said, stay away from Warty's punch."

"I'm convinced."

Bella squeezed Harold's hand. "What did you do this afternoon after I last saw you?"

"I helped out with the open house and took a walk. I also saw one of your old friends. Detective Deavers was here."

"What brings him to Mountain Splendor?"

"We had a suspicious death in the lobby. A woman named Alice Jones, a resident of the Front Wing, died. He was here to investigate."

"Tell me the particulars."

Harold recounted all that happened. "One other minor incongruity. At the open house I helped by manning a table for people who wanted their names added to the waiting list when vacancies arise here. I left that list with Andrea at the front desk and she made a copy for Peter Lemieux. Peter couldn't find that copy later."

"And knowing your suspicious mind, you think this might relate to the death of Alice Jones."

Harold gave a sheepish grin. "You know me so well. I guess I hadn't consciously voiced that concern, but you're right. There is something here tied to the waiting list."

"I think you and I should look into it tomorrow," Bella said. "I'll make arrangements for us to help in the office, and we can snoop around. They're always looking for volunteers to supplement the paid staff."

# CHAPTER NINE

Viola pulled Bella away to discuss some important female topic, and Harold used the opportunity to look around the room. Who would have figured the types of friends he had made? He never imagined the variety of hu… ah… creatures he'd meet. He watched Tomas scratch behind his ear and transform into a mutt. Bailey quickly led the dog out of the room. Harold gave a sigh of relief. He didn't want his rug spotted.

A moment later, his wary eye caught Warty. The short warlock with his wild, spiky hair was waving his wand at the green, steaming bowl of punch. "Alla ka jabbers," Warty shouted. Nothing happened.

Warty shook his wand and peered at the end of it. There was a puff of smoke, and Warty let out a gasp as a ring of soot appeared around his right eye.

Harold sauntered over. "Problem?"

"Dang wand is misbehaving." Warty pointed it again at the bowl of green punch. "Bibble, bibble bab." This time a water spout formed over the punch. Tadpoles shot into the air and fell back into the punchbowl.

"You might want to be careful," Harold said. "The management would be upset if we messed up the carpet." To say nothing of how the resident would feel.

Warty shook his wand again. "This has never been the same since it fell into Lake Dillon."

"What happened?" Harold asked.

"I went on a field trip with Warlocks Anonymous. It's a twelve-step program for warlocks who are recovering from misdirected spells. We rented a boat to go out on the lake at the end of summer. Beautiful day with nary a cloud in the sky. One of the other guys bumped into me when we hit the wake of a powerboat, and my wand fell into the water. The jerk refused to jump in the drink to retrieve it."

"How'd you recover it?"

"I tried to cast a wandless spell but that only ended up causing the boat engine to conk out. One of the crew threw out a net which snagged my wand. It was pretty waterlogged, and it's sputtered ever since." He shook it again and a tadpole squirted onto the carpet. He reached over, picked up the squirming creature and dropped it in the punchbowl.

"How'd you get the boat back to shore?"

"We had to row. For some reason the other guys didn't invite me on the next outing when they went up to the casinos at Blackhawk. Too bad. I probably would have broken the bank at the casino."

Or broken something else, Harold figured. "These days some people are so closed minded."

Warty squinted at Harold. "You're looking a little wan. Do you need me to cast a rejuvenation spell for you?"

"That's okay. It's merely the lighting in the room."

"You sure?"

"Absolutely."

"I guess I better find Bella. I know she misses me." Warty dashed off, leaving Harold to stare at the bubbling punchbowl. Poor Bella. She detested Warty, who never got the message that she wasn't interested in him. Across the room Warty approached Bella. She turned and waggled her finger at Warty. Warty froze. Viola grabbed a balloon from the wall and taped it to Warty's forehead. He made a better decoration than a warlock.

Harold couldn't resist so he strolled over to where Bella and Viola stood admiring Viola's decoration.

"What have you done to Warty?" Harold asked.

"He made an inappropriate comment so I froze him," Bella said.

"How long are you going to keep him that way?"

"For the rest of the party, if need be."

Viola stuck another balloon to Warty's left ear. "He's looking better. One more balloon should make him more symmetrical." She added another to his right ear. "There, my work of art is completed."

Bailey came by with a tray of red and green Jell-o cubes. "Who's ready for a shot?"

Viola grabbed a red one and popped it in her mouth. "Yum."

Bailey held the platter out. "Harold, care for one?"

He took a green one.

"We've run out of counter space," Bailey said. "There's nowhere to set this tray."

"I can fix that." Bella wiggled her nose and Warty's arms raised and his palms turned upward. "Here's a perfect holding surface."

"Super." Bailey set the tray on Warty's outstretched hands.

Harold circulated and spent time discussing phases of the moon with Kendall who admitted being something of an amateur astronomer. "There's a lunar eclipse next month. I especially like when the total eclipse occurs and the moon is red with the reflected light from earth. Quite a sight."

"Does an eclipse affect your howling?" Harold asked.

"Nah. I'm off tune all the time anyway."

The next time Harold passed Warty, he noticed the tray was empty. He picked it up and set it against the kitchenette counter.

A little later Harold checked Warty and found that someone had hung a coat on his outstretched arms. Kendall came pushing up with his walker, grabbed the coat and put it on. "This is a good coat rack, but can you fix the traffic hazard? I'm having trouble navigating through here."

When Harold next encountered Bella, he said, "Warty is blocking traffic flow in the living room. Do you think you can unfreeze him?"

"I suppose it would be safe." She crinkled her nose.

Warty dropped his hands and looked wildly around the room. He spotted Bella and dashed in the opposite direction.

Bella dusted her hands together. "Mission accomplished."

"Do you think he got the message this time?" Harold asked.

"I sure hope so. I keep telling him I'm not interested in him. The next time I'll freeze him to the ceiling and leave him there for a week."

"But not in my apartment. It would ruin the ambiance."

Harold had another piece of cake, watched Pamela fly around the room. She apparently had her hearing aids in as her sonar seemed to be working this time.

The sound of a knife striking the green punchbowl caused the conversations to stop.

"May I have your attention!" Warty shouted. "In honor of Harold's three month anniversary, I have a special magic effect to demonstrate."

Groans emerged from around the room. One voice shouted, "No!" Another called out, "Don't do it!"

"Whatever you have in mind, forget it," Bailey said.

"Please spare us," Viola added.

Warty waved his arms. "You all will be pleasantly surprised this time."

"We've been unpleasantly surprised enough," Kendall said.

Warty waved his wand in a circle. "Now focus your attention on the punchbowl." He pointed the wand at the green bubbling liquid. "Ibbity, bittity, boo."

Flames shot toward the ceiling and the punchbowl exploded, showering those nearby with goo.

Viola shrieked. "My new hairdo!"

"You've gummed up the works on my walker," Kendall shouted.

The flames caught a curtain on fire, and smoke filled the room.

Bella stepped forward and breathed out, extinguishing the fire. She waved her hand and the smoke dissipated.

Harold shook his head in disgust. He had a lot of cleanup to do, and it would take days to rid his apartment of the smell of smoke.

# CHAPTER TEN ⤫

After a bat, a dog, a dejected warlock and various other creatures disappeared from Harold's room, he stood there with Bella inspecting the damage.

"Fortunately, the sprinklers didn't come on to drench your room," Bella said.

"Thanks to your quick action in extinguishing the fire and dissipating the smoke. What got into Warty anyway?"

Bella sighed. "He tried to do his magic, but he's completely incompetent. Maybe we should convince him to do something mischievous next time. Since his spells backfire, that would lead to something positive or benign."

"I think the only logical solution is to keep him away from events."

"I can assure you I didn't invite him, but he doesn't want to be left out and always shows up. He gets his feelings hurt and then does dumb stunts to attract attention."

Harold sneezed. "I can't sleep here tonight. I need to go somewhere where I can breathe. Care to invite me for a sleepover?"

Bella patted his arm. "It's tempting, but I need my beauty sleep. You wouldn't want to see what I look like in the morning. You better call Peter Lemieux and report what happened. He might have a spare room for you."

"I don't know. When I last spoke with him, he indicated we were filled to the brim with residents of both flavors."

Bella gave him a mischievous grin. "And I bet you wouldn't want to spend a night in Warty's room."

"You have that right. I might end up as a toad."

"Speaking of toads, what happened to all the tadpoles in Warty's punch?"

Harold kicked aside a green glop on the carpet. "The last I saw was they went up in the explosion. I don't see any in the mess on the rug. Anyhow, I better call Peter." He picked up the phone and Peter said he'd be up to inspect the damage in thirty minutes.

While waiting, Harold and Bella picked up the pieces of glass from the exploded punchbowl and dropped them in a trash bag.

When Peter arrived he sniffed loudly. "What happened here?"

"Do you want the full explanation or the condensed version?" Harold asked.

"I sense there's a story here."

"Yeah. You see the evidence of a Warty explosion. Unfortunately, I can't sleep in the stinky place tonight. Any other rooms available?"

Peter tapped his chin. "I knew I should have kept a guest room for a circumstance like this, but, as you know, we've had so much interest lately that I put new residents in every possible spot. The only unoccupied room is Alice Jones's old room. I don't know if you'd be willing to sleep there."

Harold shrugged. "I don't have a problem with that. Have the police released it?"

"Yeah. Since she died in the lobby, they inspected her room this afternoon and said it didn't need to be sealed off."

"Any relatives who might not want her belongings disturbed?" Bella asked.

Peter gritted his teeth. "That's not a problem either. She has no close relatives. Since with her medical condition she expected to expire at any moment anyway, she gave me instructions to donate all her things to Goodwill when she passed. Therefore, you can use her place until we can get the mitigation team in to clean and repaint your apartment."

"The only problem I see is giving up my neighbors to be in the Front Wing."

Bella gave his hand a pat. "You'll survive."

"How long do you think it will take to get my room fixed up?" Harold asked.

"I'll contact the crew first thing in the morning, and if they have no major projects, I hope they can do it in two days. The longest part will entail everything being scrubbed to eliminate the smoke aroma. They come in with a group of workers who wipe clean every object and surface in the room. After that, repainting can be done quickly." Peter paced around the room inspecting the damage. "The only other challenge will be replacing the curtains. I'll get those ordered tomorrow."

"I can move back without that completed, once I can safely breathe the air in here again." Harold also figured Bella could use her special powers to provide some temporary window covering.

Peter headed toward the door. "Go ahead and pack a suitcase, and I'll go get a spare key for you."

After Peter left, Bella said, "I'll let you take care of moving. We'll check in tomorrow." She disappeared through the wall.

Harold retrieved the small suitcase from his bedroom closet. He sniffed. It didn't smell like smoke. He packed two days worth of clothes and added the book on the history of witchcraft he'd been reading. He wouldn't bother with any food items. He'd forego snacks between meals, or worst case, he could come back up to raid the small refrigerator in his kitchenette. That would give him a chance to see Bella as well.

He had completed packing by the time Peter returned with the key. "Room five-fourteen. You'll like the view."

Harold didn't bother to mention that he preferred the view here where Bella might appear through the wall at any moment. Much more attractive.

After taking the pokey little elevator down to the second floor and transferring to the green-door elevator, he rose to the fifth floor of the Front Wing, exited and pulled his wheelie suitcase to the correct apartment. Taped to the door Harold found a chart with the acceptable weight ranges for women by age. He shook his head. Alice had definitely been wrapped up in health issues.

Inside, he turned on a light and found an immaculate living room, simply furnished with a matching couch and easy chair, an entertainment center with television and stereo, a pole lamp and a bookcase. He stepped over and peered at the bookcase. If he finished the book he brought, there would be plenty to read. Although the books were aligned neatly, it looked as if Alice hadn't dusted for weeks as a layer of dust lined the shelves, except for one place where it looked like a book had been removed recently.

He peeked in the bedroom. The bed was covered with a bright pink blanket. He groaned, but decided he could live with that for several days. In the hall closet he found sheets and remade the bed. He had a clean place to sleep.

The kitchenette had nothing out on the counter. Taped to the refrigerator door appeared two lists—one with the signs of a stroke and the other with symptoms of a heart attack. He opened the refrigerator and found bottles of pills lining the top shelf, several bottles of some dark tonic but no food. Next, he inspected the bathroom. Again, nothing on the sink. He opened the medicine cabinet and was assailed by row after row of pill bottles. Alice had certainly kept the pharmaceutical industry fully employed.

Harold wondered how much she spent on these various forms of medication. Assuming she was on a Medicare Part D plan, she must have reached the donut hole of not being reimbursed by April of every year.

Having inspected his new domain, he put his small suitcase on top of the bedroom dresser. He didn't bother to unpack anything other than his toilet kit, which he set on the bathroom sink, and his book, which he placed on the nightstand. He'd live out of the suitcase, rather than stash anything in the dresser drawers. He hoped Peter would be successful in accomplishing a quick transformation of his damaged apartment.

Although tired, he realized that he might be able to learn something more regarding the suspicious death victim. He opened the top dresser drawer, found underwear and quickly closed it. The second drawer held socks, and the bottom one had T-shirts and walking shorts. In the closet he found three dresses neatly hung on hangers, a pair of jeans, half a dozen blouses, a sweater and a ski jacket. On the floor of the closet rested a pair of tennis shoes, dark blue pumps and black high-heels. Alice certainly didn't have a shoe fetish. In fact she apparently hadn't cared much about clothes. Her interest ran to pills.

He supposed he should feel guilty rummaging through someone's personal effects, but he rationalized that he was only looking for clues that might shed light on what had happened to Alice.

Next, he opened the drawer of the nightstand. Hmm. The first interesting item. It seemed to be a journal. He opened it to find dates going back two months. Alice had written a few sentences every day describing her activities. Pretty mundane. What she had eaten, who she had talked to. Each day's entry had a list of the medication she had consumed. She didn't seem to have any hobbies other than taking pills.

# CHAPTER ELEVEN 🦇

Peter Lemieux had mentioned the view from Alice's room, so Harold parted the curtains to look outside. There was a small balcony. Down below he could see the circular driveway of the retirement home. The half moon gave a hint of the outline of the hillside. He imagined during sunlight hours, the view would be impressive. He'd have to remember to check again in the morning.

His thoughts returned to the issue of the mysterious death. Had someone killed Alice rather than her succumbing to some medical problem? Obviously Detective Deavers wasn't convinced of a natural cause. If he were trying to kill Alice, how would he do it? He never thought he'd ask such a question, but after his experience during the summer, he certainly had looked upon the human race from a different perspective. During his career as an insurance salesman, he only thought of death in terms of actuarial tables, insurance rates and compensation. How his perspective had changed. To answer his own question he ruminated for a moment. Then a clear answer emerged. With all the medication the woman took, messing with her pills might be a way to dispatch her.

Now fully awake, Harold made another quick scan of the apartment and decided to take a short walk before turning in. He exited and locked the door. No one else around. As he headed to the elevator the Front Wing green door opened and a woman shuffled out. She used a cane. One of Alice's neighbors.

"Good evening," Harold said.

The woman looked him up and down as if inspecting a bottle of bug killer. "What are you doing here?"

*Real friendly.* "I'm staying in room five-fourteen."

45

"That's Alice's room. She's dead. Why would you be staying there?"

"I'm only in the apartment temporarily."

She tapped her cane on the floor. "You haven't answered my question. Why are you in her room?"

"My place had a little... uh... problem tonight. This was the only open apartment to use overnight, so Peter Lemieux told me to use it."

She gave Harold the evil eye. "You don't look familiar, and I know nearly everyone in the Front Wing."

Harold forced a smile. "That may explain it. I live in the Back Wing."

The woman's eyes grew wide. She crossed herself and hobbled past Harold.

He spun to see her reach a room, frantically work her key and disappear inside to the sound of the door slamming.

No love lost between the Front and Back Wings. Harold decided if he wanted to carry on any conversation with Alice's neighbors, he would have to refrain from mentioning where he had come from.

Harold found a small couch near the elevator and sat down. He figured he didn't have to worry that it would transform. He thought over what he had heard. His contemplation was interrupted by the elevator door opening again. This time a man his age stepped out. Harold thought he'd try to engage this man in conversation. "Evening to you."

The man squinted at Harold. "Who the heck are you?"

*Great. Another friendly resident.* "I'm... uh... Alice Jones's cousin. I'm staying in her room after her unfortunate death today."

He peered intently at Harold. "I didn't know she had a cousin."

"Long lost third cousin from Fort Collins. I'm only staying for a few nights. Did you know her well?"

"What are you implying? I don't know any of these old dames around here. I keep to myself."

Harold searched for something to keep the conversation going. All he could think of was what he had seen in her apartment. "Alice seemed to take a lot of pills."

"Everybody knows that. She is, or was, a walking pill dispenser. Why do you mention it?"

46

"Only a comment."

The guy gave Harold a withering stare. "Now, I need my sleep." Without so much as a nod, he pushed past Harold.

Harold watched as the man let himself into a room at the end of the hall. Shaking his head at the unfriendly encounter, he lowered himself to the couch again. He wasn't used to sofas near elevators that didn't sigh when you sat on them. After waiting another fifteen minutes, Harold yawned, stood and moseyed back to his room. He'd try to talk to more people in the morning.

Back inside, he locked the door, slid the security chain, put on his pajamas, brushed his teeth and got in bed to read. The book on the history of witchcraft described the Salem witch trials. Most of the people convicted were hanged. No one was burned at the stake. Interesting how folklore doesn't reflect reality.

After two more pages, instead of his usual reaction of getting sleepy, he felt more awake than he had earlier. *Must be thoughts of Alice's demise.* He set his book on the nightstand and slid out of bed.

Turning on the living room light, he paced around. After he circled the living room twice, his gaze focused on the bookshelf. He regarded the neatly lined up books, all hard covers, not an earmarked paperback in sight. He ran his finger along the spines. Several cooking books, one on knitting, another on national parks. Boring. Next, he surveyed a section that contained all sorts of historical novels. Most appropriate for a little old lady. Then he did a double take. Auto mechanics? That seemed out of place.

He grabbed the book from the shelf and began leafing through it. Sure enough, a ten-year old tome on lube jobs, carburetor adjustment and engine tuning. What the heck? He returned it to the shelf. He scanned other books. An inconsistency caught his eye. He had noticed before that the bookshelf had been covered with dust except for one spot. He pulled out a book from that location, one on the history of France, and discovered a folded sheet of paper had been left between this book and the one to its left.

Some secret note?

Now in full snoop mode, he unfolded it and stared in disbelief. It was a copy of the waiting list that Harold had overseen during the open house that afternoon. How the heck had this ended up here?

Pieces of the puzzle swirled through Harold's brain. Alice dying in the lobby. This list showing up in her apartment.

Only one thing to do. He placed the list on the kitchenette counter and picked up the phone to call Detective Deavers. He had to pause for a moment to recall the number, but from his previous interaction with the detective, he was able to dredge the right digits from his memory.

At this late hour the call cut over to voicemail. "Detective, this is Harold McCaffrey at the Mountain Splendor Retirement Home. I have some information for you regarding the death of Alice Jones. There was an accident in my apartment, and Peter Lemieux put me in the only space available, Alice's old room, number five-fourteen, in the Front Wing. Two things. First, Alice took many medications. I'm wondering if her suspicious death might have had anything to do with someone switching some of her medication." Harold paused. That should catch the detective's attention.

"Second, at the open house this afternoon for prospective residents, people signed a waiting list. Peter couldn't find his copy earlier, but I discovered a copy on the bookshelf in Alice's room. Doesn't make any sense, but it might somehow be linked to her death. I thought you'd want to check it out tomorrow. Stop by when you get a chance."

Harold hung up, wondering if he babbled too much. Hopefully, he had left the pertinent information. He'd await the detective's arrival the next day.

# CHAPTER TWELVE

Harold awoke with a start. He heard a door creak and a chain rattle. Where was he? It was pitch black. Then he remembered the fiasco the night before with the Warty-caused explosion in his room and his exile to the apartment of the woman who died. He thought he heard footsteps. He jumped out of bed. "Hello?"

The sound of a door closing. He turned on the light and went into the living room and flicked on another light. "Anyone here?"

No sounds. It wasn't like his apartment where Bella could show up at any time by coming through the wall.

He checked the door. The key on the stretchy band was there, and the security chain was in place. He must have imagined it. He checked his watch. Four-thirty. Dang. He'd have trouble getting back to sleep.

He tossed and turned but eventually fell asleep, only to be awakened by a dream of strange people invading his apartment. Too much circulated through his mind to consider going back to sleep. Instead, he set his feet firmly on the floor, pulled up the pink cover to accomplish a man's version of making the bed, and padded to the window to draw the curtains. Even though the view of the hills in early morning sunshine was spectacular, he would have preferred to be back with his friends in the Back Wing. A shave and splash of water on his face sufficed, and once dressed, he checked the top of the kitchenette counter to see the waiting list there. He locked up and headed along the hallway to go down for some breakfast.

While waiting for the slow elevator, a woman shuffled up with a walker. The walker had a shelf in front with an open box of dark chocolates. She popped one in her mouth.

"Good morning." Harold graced her with his best insurance salesman's smile.

"Harrumph. What's good about it?"

Harold waved his arms. "It's a sunny day, and we're alive."

The woman stared at him. "Are you nuts? Say, I don't recognize you."

"My name's Harold McCaffrey. And yours?"

She picked up another piece of chocolate. "Betty Buchanan. What are you doing here?"

"I'm in Alice Jones's apartment."

Betty flinched. "How come?"

"It's only temporary. Probably only two nights or so. Did you know Alice?"

"The pill lady. I understand she bit the dust. Why are you in her room?"

Harold remembered the problem he had caused the night before by mentioning he had come from the Back Wing so decided to use the ploy he'd tried with the man he'd met. "I'm her cousin."

The woman squinted at Harold. "You don't look anything like her."

"Cousins by marriage."

The elevator arrived, and they both entered. Harold decided he'd try again to get some more information about Alice. "You called her the pill lady. Why did you use that phrase?"

"Your cousin had more pills than a rabid dog has slobber. Always taking them and yammering to everyone how close to death she was. Apparently, it finally happened."

"Did she have any enemies?"

"Nah, nobody liked her very much, but I can't say we hated her. Too bad she didn't mention anything but her ailments. I think she took pride in being a sicky. You aren't a pill popper yourself, are you?"

"Nope. I avoid doctors and medication as much as possible."

"A good policy."

The door opened. Rather than getting out, Betty said. "Whoops. I forgot my comb. I better go back up to my room."

Harold inched past her. "Nice meeting you, Betty."

She only snorted.

Harold left the elevator, and the door closed. Another surly resident of the Front Wing. One of the reasons he preferred the Back Wing—more friendly residents there.

Harold entered the dining area and spotted Ned Fister sitting by himself and shoveling oatmeal into his mouth.

Ned looked up as Harold approached. "Ah, company. Plunk your behind down and join me in this gourmet meal. What have you been up to?"

Harold lowered his aging body into the chair. "I've come over to the dark side. I'm a temporary resident of the Front Wing."

"Why'd you go and do that? You nuts?"

"No choice. There was a little accident in my room last night, and I needed a new place to stay for a while. I'm in the room that Alice Jones used to reside in."

"No kidding. The dead lady. That creep you out?"

"No. I didn't find any ghosts floating around the room."

"You're probably immune anyway if you've been living in the Back Wing."

Harold nodded his agreement. He was used to bats and other strange creatures.

Ned speared a piece of sausage with his fork. "I heard there's going to be a little service for Alice after lunch this afternoon. You attending?"

"Hadn't heard about it but will try to get there."

"One o'clock in the Front Wing lounge. I'm in charge of putting together a bouquet of flowers."

"Won't that destroy your garden?"

"Nah. I'll selectively pick some flowers. They won't be missed. It's also the end of the season so they won't last much longer anyway. I'll supplement what's there with a trip to the florist this morning."

Harold ate scrambled eggs, bacon and toast, and once filled, dropped his napkin on the table. He prepared to leave the dining room when the four women bridge players at their breakfast table began to shriek.

"What's the hubbub?" Ned asked.

More screaming came from around the room. Several women stood up on their chairs. A woman at the nearest table pointed and shouted, "Get those things out of here."

51

Harold looked at the floor and saw hundreds of baby frogs hopping around. The wait staff came running over with brooms and dustpans. They swept the frogs up, but most of them hopped out of the dustpans. One landed on a table. A woman jumped and knocked the table over as plates and silverware clattered to the floor. People raced for the door as fast as their old legs and walking-assistance devices could carry them. The woman from the elevator, Betty Buchanan, set a record for the fastest walker exit Harold had ever seen.

"Why all the ruckus?" Ned asked. "I think they're kind of cute. I see those in the garden all the time."

"Some people don't appreciate wildlife."

"I wonder where they came from?"

Harold knew but didn't want to discuss what had started as tadpoles in Warty's punch. "Maybe we'll have a plague of locusts next."

"Hope not. Those would eat my flowers. Frogs don't cause a problem. They need to find a home in a pond somewhere."

Harold and Ned watched as the wait staff succeeded in sweeping the frogs out the door.

"This place will be hopping for days," Harold said.

"Should be entertaining," Ned replied. "Maybe we'll have frogs' legs for dinner in the near future. Well, back to the garden for me."

Harold and Ned left the dining room and took the stairs to the lobby level. Ned headed out to the garden, and Harold stopped to chat with Andrea at the reception desk. "I think I found the missing waiting list copy."

"Oh, good. Where was it?"

"In Alice Jones's room."

Andrea bit her lip. "That doesn't make any sense. I left it in Mr. Lemieux's office."

"I know. It's strange. Did you happen to notice anything unusual right before Alice Jones died in the lobby?"

"It was really busy. I didn't pay too much attention. The detective asked me the same question."

"Sometimes you recall things later. Try to visualize exactly what transpired."

Andrea closed her eyes and then popped them open. "One thing. I saw her reach in her purse, pull out a bottle and take a pill."

"That's worth mentioning to Detective Deavers. I left a message for him. I'm expecting him to stop by this morning."

Her eyes lit up. "He arrived a few minutes ago. He went to Mr. Lemieux's office. You should be able to find him there."

Harold thanked Andrea. Rather than an after breakfast stroll, he headed to Peter's office and found the detective there. Harold stuck his head in the office. "Detective Deavers, I'd like a word with you when you're done."

"Be right with you."

Harold waited outside the office, and shortly, Deavers joined him. "Interesting message you left last night, Mr. McCaffrey."

"Yeah. Let's go up to my temporary apartment, and I'll show you what I found."

As they waited for the elevator, Deavers asked, "Your message mentioned a waiting list."

"Yes. I had been in charge of manning a table at the open house yesterday. I watched over people signing a waiting list to become residents here."

"Mr. Lemieux indicated that he couldn't find a copy of this list."

"The receptionist, Andrea, said she left it for him, but it disappeared. I think it's somehow linked to the death of Alice Jones."

"Why'd you reach that conclusion?"

"A gut feeling. I found a copy of the list in Alice's room. I can't explain how it ended up there. The other thing I've learned is that Alice was a medicine fanatic. She had all kinds of pills in her room and told everybody her medical problems. There's a chance that her death might be tied to improper medication somehow. You'll want to check with Andrea. She saw Alice take a pill shortly before she died."

"The ME will be running a toxicology test. We'll see what shows up."

After the interminable wait by the green door, they reached the fifth floor, and Harold led Deavers into room five-fourteen. "I found the copy of the waiting list on the bookshelf here. It will have my fingerprints on it because I picked it up. You can check for other prints as well."

Harold stepped over to the kitchenette counter where he had left the waiting list. It was gone.

# CHAPTER THIRTEEN 🦇

Detective Deavers pointed to the empty kitchenette counter top. "You're sure you left the waiting list copy here?"

"Absolutely." Harold put his hand to his forehead. "I'm not getting senile. It was on the counter when I went down to breakfast."

Deavers's cell phone rang, and he stepped away from Harold to take the call. "Right away." He stashed his phone. "I have an emergency to take care of. When I get back, let's track down another copy of this waiting list."

Harold gulped. "I'll see what I can do."

Deavers strode out of the room, and Harold immediately began searching for the missing waiting list. Wondering if it might have blown off the counter when he left for breakfast, he checked the kitchenette floor and all over the living room. Nowhere in sight. Had someone been in this room? He had left the door locked.

Not wanting to be in this apartment another minute, Harold raced down the stairs and dashed through the lobby. He figured he could enjoy a little sunshine and think over the events of the last day.

He headed along a social trail that skirted the retirement home property, and kicked a pebble to the side. What had happened to Alice Jones and where had the missing waiting list gone to? The medical examiner and police would take care of the first question, but Harold couldn't figure out the answer to the second. Someone had entered the apartment between the time Harold left for breakfast and when he returned with Detective Deavers. He had found no signs of a forced entry so someone had unlocked the door. He remembered the sounds during the night. Had someone tried to get into the room then? One other question occurred to him. What had happened to Alice's key?

Had whoever invaded the apartment taken it? He'd ask Deavers the next time he saw him. The other possibility was that someone on the staff had entered the room. Did Peter Lemieux have a problem with an employee misusing a master key? He'd have to ask him. Several avenues to pursue.

With no immediate answers, Harold walked for an hour. He came to a spot where the trail crossed a ravine with water still trickling from the last rain storm. Looking carefully at the mud, he spotted the hoof marks of deer. They roamed all through the foothills and had multiplied. Next, there would be a rash of mountain lion sightings as the predators pursued the plentiful prey in the area. Harold shivered. It made him think of someone sneaking into his temporary room.

He retraced his steps, and when he reached the building, he had no desire to return to Alice's room. Instead, he headed up the red elevator to the fourth floor. One person he wanted to see — Bella.

Realizing it was early for her, he bit his lip and knocked. He heard a rustling sound inside and the door opened.

"Good, you're up," Harold said.

"Yes. I got going early this morning. Come on in."

They settled in her living room. Harold looked around at the eclectic decorations. A number of interesting vines and bulbs hung from hooks in her kitchenette. A large black kettle rested on a hotplate. A photograph of Stonehenge and several other pictures of wooded scenes graced the walls.

"How are your new accommodations?" Bella asked.

"All right, I guess. The people in the Front Wing are as friendly as wolverines, and some strange things occurred."

Bella arched an eyebrow. "Oh?"

"I think someone might have tried to get into my room last night."

"And not going through the walls, I trust."

"No. The conventional way. Opening the door. But I don't know who or how the person obtained a key. I discovered a copy of the waiting list in Alice Jones's bookshelf. I brought Detective Deavers up to the room this morning to show it to him, but the list had disappeared."

"So someone is definitely getting into the apartment. Interesting. That must make you feel uncomfortable being there."

56

"Exactly."

"On another subject, I have a project for us this afternoon. I arranged for you and me to help in the office. That way we can check the original waiting list."

"There's another event I want to go to. The administration is holding a service for Alice at one this afternoon. You want to join me?"

"Sure. We might pick up some suspicious behavior. Besides, my presence will make some of the Front Wingers uncomfortable. No sense wasting the opportunity. We'll go to the ceremony and afterwards do our volunteer and snooping work."

\*\*\*\*\*

After lunch, Harold retrieved Bella, and they entered the Front Wing lounge where rows of chairs had been set up. One couch looked out of place. Harold went over and said, "Alexandra, is that you?"

A whispered reply, "Bella said I should come spy."

Harold looked up at the ceiling. He spotted a bat on a beam. Bella had marshaled the troops.

Bella and Harold took seats next to Ned Fister in the last row so they would be able to watch the other attendees.

A lectern and microphone had been set up in the front of the room. Two vases held a collection of yellow, pink and white flowers.

Harold leaned toward Ned. "Your flowers look great."

"Yep. I put together a good collection including Creeping Baby's Breath, Shasta Daisies, Beard Tongue, Sun Roses and Yarrow."

People began to file in and take seats. At exactly one, a woman sat down at the piano and played *Amazing Grace*.

When she finished, Peter Lemieux strode to the lectern and leaned toward the microphone. He tapped it once and began. "Thank you all for coming. It's a sad occasion when one of our own passes away, but it's important for us to acknowledge someone who was a member of our community. We will miss Alice Jones, and I know several of you have expressed a desire to pay her a final tribute. Although a recent addition to Mountain Splendor, Alice made a number of friends here. She will be remembered. Who would like to say a few words?"

The man Harold had spoken with last night stood, limped up to the lectern and took the microphone. "I was on the same floor with Alice. Although she took too many pills, she didn't cause any problems."

A woman who Harold didn't recognize was next. The bottom line of her tribute, "Not a mean bone in her body."

Harold looked around the room again. No sign of Detective Deavers. He must be tied up with his emergency.

One of the maids took the microphone and mentioned that Alice left candy for the housekeepers. A man said she was friendly to the wait staff.

Harold whispered to Bella, "All positive but kind of innocuous. Although people seemed to like her, no one has said anything very personal about her."

"Maybe she didn't share much."

Harold thought that was possible. From what he had read in her diary, her activities and thoughts were pretty mundane. But, of course, if he had kept a diary, his comments would have been very similar in the last several years—that is, until he moved into the Back Wing.

The two women Harold had talked to, Betty Buchanan and the one he had scared, didn't step forward to say anything.

Peter made some final remarks to the effect that he appreciated everyone attending, the pianist played her rendition of *Morning Has Broken*, and people filed out of the room.

Ned said he would go do some more gardening, and Harold and Bella remained seated until everyone had left. The bat flapped down to the floor and transformed into Pamela Quint. The couch changed into Alexandra Hooper, and she strolled over to join them.

"Any observations?" Harold asked the group.

Pamela cupped a hand to her ear. "Whadya say?"

"Turn up your hearing aids," Bella shouted.

Pamela tweaked the devices in her ears. "That's better."

"We were discussing if you had any observations on the group attending the memorial service."

Pamela stretched her arms. "Lots of hair I'd love to mess up. Nothing else."

Alexandra waved her hand. "Ooh. Ooh. I noticed one man with a big tush."

"That's not helpful," Bella said. "I didn't pick up any clues, but I wouldn't trust these Front Wing people."

"You think one of them could have done something to Alice?" Alexandra asked.

"It's possible. Let's see if Harold and I can learn anything from our office work. It's time to do our civic duty... and snoop."

# CHAPTER FOURTEEN 🦇

Harold and Bella spent an hour helping the office manager catch up on sorting correspondence and filing reports. Once they completed the initial wave of work, Bella motioned toward one of the cabinets. "That's where the waiting list and applications from yesterday should be stored. What do you say we have a little peek?"

"Can't argue with that," Harold said.

Bella wiggled her nose. The drawer opened, and a manila folder flew into her hand. "Imagine that. Here's exactly what we want to see." She set it down on a desk.

Harold reached over and opened the folder. The waiting list original rested on top. He grabbed it and stepped over to the copier to make two copies. "I'll keep one and give the other to Detective Deavers when he next shows up."

"As long as we're here, let's take a look at the application forms," Bella said. "First on the list, Henrietta Yates."

They read through and found a very innocuous set of information — age seventy-seven, widow, two grown children living in California, work experience as a clerk in a hardware store for thirty years, hobbies knitting and scrapbooking.

Next, Frederick Jorgenson. Age seventy-six, widower, no children, retired chiropractor, hobbies included tennis, hiking and stamp collecting.

"So far nothing suspicious," Bella said. "I suppose Detective Deavers can do a background check on these people."

Harold picked up the application for Edgar Fontaine, retired dentist, age eighty-one, widower, avid hiker, president of the Senior Sneaker hiking club. "I remember him from the open house. He also

60

tells dumb jokes."

"He'd fit right in around here." Bella cleared her throat and read out loud, "Here we have Celia Barns, two grown children and four grandchildren on the East Coast, retired actress, age eighty-two."

Harold rolled his eyes. "She *acted* like she was still in her twenties."

"Maybe we can fix her up with Edgar Fontaine. She can act young, and he can entertain her with his jokes."

Harold leaned over Bella's shoulder to continue to read Celia's application. "It looks like they know each other. She's also a member of the Senior Sneakers hiking club."

He picked up the next application. "Duncan Haverson, retired engineer, age seventy-nine. I remember he had a very precise signature. The consummate engineer. Hmm. A pattern here. Another hiker. I wonder if this whole hiking club decided to move to Mountain Splendor."

Bella waved the next form. "And on to Phoebe Mellencourt— eighty, retired secretary."

"She wore a red hat at the open house and asked a question about the food here."

Bella tapped the application. "A subject on which, given that I don't eat in the dining room, I wouldn't have an opinion."

"It's not bad, actually. Phoebe didn't list any hobbies on the application form so don't know if she's connected with the hiking club."

Bella raised another application. "And here we have Gertrude Ash, eighty-three, worked in the non-profit world, no hobbies mentioned. Maybe she can replace us as volunteers when we burn out." Bella leafed through two remaining applications. "Here's an interesting one: Cassandra Lemieux. Same last name as Peter's. Doesn't list an age or previous occupation."

Harold stared at the waiting list. "Not someone who signed up at the open house. I'll have to ask Peter."

"And one final one. Bartholomew Sampson. Again little information. But someone wrote in pen, 'Back Wing.'"

"Also not on the waiting list. Peter must have a separate list for the Back Wing, since the open house was geared toward Front Wing residents."

Having reached the end of the applicant file, Harold took all the applications to run copies to give to Detective Deavers, and they returned the originals to the manila folder and stashed it back in the file cabinet.

The office manager gave them several more assignments and at four thirty indicated that they could call it quits.

Bella decided to head to the Back Wing, but Harold said he wanted to speak with Peter Lemieux.

Peter was on the phone when Harold stuck his head inside the office, but Peter waved him in and pointed toward a chair, so Harold sat down to listen to one side of a conversation concerning ovens.

After Peter hung up, Harold asked, "Renovating the kitchen?"

"The head of food services has a bid out for replacement ovens. He asked me to speak to one of the bidders. What brings you here?"

"I want to give you an update on several items. I had a conversation with Detective Deavers and want to make sure you're aware of it. I encountered something strange. I found a copy of the waiting list from the open house hidden in a bookshelf in Alice Jones's apartment. I thought it might relate to her suspicious death and tried to give it to Deavers, but between the time I went down to breakfast and when I brought Deavers up to the room afterwards, it disappeared."

Peter chuckled. "Something that might happen in the Back Wing."

"Possibly. Someone must have come into the apartment while I went to breakfast. I want to bring it to your attention in the unlikely chance that someone on the staff used a master key to get into the room."

Peter bit his lip. "We've done a careful job of screening employees. I hope it wasn't one of our people."

"I'm not accusing anyone on the staff, but someone has a key to Alice's room. The other possibility is that someone took Alice's key. I'll mention that to Deavers when I next talk with him."

Peter nodded his concurrence. "I have a piece of news for you. Maintenance completed painting your apartment. You can move back tomorrow morning."

"That's good. I look forward to returning to the Back Wing."

Peter tsked. "You're the only person in the Front Wing who would say that."

"I like the people better in the Back Wing. They're real, not the stuffed shirts living in the Front Wing." Harold snapped his fingers. "One other thing. When Bella and I worked in the office this afternoon, we came across an application for a Cassandra Lemieux. Any relation?"

Peter's eyes lit up. "That's my mom. She's interested in moving in here."

"That explains it, but I didn't meet her at the open house, and she didn't sign the waiting list."

"That's because she'll become a resident of the Back Wing."

Harold blinked. "Like I did, or does she have some special power?"

"She has one unique attribute that qualifies her for the Back Wing, but I won't get into that at the moment. Needless to say, she'll be moving in tomorrow."

"I thought we didn't have any Back Wing openings."

"A Back Wing resident left today who… uh… made a quick decision to visit Eastern Europe for an extended period of time. We've had a separate list of people interested in the Back Wing. My mom is first on the list with Bartholomew Sampson next. My mom is so anxious to move in that she didn't want the apartment repainted, so she'll be here in the morning. I hope you'll welcome her."

Harold wondered what Cassandra's special power was, but since Peter didn't want to elaborate, he'd have to wait to find out. "Be happy to. Bella and I will make sure she meets everyone in the Back Wing."

Peter let out a sigh. "Thanks. She should fit in well."

A thought pulsed though Harold's mind. "You don't seem to exhibit any special powers, but you indicate your mom does. How come?"

"My dad was as normal as you, Harold. My sister inherited a streak from my mom, but I took after my dad."

"And with the family connection, is that why you've been so understanding of the Back Wing lifestyle?"

Peter gave a sheepish grin. "Busted."

"You've done a great job turning around this place, and there's nothing wrong with finding a residence for your mother. I look forward to meeting her."

# CHAPTER FIFTEEN 🦇

Harold returned to his temporary apartment and hid the copies of the waiting list and applications in a kitchenette drawer under a dishcloth. Then he phoned Detective Deavers. The call cut over to voicemail. "Detective, this is Harold McCaffrey. I located the master waiting list this afternoon and made a copy for you. Let me know when you can stop by so I can give it to you. I also have copies of the applications from those people and two others who may become residents in the future." He left the phone number of Alice's apartment.

It surprised him that Detective Deavers hadn't stopped by again today. Harold would have thought that the suspicious death would be a top priority for him. Oh, well. The police had their way and timing for dealing with these things.

Harold scanned Alice's apartment again. Nothing out of order. Whoever had taken the waiting list hadn't ransacked the place. His gut tensed at the thought that someone had a key and had invaded his space, temporary as it might be. And twice. Once to hide the list in the book on the shelf and the second time to remove the list from the kitchenette counter. Very weird.

Harold picked up his book to read, checking his watch every fifteen minutes. He finally threw it down, realizing that he couldn't concentrate. He'd head down for dinner on the early side.

In the hallway he encountered Betty Buchanan, moving toward the elevator with her walker.

"Good evening," Harold said.

"You again."

"Nice to see you, too." Harold gave his professional smile.

"Can't say it's mutual."

Harold scowled. He didn't like rude people. "I don't know what's eating you, but I was taught to be friendly to my neighbors."

Betty didn't even look toward Harold but kept plodding toward the elevator. "You don't belong here. I don't consider you a neighbor."

"Did you consider Alice Jones a neighbor?"

Betty reached the elevator and punched the down button. "Not much of one. She kept to herself."

"Ever been in her room?"

Betty turned and squinted at Harold. "What do you mean by that?"

"If you live on the same floor, I'd think you'd visit each other."

"No way. I don't invite people in and don't go snooping in other people's apartments."

The elevator arrived and Betty pushed herself inside. Harold decided to take the stairs. He'd had enough of unfriendly people. As he descended the stairs, he realized Betty had never directly answered if she'd been in Alice's room. And the comment about not *snooping*. Strange word to use.

Harold entered the dining room, sat and received a plate of ham, scalloped potatoes and peas from the waiter, a young man with short-cropped blond hair. "Here you go, Mr. McCaffrey. Have a good dinner."

"Thanks."

The wait staff was friendly here, not like the Front Wing residents.

Harold cut off a piece of ham and ate it. Not bad. He tried to avoid salty food, but once in a while it was okay. No Ned Fister in sight, but Harold had arrived right after food service began. Ned probably had to clean up after an afternoon in the garden. Harold had done yard work for years but lost interest when his wife died. He had lost interest in everything at that point. Good thing he'd ended up in the Back Wing. That had definitely revived him.

He had almost finished his meal when Ned entered the dining room and made a beeline toward Harold.

Harold waved a fork at him. "About time you arrived."

"Hey, some of us have work to do, not sit on my backside all day staring at the ceiling. I had to fight the aphids, not laze around like you, Harold."

"I'll have you know I did my civic duty and helped out in the office today. I'm amazed I survived all the paper cuts."

Ned chuckled. "Can't be as bad as getting scraped by rocks in the garden and bitten by ants."

"Okay. We're both heroes. Tell me what you did today. Any more seven in one blow experiences?"

"Nah. Today it was the dang ants. I had to get rid of a colony that decided to take over near a lilac bush. Couldn't let that happen without a fight." Ned picked up his knife and fork and dove into the plate that had been delivered by the waiter.

Harold took a sip of water and put the glass down. "I had a strange thing happen after breakfast. I discovered someone had snuck into my temporary room while I was down here jawing with you."

"No kidding? Steal some of your stuff?"

"No. I didn't take anything of value into my interim digs. But I had found a copy of the waiting list from the open house yesterday. That disappeared."

"Sure you didn't misplace it?"

"You sound like Detective Deavers. The answer is I left it on the kitchenette counter, and it walked away."

"Wouldn't put it past some of these Front Wingers. If it isn't nailed down, the sticky fingers will commandeer it."

"But someone had to get into the apartment. I left it locked."

"Hmm. That doesn't sound good. The detective investigate?"

"Not yet. He's off on some higher priority case. I hope to hear back from him soon." Having finished his meal, Harold excused himself and headed back to the fifth floor of the Front Wing.

At the elevator with the green door, Harold waited with a man and a woman he didn't know. The woman said to the man, "Can you believe that Alice Jones died? Must have been from an overdose of medicine."

"That woman could sure pack away the pills."

Harold's ears perked up. "Did both of you know Alice?"

The man crinkled his nose at Harold, and the woman gave him a withering stare. "This is a private conversation."

Harold forced a smile. "I'm not trying to interfere, but I happen to be staying in Alice's apartment for a few days."

"And why are you doing that?" the man asked.

Here we go again. Harold decided to continue with his ploy. "I'm her cousin. I came for the ceremony today. Probably be leaving tomorrow. I'll sure miss Alice."

"She was okay," the woman said.

"She have any enemies?" Harold asked.

The woman snorted. "Too mousey for that."

The man nodded. "She didn't bother people."

The elevator arrived, and they all got in. No one said anything. The other two exited on the third floor, and Harold continued up to the fifth. All he had learned thus far about Alice was that she took too many pills and didn't hassle people. No enemies uncovered yet. She might have been in the wrong place at the wrong time or had there been some nefarious motive behind her death? He didn't know. He could picture her gravestone: "Here's lies Alice Jones. She popped pills but didn't pop off at the mouth."

He definitely needed to return to the Back Wing. The Front Wing wasn't good for his mental health.

Back in Alice's apartment, Harold sat in the easy chair to read. After a page he threw his book down again. He couldn't concentrate. His mind continued to swirl with the Alice Jones affair. What had happened to her and who had taken the waiting list?

His lack of answers was interrupted by the room phone ringing. He picked up to find Detective Deavers on the line.

"You left a message for me, Mr. McCaffrey."

"That's right. I found the master of the waiting list as well as filled-out applications and made copies for you. When can you stop by?"

"You sure seem obsessed with this waiting list."

"I can't be sure, but it may tie to Alice's death. You shot out of here this morning like your mother had died. Big case?"

Deavers sighed. "Yeah. A murder. A woman's body was found near a dumpster. She had been bludgeoned."

"I guess that takes priority over the suspicious death of Alice Jones."

"Unfortunately true. I have to juggle both cases right now. But I'll see you sometime tomorrow."

Harold signed off. He didn't envy Detective Deavers. It would be a heck of a life to shift from one death to another. And to go home and have to think about these victims in off hours. Wait a minute. He was doing the same thing.

# CHAPTER SIXTEEN 🦇

The next morning, Harold overslept, unusual for him. He quickly dressed and made it down to breakfast right before the seven thirty cutoff time. Given his late arrival, he missed Ned Fister so he sat by himself as he gobbled a waffle and downed his orange juice and coffee. The wait staff had cleared off most of the tables by the time Harold left the dining room.

Harold spotted Peter Lemieux strolling through the dining room and waved him over. "Still okay if I move back into my room this morning?"

"Go for it. Everything has been fixed."

Harold's spirit soared. He could go home—to the Back Wing.

Returning to the fifth floor of the Front Wing, Harold stripped the sheets and remade the bed with fresh linen from the hall closet before he packed his stuff and double-checked to make sure he hadn't left anything. From one of the drawers of the kitchenette, he retrieved the copies of the waiting list and application forms. Good thing he hadn't left those. He thought of knocking on the doors of his temporary neighbors to say how much he had enjoyed their company—not.

He wheeled his small suitcase along the hallway, thankful that he didn't have to witness the glares of any Front Wingers. Then he completed the elevator shuffle, taking the green elevator down, transferring to the red elevator and rising to the fourth floor of the Back Wing.

After unpacking and stashing his clothes and toilet articles where they belonged, he set the waiting list and application copies on the kitchenette counter and strolled into his living room to check on the repainting. He sniffed. A faint aroma. The wall bore a fresh sheen from the new paint, and the curtain had been replaced.

His thoughts turned to the waiting list. He needed to follow up on one item. He checked his watch. After nine. Not too early to call. He moved his finger down the list and found the phone number of Edgar Fontaine.

He called and reached voice mail. "This is Harold McCaffrey. I understand you're the president of the Senior Sneakers hiking club. I'm interested in joining your group for some exercise. Please give me a call when it's convenient." After leaving his number, Harold clicked off.

He considered reading his book on witchcraft but wondered if Bella might be awake. It would be more interesting to do live research. He tapped on the wall and waited. In a few moments he heard a rustling sound, and Bella's head poked through the wall followed by the rest of her. She wore a black robe.

"Hope I didn't wake you."

She stretched her arms and yawned. "Not a problem. I went to sleep early last night. Without you here, I had no distractions."

"I'll take that as a compliment."

"Welcome home." Bella put her arms around Harold's neck and gave him a kiss.

"Wow. I could get used to a greeting like that."

"I considered putting on a welcome home party for you, but after the last debacle decided not to risk it."

"Yeah. No more parties unless Warty is prohibited from performing his so-called magic. After the snobby people in the Front Wing, it's good to be back with my people."

Bella stepped back and took Harold's hand. "Are you sure you don't really have some special powers? You fit in here so well."

"Nope. All I can conjure up are warm feelings for one special witch."

Bella put her arms around his neck again. "That's good to know. How are you enjoying the book on the history of witchcraft?"

"It's interesting. So many myths about witches are nothing more than that, myths. I like the real thing."

They were interrupted by the phone ringing.

Harold reluctantly disengaged from Bella and grabbed the phone. "Harold McCaffrey, please."

"Speaking."

"This is Edgar Fontaine. You had called to inquire about the Senior Sneakers hiking club."

"Yes. I met you during the open house at the Mountain Splendor Retirement Home. I was taking names for the waiting list."

"That's right. You were the guy sitting behind the table."

"I enjoy walking and would like to participate in your outings. How often does your hiking group meet?"

"We're a very active group of seniors. We often schedule up to three hikes a week. Our next one is ten a.m. on Saturday. We're going to take an easy trail up South Table Mountain. Would you care to join us?"

That's what Harold wanted to hear. He'd have a chance to talk informally with a number of the people on the waiting list. "I would like that. May I bring friends?"

"Absolutely. We welcome people of all ages. Although we're a senior group, we've had kids and younger adults join us. We often have to wait for the younger people, though." He chuckled. "They're not in as good shape as we are."

*Perfect.* He would bring his grandson, Jason, along. Jason enjoyed excursions and was a good observer. "Give me directions to the meeting place."

After hearing how to find the trailhead, Harold signed off.

Bella arched an eyebrow. "What did you line up?"

"With this connection to the waiting list and since there are several people on the list who belong to a senior hiking club, I inquired and found out I could go on one of their hikes. Would you like to join me?"

Bella frowned. "I don't usually enjoy Front Wing types."

"This will be a chance to do a little snooping. I know you enjoy that."

"If you put it that way, how can I possibly resist? And besides, I need to keep my figure trim."

Harold waggled his eyebrows. "And I must say you're doing a good job."

"Okay if I ask Bailey? She could use some exercise."

"Edgar Fontaine said they welcome any new people, although he might be a little surprised with you and Bailey. Also, Jason will be here for the weekend, so we'll make it a foursome. Jason likes both you and Bailey."

"Sounds good. But something I don't understand—your obsession with the waiting list."

Harold grinned. "You sound like Detective Deavers. It's my intuition acting up. The timing of Alice's death after the open house, the disappearance of the waiting list left for Peter and it turning up in Alice's apartment and then disappearing again. Something's fishy." He held out his open hand. "Therefore, I figured it was time to learn more about the people on the waiting list, and as we discovered yesterday, a number of them hike together. Simple as that."

"I've learned that nothing is simple when *you* start looking into it. But I'm game for an expedition. I hope it isn't too early in the morning."

"If you got going by a little after nine today, you should be able to make ten on Saturday. But stay away from late night coven activity Friday night."

"Nothing scheduled until the end of October."

"Will you invite me to one of your ceremonies?"

Bella wagged her finger at Harold. "You're as bad as Jason. When he was here during the summer, he pestered me to take him to a coven gathering."

"If we bring you along on hikes to mingle with our kind who lack special powers, you can reciprocate. I'm reading the book you gave me and want to know as much about your lifestyle as I can."

"We'll see."

"I'll take that as a definite maybe. Let's go see if Bailey will join us on Saturday."

Bella checked her watch. "She won't be up yet. I'll speak with her this evening. She bought a new Thermos yesterday and will want to bring it along for her… uh… liquid refreshment."

# CHAPTER SEVENTEEN

Harold puttered around his apartment during the morning, glad to be back in the Back Wing and out of the clutches of the churlish people in the Front Wing. What a contrast. Maybe some of the people on the waiting list would be friendlier. Those he talked to at the open house had yet to be tainted with the Front Wing stamp of scorn. The waiting list. He went into the kitchenette and removed it and the applications. He scanned the names again. Could one of these people be somehow tied to the murder of Alice Jones? Harold had no definite reason to think so, but he couldn't rid his mind of the idea that somehow this list provided a connection to the suspicious death. Once Detective Deavers showed up and had some time from his priority interruption, they could discuss Harold's theory. Theory. That's all it was so far. He dropped the sheets on the kitchenette counter.

Harold paced around his room before settling into his easy chair to read a chapter on the history of witchcraft. He realized Bella came from a long line of very unique people. All the hubbub over warty-nosed, green-faced women in pointy hats with broomsticks. The reality as described in this book appeared very different. Sure, there were spells, incantations and brews, but many witches were expert herbologists. They came from a tradition of cures, not only curses. At first he couldn't picture Bella putting a curse on someone, but he remembered what she had previously done. Her curses were reserved for serious miscreants, like when she had frozen Warty. The guy deserved it. And she also helped people whenever she could.

Harold's tummy rumbled, so he went to his refrigerator to help himself to some fruit. He bit into a crisp Gala apple. An apple a day keeps the warlocks away. He hoped he'd never have to deal with Warty coming to his apartment again. The guy tried, but his magic could only be described as hopeless.

Harold threw the apple core in the trash and grabbed a banana, which he quickly chomped through. He patted his stomach. He had consumed a healthy mid-morning snack that would tide him over until lunch.

Before he could return to his reading, the doorbell rang, and Harold moseyed over to find Detective Deavers standing there.

"I had to search for you," Deavers said. "You weren't in that room we went to yesterday."

"Nope. I'm back from exile. Have a seat. Can I get you coffee, tea, water or a soft drink?"

Deavers waved away the offer with a flick of the wrist and dropped heavily onto the couch.

Harold sank into his easy chair. "You've become a busy fellow with a murder as well as the suspicious death of Alice Jones. Quiet little Golden has become the crime capital of Colorado."

"Things seem to go in cycles. We had this wave of crime during the summer that you're familiar with and then nothing until this week. Now all hell has broken loose again. And some of it centered around Mountain Splendor."

"And usually senior citizens are the calm, law-abiding types."

"That's what I used to think." Deavers's lips curled slightly. "That is until I met you and your cohorts."

"Hey, I don't cause crimes. I only try to help solve them in my small way."

"So, let's get to this phone message you left me. Tell me what's on your mind, Mr. McCaffrey."

Harold tapped the table where his book rested. "I spent two nights in Alice Jones's room, out of necessity because of some accidental damage to this apartment. As I told you before, I discovered a copy of the waiting list compiled during an open house two days ago. A copy of this same list had been left for Peter Lemieux by Andrea, the receptionist. Peter never found the copy, and I suspect the one I discovered in Alice's apartment was that same copy. Later it disappeared between the time I left the apartment and when I tried to show it to you."

"Yeah, we've been over this before."

Harold held up his hand. "Bear with me for a moment. I want to set the stage for you, that's all. Anyway, I'm concerned that someone has a key to Alice's room and used it to sneak in when I was down at breakfast yesterday and that they took the waiting list I left in Alice's apartment. Peter Lemieux doesn't think it could have been done by an employee. By the way, did you find Alice's room key in her purse?"

Deavers blinked. "Interesting question, but we did find her key."

Harold sagged as if air had been let out of a balloon. So much for that part of his theory. "Someone must have obtained a master key. It could have been a member of the staff or the result of a theft."

"I'll take that into consideration. Let's revisit your obsession with this waiting list. What leads to your suspicion?"

Harold considered how he wanted to address this subject. Time to wade into the pool. "Bear in mind this is only my own opinion without any supporting proof. I find the timing very suspicious that right after the open house, Alice is found dead. If she didn't die of natural causes, her death might have been caused by one of the visitors that afternoon. I happened to be manning the table when people signed up for the waiting list during the open house that afternoon. There may be some connection, particularly since strange things happened to a copy of that list afterwards."

"Pretty flimsy connection."

Harold bit his lip for a moment and continued. "I grant you that, but since I believe you don't yet know who might have contributed to Alice's death, it gives you another avenue to pursue."

Deavers's cell phone buzzed, and he grabbed it out of his pocket. "Yeah... okay... I'll be there shortly." He snapped it shut and stood.

"Another emergency?"

"The Chief wants me back at headquarters. He has a task force meeting about the recent murder."

Harold raised himself out of his chair. "Before you leave, let me give you the copy of the waiting list for the Front Wing I made for you. You might want to run background checks on these people. I also made copies of the applications, which include two other people who are waiting to become residents of the Back Wing."

"What is this, a two class facility?"

"Usually people prefer one wing over the other. The open house was only for prospective residents of the Front Wing. The other two people signed up separately for the Back Wing. Peter Lemieux tries to accommodate potential residents' preferences on which location to live in."

"The rooms and surroundings don't seem that different to me," Deavers said.

Harold decided not to pursue that line of discussion on the differences between the two wings. Instead, he strode over to the kitchenette counter, grabbed the collection of papers and handed them to Deavers.

Deavers crinkled his nose as if he had been handed something stale and unseemly.

"Don't look that way, Detective. This might be useful."

"Yeah." Deavers glanced down at the top sheet and did a double take. "You've got to be kidding me."

"What is it?"

Deavers waved the papers in his hand. "The first name on this waiting list is Henrietta Yates."

"That's right."

"Do you know who she is?"

Harold nodded. "Sure. I met her at the open house. A short, skinny woman who wore tennis shoes. Nothing really distinctive. She's eager to become a resident of the Front Wing here at Mountain Splendor. Practically beat a speed record to be the first person in line to sign up for the waiting list."

Deavers turned a steely stare on Harold. "She's also the murder victim who was bludgeoned to death yesterday."

# CHAPTER EIGHTEEN

After Deavers left, Harold sat in his easy chair digesting this latest piece of information. A second death connected to the waiting list for the Front Wing. How did this all play together? He reviewed what he knew. Alice Jones found dead in the lobby. Deavers had shared nothing specific yet as to whether her death was the result of a murder or an accident or natural causes. But Henrietta Yates had definitely been murdered. The first person on the waiting list. Harold went over to look at the copy of the waiting list he had retained. Next person in line, Frederick Jorgenson. The detective had indicated he would be contacting Jorgenson. Deavers was taking Harold's hypothesis seriously.

Harold shivered. He wouldn't want to have his name on that list. Nothing he could prove, but the connection between crimes and the Front Wing waiting list definitely appeared suspicious.

He was saved by the bell when his room phone rang. He picked up to be greeted by Peter Lemieux. "I have a favor to ask, Harold."

"As long as it doesn't entail signing people up for another waiting list."

"No, nothing like that. My mom has arrived. I thought you might join us for lunch in the dining room. Afterwards, if it's not too much to ask, could you show her around the Back Wing, you know, kind of take her under your wing, so to speak. You're one of the few residents of the Back Wing who comes to the dining room and are up at this time of day."

"Be happy to."

"Good. We'll see you there at eleven thirty."

*****

After another unsuccessful attempt to read and not wanting to turn on the television, Harold resisted the urge to take a nap but finally roused himself from his chair and moseyed down to the dining room, taking the stairs to stretch his legs.

He spotted Peter sitting with an attractive older woman at a four-person table. He joined them and after introductions, Cassandra Lemieux put her hand on Harold's wrist and looked in his eyes. "Do tell me your life story."

Harold shrugged. "Pretty basic. I sold life insurance, lived in Denver, my wife died, and I came here."

Cassandra smiled. "A man of few words."

"Don't let him fool you, Mom. He can ask some pretty tough questions. We had a little situation this summer with two women going missing. Harold helped the police solve the case."

"Sounds like a good story." Cassandra grabbed Harold's hand and squeezed.

He gulped. She was a good-looking woman. He wouldn't want Bella to see them together and get the wrong impression.

Cassandra laughed. "I can see you're uncomfortable. I'm a touch type of person. I can sense that you have a lady friend. I'm not going to interfere in any way."

"She's always been that way," Peter said. "Picking up cues. She knew when I did something wrong. The proverbial eyes in the back of her head. I could never put anything over on her when I was a kid."

"Nor now either." Cassandra graced Harold with a demure smile.

Harold coughed and cleared his throat. "Thanks for what you said, Cassandra. I do have a girlfriend, named Bella Alred. I'll introduce you two this afternoon."

Cassandra gave Harold's hand one more squeeze and released it. "I look forward to it. She's a lucky woman."

Harold wondered what Cassandra's special power might be, other than intuition. He didn't feel this was the time to inquire. Instead he asked, "Tell me about yourself."

"Like you, it's pretty basic. "I married Peter's father right out of high school. We had Peter and his two sisters bing, bang, boom. My husband was a physicist, and I became a stay at home mom."

"Not exactly stay at home," Peter interjected. "She ran the PTA, coached soccer, directed a children's choir group and joined the school board."

Cassandra flicked her wrist. "Oh posh. Only things to stay involved with my kids' activities and interests. After Peter's father died, I traveled and then was elected to the city council. When I became term limited, I decided to come here to keep an eye on Peter." She winked.

"I thought I was keeping an eye on you, Mom."

"Whatever. Tell me what I should know about this Back Wing."

*****

After lunch, Peter excused himself to attend a staff meeting, and Harold offered to give Cassandra a tour of the Back Wing.

"I take it that your husband didn't have any special powers," Harold said as they stopped at the Back Wing lounge, unoccupied as was typical for daylight hours.

"That's right, and Peter inherited his lack of unusual abilities."

"And your special power?"

"Quite simple. I can time travel back up to an hour but no more." She gave a sly grin. "That's why I'm intuitive. I asked you a lot of questions the first time I had lunch with you and Peter. Then I went back an hour and changed the situation slightly without having to ask the questions."

Harold scratched his head. "Doesn't that do something weird to the space-time continuum, as they say in science fiction movies?"

"Nope. We proceed with the new path, and the old one disappears into universal dust."

"But you could change history that way."

"Minor history. It's like a governor or speed limiter on a car. I can make miniscule mischief and only where I am. Nothing big time like killing someone or preventing a murder in another place."

"Too bad. We could use your talent around here. There's been a suspicious death and a murder possibly linked to Mountain Splendor."

Cassandra rubbed her hands together. "Tell me more. I love mysteries."

Harold explained what had happened to Alice Jones and Henrietta Yates.

"Interesting. That was insightful of you to first identify the waiting list. Maybe you do have special powers after all."

"No. I think it's nothing more than my suspicious mind. But one more question. Why can you only change things back one hour?"

"Good question. I could never figure that out. I discussed it with my husband, and he thought it might have to do with the half-life of some radioactive material, the name of which I can never remember. As it degrades, my power dissipates. In any case, I experimented and discovered that the approximate one-hour deadline held consistently. For whatever reason, that's the way my special power works. Next, onto the subject of this Bella of yours."

Warmth rushed through Harold's chest. "She's a beautiful witch and my neighbor. She can do all kinds of magic, including freezing people who misbehave."

"I want to go meet her."

"I'm not sure she's up yet."

"Oh, I'm sure she is."

Harold regarded her askance. "You know something I don't?"

A Cheshire Cat grin appeared on her face. "Let's go see."

They took the elevator to the fourth floor and sauntered along the hallway. Harold knocked on Bella's door.

She answered, fully dressed in a slinky black gown.

"Bella, this is our new Back Wing resident, Cassandra Lemieux, Peter's mother."

"Come in. I'm brewing some of my special tea."

They entered to an aroma that Harold tried to place. He took a deep whiff and thought of meadows, fresh breezes and pine forests.

"We've met before, Bella," Cassandra said.

Bella crinkled an eyebrow and regarded her carefully. "That's strange. I don't remember you, and I have a good memory for people."

"You wouldn't remember." Cassandra regarded her watch. "I met you exactly forty-three minutes ago. My special power is that I can go back in time up to an hour."

"That's unusual," Bella said. "I've never heard of that special power before."

"Yes. It's my unique ability. I also have a confession to make. I played a little prank on both of you. The first time Harold brought me to your apartment, I pretended to be stealing Harold from you. You became very incensed and threatened to turn me into a frozen statue. I've enjoyed meeting Harold, but I can see that you're right for each other."

Harold went over and gave Bella a hug. "You'd do that for me?"

Bella returned the hug. "Of course. But if you mess around with Cassandra, I'll turn *you* into a statue." They she burst out laughing, released Harold and stepped over to take Cassandra's hands in hers. "I think we're going to become great friends."

Cassandra let out a breath. "Whew. I'm glad my prank didn't backfire. I sometimes get myself in binds by messing with my special power."

# CHAPTER NINETEEN 🦇

After an uneventful rest of the day and a lonely dinner because Ned Fister had gone to visit a nephew, Harold returned to the fourth floor of the Back Wing to find the place alive with his friends. Viola and Bella stood outside Harold's room debating the nutritional value of blood versus lotus roots. Pamela Quint flew through the hall, bouncing off the wall, as she tested different settings for her new hearing aids. Kendall Nicoletti and Tomas Greeley discussed a book they were both reading in their book club titled, *Neither Wolf Nor Dog*. And not a sign of Warty with anything that bubbled or exploded.

Bailey raced up and grabbed Harold's arm. "Don't forget. Tomorrow night you're helping us with takeout. We have to stock up for the next month."

"I haven't forgotten, and as I told you, Jason will be here, but I'm not sure we should involve him in this escapade."

"He'll provide another pair of strong arms. I like the little tyke."

"Not little. He's taller than you."

"He's drafted. We need him to join us."

"But something might happen."

Bailey crossed her heart. "I personally guarantee there will be no problem."

Harold paused. He wasn't completely convinced but knew Bailey would keep after him unless he agreed. "I guess he can join us."

"Good. Oh, there's Cassandra. What a delightful addition to the Back Wing." She waved and dashed over to speak with Peter's mother.

Cassandra hadn't wasted any time getting to know her wing mates. Quite a social butterfly.

Harold shook his head in amazement. Here he was in the middle of all this hubbub with all his new and interesting friends. He checked the hallway again. Good. No Warty in sight. Things would be safe.

He stepped over to Bella and whispered in her ear. "When you and Viola are finished, would you like to join me and take a moonlight stroll?"

"Why yes." She pivoted back toward Viola. "If you'll excuse me, Harold and I will be going outside for a while."

Viola squinted. "Who's Harold?"

"He lives in the room between us."

"Oh, yeah. The dingbat who took over our meeting room." Viola shook a fist at him. "Usurper. Stealer of all that's sacred. Violator of women's rights. You should be banned for life from the Back Wing."

Bella patted Viola's hand. "Don't get carried away. It's his apartment, and we all like Harold."

Viola poked a finger into Harold's stomach, causing him to exhale loudly. "If you say so, I guess he's okay. Kind of soft in the gut, though."

Bella grabbed Harold's arm and led him away. "We better get out of here before Viola tries to nibble on your throat. She has her false fangs in her mouth this evening. Earlier, she forgot she left them in the dish drainer. I had to help her search. She has more ways of misplacing those teeth."

As they waited for the elevator, Harold said, "Let me give you an update on Detective Deavers's investigation. The plot has thickened. The first person on the waiting list, Henrietta Yates, has been bludgeoned to death."

Bella put her hand to her mouth. "That's horrible. The poor woman. And a connection to Mountain Splendor."

"Exactly. Deavers is taking seriously my concern about the waiting list."

The elevator arrived, and they went inside. Harold continued. "Our outing on Saturday will provide a good opportunity to investigate the people on the waiting list. It's become more critical with this latest death."

Outside, they stopped at a bench near Ned Fister's neatly trimmed hedges and sat. A gentle breeze caressed a nearby pine tree causing the branches to dance. The moonlight cast shadows across the Ned-tended flowerbed. Harold never thought he'd be attracted to someone again after his wife died.

Bella took Harold's hand. "It's a beautiful night. Still warm from the heat of the day. Soon it will be getting colder."

"I love this time of year. The leaves have fallen. I dreaded doing all the raking, but once it was done, I could relax... until I had to start shoveling snow."

Bella gave his hand a squeeze. "I never had to shovel. For some reason, if I spoke nicely to the snow, it blew away from my sidewalk all by itself."

"I must have been surrounded by witches, because the snow blew from everywhere around the neighborhood and accumulated in huge mounds on my sidewalk and driveway."

"Your only problem—you didn't know how to talk to the snow."

"That's for sure. Speaking of which, there was the discussion this afternoon about turning me into a statue. I'd consider it very inappropriate if you get mad at me sometime and attempt to use your special powers against me."

Bella pulled her hand away from Harold's. "Really?"

Cassandra came running up, forming a T with her hands. "Wait. Time out. Stop this conversation."

Harold gave a start. "Huh?"

"Hello, Cassandra." Bella leveled her gaze at the interloper. "What brings you out here at this time of night?"

"I know I'm interfering, but I can't help myself. I don't want you two to get in an argument."

Bella crossed her arms. "What makes you think we'd do that?"

Harold chuckled. "Cassandra is very intuitive. And, Bella, you did have a negative reaction to my comment."

Cassandra swatted at Harold. "Don't say any more."

"Are you taking my side?" Bella asked.

"I'm taking both of your sides. You got in a big row when I found you here thirty minutes ago, and you both went stomping off. It's such a nice romantic evening that you shouldn't waste it. Maybe I shouldn't have, but I reset time so you wouldn't have the argument. So change the subject."

Bella broke into laughter. "Your special power."

"Yes. So please set aside, for the time being, any discussion of Bella's use of magic and ability to freeze people. It's too nice an evening to be in disharmony. And I don't want to have to keep coming back and resetting time. I'll be on my way. Bye." With that she gave a finger wave and flitted back toward the lobby.

Harold took Bella's hand. "If Cassandra went to all that trouble, I guess I won't pursue the subject. You okay?"

"Yeah. I got my hackles up, but I agree. We might as well take advantage of the moonlight." She rested her head on Harold's shoulder. "It's so peaceful and quiet out here, particularly since it's too early for Kendall to howl."

"I'm sure glad I moved into the Back Wing," Harold said. "And ending up with the most attractive neighbor in the whole building."

"You mean Viola?"

He gave her a nudge. "You know who I mean. If I had ended up in the Front Wing, we might never have met."

"That's true. There's so little interaction between the wings."

"Other than when you scare the bejabbers out of some of them."

"Only when they deserve it."

Harold chuckled. "Oh, they often deserve it. Too many snobs in the Front Wing. The two nights I stayed in Alice's room definitely reinforced that viewpoint. I tried to reach out to people, but the ones I met on her floor were downright hostile. And compare that to the Back Wing. Cassandra moves in today, and everyone greets and welcomes her. And here she is trying to help people."

"We all have a bond of special powers."

"I don't. You welcomed me and have been friendly toward me."

"You're special, so to speak. Your special power includes accepting people from all walks of life."

"It also served me well as an insurance salesmen. A lot of people reacted negatively to my occupation. Eventually, I succeeded because of my willingness to reach out to people without being pushy. It had to be the right combination of persistence and truly liking people."

"Your special power."

Harold shrugged. "That's the way my parents brought me up."

"Now enough talk. Let's not waste the moonlight." Bella turned her head, and their lips met.

# CHAPTER TWENTY

On Friday afternoon at 4:10, Harold's doorbell jangled. He stashed his book on witchcraft face down so it wouldn't attract any comment from his son, Nelson, or daughter-in-law, Emily, and leaped up to answer. They stood there along with his grandson, Jason. "About time you got here."

"We ran into a lot of traffic." Nelson regarded his watch. "I hope we can get on I-70 before the real crunch."

"I don't envy your drive," Harold said.

"It will be worth it. Emily and I will be soaking in the hot pools at Glenwood Springs all day tomorrow and Sunday morning."

Jason stepped forward, holding a duffle bag. "Are all my friends still living here?"

"You bet. They're looking forward to seeing you after dinner tonight."

"Friends?" Emily asked.

"Yeah, cool people."

Harold winked at Jason. "He made quite an impression on my fellow residents when he stayed here during the summer."

Nelson arched an eyebrow. "I can't understand it. We told Jason he could come with us to Glenwood Springs, but he said he'd rather come visit you."

Harold held his open hands out. "Hey, what do you expect? Things really rock around old people."

Nelson coughed. "Don't overplay it, Dad."

"Grandpa's right," Jason said. "His friends have so much going on here. Much better than sitting in boring pools."

"You used to like going down the slides." A wistful expression crossed Emily's face.

"That's okay, Mom. When I went to Waterworld in August, I had a chance to go on plenty of waterslides."

"Besides," Harold added, "it will give the two of you some time together."

Nelson's and Emily's eyes met. Harold decided this weekend would be a win-win for all involved.

"Now get out of here." Harold waved toward the door. "My grandson and I have some catching up to do."

Emily looked over her shoulder, displaying quirked eyebrows, before Harold closed the door.

Jason rubbed his hands together. "Now give me a full report on everyone. How's your girlfriend, Bella?"

"She's great. We're seeing a lot of each other."

"Hah. I knew it. You didn't deny that she's your girlfriend this time."

"Things have changed. What about you?"

A huge grin spread across Jason's face. "I have a girlfriend, too. Jessica and I have been on two dates."

"Aren't you a little young to be dating?"

Jason gave his grandfather a playful fist bump on the shoulder. "Aren't you a little old to have a girlfriend?"

"Touché. But won't you miss seeing your girlfriend this weekend?"

"Yeah, but she has a Girl Scout campout so won't be around anyway. Next best thing is being in the Back Wing."

"Two hot dates so far. Where'd you go?"

"Our first date was grabbing some hamburgers. Our second, to the movies. We saw a really bloody horror flick."

"Sounds so romantic."

Jason gave a disgusted grunt. "Come on, you know what happens when there's a scary scene. Jessica wanted me to put my arm around her shoulders to protect her."

That brought back memories of the night before when Harold had his arm around Bella as they sat outside. "Maybe we could go on a double date sometime."

Jason laughed. "As my dad said, don't overplay it, Grandpa. Now, give me an update on Tomas. He still like chasing Frisbees?"

"You bet. He'll want you to toss for him while you're here. Oh, and later tonight we have a secret mission that includes you."

Jason bounced from foot to foot. "Some cool detective work? Solving crimes? Searching for missing women again?"

"No, nothing that sinister. We have to help Bailey and Viola with takeout. Bella will also be joining us."

"I can handle that. I noticed there was no one in the hallway when we came. Everybody resting up for tonight?"

"Exactly. After dinner you'll get reacquainted with the old gang. They'll all be roaming the hallways."

"And Kendall, Alexandra and Pamela?"

"All in good health. You can probably join Kendall for howling tomorrow night. Alexandra is busy with new couch patterns, and Pamela is flying straighter when she remembers to use her hearing aids. We also have one new resident, Cassandra Lemieux."

"Same name as the guy who runs this place."

"Good memory."

Jason tapped his forehead. "I take after my grandpa."

"Cassandra is Peter Lemieux's mother."

Jason stretched his arms. "What's her special power?"

"I'll leave that for you to find out."

"A puzzle. I'll see if I can figure it out. And Warty?"

Harold grimaced. "A problem. He caused an explosion in this apartment, and I had to spend two nights in the Front Wing."

"With all the snobs."

"Yeah, but I survived. I actually stayed in the apartment of a woman who died."

"That's creepy."

"And you're the one going to horror movies?"

"Well, yeah. They're make-believe. But being in a dead woman's room."

"Her body wasn't there or anything. Enough of that subject. Tell me more how school has been going."

Jason shrugged. "Same old, same old. Teachers giving too much homework." Then his eyes lit up. "But I'm in the high school band. I'm a drummer. I should have brought my drum set to practice while I'm here."

"No way. It would disrupt the whole place."

"I remember the parties you had here. There was lots of noise. My drums would fit right in." He rapped his fingers on the kitchenette counter top. "What else exciting has happened since I was last here?"

Harold paused for a moment wondering how much he should mention, but then again, Jason had helped with the difficult situation during the summer. "The woman whose room I stayed in died in the lobby under suspicious circumstances. Another woman was murdered who was on a waiting list to move in here."

Jason sucked on his lip for a moment. "The waiting list links her, huh?"

"Yes. Detective Deavers is investigating."

"I remember him. A really intense dude."

"That's the one. I think the waiting list is a key, and you'll have a chance to join us tomorrow to do a little investigating. Several other people on the waiting list belong to a hiking group. You, Bella, Bailey and I are going to join a hike in the morning."

"I hope not too early."

"You'll be able to get a good night's sleep after our project this evening. And on the hike we can chat with some of the potential Mountain Splendor residents."

"I get it. We can grill the suspects."

"Let's just say we're getting to know some of the people and watching them."

Jason tapped his right eye. "Private eye, ready for duty."

# CHAPTER TWENTY-ONE 🦇

"Come on, Grandpa, I'm going to challenge you to a game of shuffleboard. There's plenty of time before dinner."

"Do you think you're up to it, young 'un? Last time I whooped you pretty bad. It could happen again."

Jason grinned broadly. "Maybe I've been practicing."

"Maybe so have I. Let's go downstairs and test your abilities." Harold grabbed the squishy key cord on the inside of his doorknob, locked the door and led Jason to the elevator.

Jason paced in circles while they waited. "Your elevator is as slow as ever."

"Yep. Like most of the people around here."

Jason pointed to a bright green convertible Bahama sofa and went over and tapped it. "Is that you, Alexandra?"

The couch vibrated and turned red.

"I thought so."

The sofa transformed into Alexandra, and the short stout woman padded over and gave Jason a hug. "Welcome back. While you're here I can show you some new shapes. I'm practicing sofa beds."

"That's cool. Have you ever done a bunk bed?"

She shook her head. "That would require me cloning myself."

The elevator arrived, and Alexandra changed back into a coaster futon sofa bed.

Once downstairs and outside, they stopped at a hedge that Ned Fister was trimming.

"Hey, look who's back," Ned said.

"Yeah. I'm here to visit Grandpa for the weekend."

"You two going to join me for dinner?" Ned asked.

"Once I give Jason a shuffleboard lesson."

Jason grinned. "Or maybe I'll give you a lesson."

They proceeded to the shuffleboard court. Jason collected two shuffleboard sticks and the discs and set them up on one end of the court. He pumped his fist in the air. "Prepare to meet your doom."

"Oh, yeah. By you and who else?"

Harold won the first game and Jason the second.

Jason set up for the third game. "All right. This is for the world championship."

At that moment, two women, one of whom Harold recognized as Betty Buchanan from the fifth floor of the Front Wing, approached the court. Betty pushed her walker to within inches of Harold's feet. "Move on, we're here to play."

Harold eyed the woman. "We're in our final game, and after that you can have the court."

"Speed it up. It's our turn."

Harold recognized that this woman had a very strong frame of reference. Everything was about her.

Instead of playing rapidly, Harold purposely took extra time before each shot. The woman with Betty stood watching quietly, but Betty began slamming the front of her walker onto the cement. "Could you play any slower?"

"Sure," Harold replied. On his next turn, he took twice as long before sending the puck down to nudge Jason's biscuit out of the eight-point trapezoid and into the minus ten-point trapezoid.

Jason gave a disgusted grunt. "How do you do that?"

"Age and cunning."

They continued their game, with Harold deliberately taking as long as he could while delighting in Betty's frustration. Finally, he decided not to toy with her any longer because he didn't want her to suffer a heart attack. He finished off the game by beating Jason by three points.

"I guess you're the world champion, Grandpa."

Harold put his arm around his grandson. "Don't be so sullen. I'll give you a rematch another day."

Jason's eyes lit up. "Cool. I'll get you next time."

"One of these times you will."

"Are you two going to stand here yakking all day?" Betty grabbed the stick out of Jason's hands.

"Whoa, lady. Don't be so pushy."

"Pushy. I'll show you who's pushy." She rammed her walker against Jason's tennis shoe.

He hopped away.

Harold stepped between the two of them. "Betty, it's your turn, but making threats to my grandson is unacceptable." He turned to the other woman. "You're free to play."

The other woman forced a smile. "Thanks."

Without another look at Betty, Harold led Jason back to the lobby.

"What was eating that wild lady?" Jason asked.

"Usually older people aren't so impatient. She definitely has a gruff disposition."

"I'll say. She creeped me out."

They returned to Harold's apartment to wash up for dinner. Once cleaned up, they gathered in the living room.

"Is Bella going to join us for dinner?" Jason asked.

"She doesn't usually go to the dining room, but maybe since you're here she'll come. Why don't you rap on the wall?"

Jason banged his fist hard enough to cause a nearby picture of a mountain scene to jiggle.

In a moment, Bella's head peeked through. "What's all the commotion? Oh, hi, Jason."

"We want you to come down to dinner with us," Jason said. "Grandpa and I would both like that."

"I guess I could this one time. Give me some time to change." She disappeared and five minutes later came through the wall. "There. I'm ready."

At the elevator, Harold saw no couch.

Jason hopped from one foot to the other. "Tell me more about this investigation."

"Bella helped me track down a copy of the waiting list that was in the files in the office. A number of the suspects are in a senior hiking group. I contacted one of the people in that group, which we'll join tomorrow. Maybe we can learn something."

"Cool. I'm ready to check them out."

"That's a good idea," Bella said. "We'll have to take a look at the waiting list and see who might be on the hike. We can divide up which of us gets to interrogate specific suspects."

"But we can't be too obvious," Harold said.

Jason grinned. "Yeah, but I can get away with asking them dumb questions. I can hardly wait."

Down in the dining room they took a four-person table and were soon joined by Ned Fister.

"Hey, this is quite a treat with Bella and Jason here," Ned said.

"We get to take a break from two geezers grousing and complaining to each other," Harold said.

Bella looked around the room. "The four women at that next table are staring at us."

"Those are the bridge fanatics," Harold said. "Maybe you can put a spell on them to have bad bridge hands."

"Not worth the effort."

"There was one obnoxious woman when we played shuffleboard," Jason said. "You should turn her into a statue."

"I only save that for special occasions. Let's see what this Front Wing food tastes like."

"It's not Front Wing food," Harold said. "It's available to everyone. It happens that I'm the only Back Winger who eats here."

Bella added some mint jelly and took a bite of a lamb chop. "Not bad."

Harold took her free hand. "Maybe you'll join me on a regular basis."

"It's possible. Not for breakfast or lunch, but I could make dinner once in a while."

Jason pointed. "There's the uncool woman."

Betty Buchanan pushed her walker up to the table and shook her fist at Harold. "Don't hog my shuffleboard court again."

Harold threw his napkin down on the table. "It happens to be for everyone."

Betty pointed at Bella. "And we don't need your kind in our dining room."

"My kind as in a pleasant personality versus obnoxious as in you?" Bella graced her with a beatific smile.

Betty snorted, wheeled her walker and headed toward the exit.

Bella wiggled her fingers. Cockroaches ran out of the rails of the walker and scampered up Betty's arms.

Betty shrieked, pushed away her walker and ran out of the room.

"Interesting," Bella said. "She doesn't really need a walker."

# CHAPTER TWENTY-TWO 🦇

"That was a cool move, Bella," Jason said. "That lady got what she deserved."

"I only hope no one from the health department finds out about the cockroaches," Harold said.

"Not a problem. No one else saw them besides Betty and our group. The cockroaches have all evaporated." Bella dusted her hands together. "All the evidence is gone."

"Can you show me how to do that?" Jason asked. "I've been practicing card tricks, but what you did would be great to use at school."

"No. I only apply these techniques to people who really deserve it."

"There's a guy named Butch who bullies all the kids. He deserves it. I'd love to zap him with cockroaches or frogs."

"Don't mention frogs," Harold said. "We had a little frog problem because of Warty."

"Sounds like a good story," Jason said. "But more important. Can you share a small amount of special magic with me, Bella?"

"You have to be a member of the witches' guild to use this type of magic."

Jason's eyes lit up. "Wow. Think of all the money you could make. You could set up a service and call it Rent-a-Witch."

"For the time being, I'll limit my special powers to Front Wing bullies. Who's ready to head back upstairs?"

Ned excused himself to make one more pass through the garden, saying he wanted to make sure everything was winterized before the first hard freeze hit. Harold, Bella and Jason returned to the fourth floor of the Back Wing.

When they exited the elevator a crowd greeted them, holding a sign that read, "Welcome back, Jason."

"Cool." A wide grin spread across his face.

Kendall blew a toy horn and then went into a coughing fit. Tomas whacked him on the back.

A card table in the hallway contained an assortment of snacks on paper plates along with two punchbowls, one red and one pale yellow, accompanied by a stack of paper cups. "Stick to the lemonade," Bailey said. "The red punch is for Viola and me."

"Does it have wine in it?" Viola asked.

"No. It's our special nourishing recipe made from the last of our takeout. Besides, you pass out if you drink wine."

Viola hiccupped. "I'm thirsty. I better have a cup."

Tomas held out a Frisbee. "I bought a new one for your visit, Jason. We can try it out tomorrow. I thought of getting a Launch-a-Ball tennis ball launcher, but decided to stick with the Frisbee."

Warty came along the hallway, waving a wand. "I'm here with entertainment. The party can start."

Everyone groaned.

Alexandra put her hands on her hips and glared at him. "You didn't bring any punch this time, did you?"

Warty lowered his wand. "Bella threatened to turn me into a frozen statue if I did. You can blame her if we don't have enough liquid refreshment."

"It looks like we have plenty," Bella said. "And no destructive spells or I *will* turn you into a statue, permanently."

Warty gulped. "I'll try to be careful, but I can't be held accountable. My wand has been misfiring lately."

"Your wand has been misfiring ever since you moved here," Pamela said. "I think it has more to do with the warlock holding the wand."

Warty hefted the wand. "I beg to differ. Look at that crack in the handle."

Pamela flicked her wrist in a dismissing fashion. "Get a new one."

"I like this one."

Bella brought a bottle of wine out of her apartment and filled two cups for her and Harold and set the bottle down on the table. They raised their glasses in a toast to Jason.

"Jason gets to load up his plate first," Bella called out.

"Cool." He dashed over and piled his plate high with chips and cookies and began munching.

The rest of the crowd descended on the snack table.

Bella clapped her hands together. "I'd like everyone's attention." A deck of cards materialized in her hand. "I want to ask Jason to perform a magic trick for us." She handed him the cards.

"Okay, here's a new one since I last saw all of you." Jason took the deck and put a card in his left hand, face up, showing the ten of diamonds. He placed his right hand over the card and rubbed it back and forth. He removed his right hand. A six of clubs rested in his left hand.

Everyone applauded, and Jason bowed.

"More, more!" Tomas shouted.

"Okay. I'll do one other trick." Jason picked a card out of the deck and held it between his thumb and fingers. He jiggled his hand back and forth and the card disappeared. He moved his hand again, and the card reappeared.

Kendall put his fingers to his mouth and whistled.

Harold felt a tinge of pride. He'd never been able to do magic tricks. He tried to put on magic shows when he was a kid, but they always flopped. But his grandson had mastered sleight of hand and could perform the tricks flawlessly.

"I can do better than that." Warty grabbed the deck. "I'll make all the cards disappear." He held the deck in his left hand and waved his wand at it. "Now watch carefully." He intoned, "Ala ka zappo!"

Cards shot out, spraying everyone.

"Oops." Warty shook his wand. A puff of smoke came out of the back hitting him in the face.

Warty wiped the soot off his cheek. "Okay. Everything is unclogged. I'm ready to do a really good trick."

Cassandra came running along the hallway. "Wait! Don't use your wand again."

Warty flinched. "Huh?"

Cassandra grabbed the wand out of his hand and handed it to Bella. "Whew. I made it in the nick of time."

"Did you come back in time?" Harold asked.

"Yes." She wiped perspiration off her brow. "Warty burned down the whole building. I had to prevent that from happening."

Bella pointed her right index finger at Warty. "Should I permanently freeze you?"

He held his hands up in a defensive position. "Not that. I promise to be good. Anything but the Bella freeze."

Bella broke his wand in two and handed him the pieces. "That's it. You cause too much damage around here."

Warty took the two pieces and stared at them as his lower lip quivered. "I hope superglue will work."

"Don't even consider it," Bella said. "You're out of commission." She flicked her wrist and the pieces of the wand disappeared. "Have something to eat and don't cause any more trouble. Remember. Frozen."

Warty muttered, "I hope I can find my spare wand."

"I wouldn't advise that," Bella said. "Remember the operative word. Frozen."

Warty slunk toward the snack table and helped himself to the potato chips.

"Thanks, Cassandra," Bella said. "We would have been homeless if Warty destroyed the Back Wing."

Cassandra nodded. "I know what you mean. It's so difficult to find good housing these days."

# CHAPTER TWENTY-THREE 🦇

People began drifting back to their rooms, leaving Bella, Harold, Bailey and Jason standing by the snack table.

Bailey pointed to a figure slumped against the wall. "Uh-oh. Looks like Viola took a nip of your wine, Bella. I don't know how many times I've told her to stay away from red wine. She gets confused by the color."

Harold and Jason offered to help, so they picked her up and carted her back to her room. When they returned Bella and Bailey stood next to the table.

"Who's going to clean up this mess?" Bailey asked.

"If you can take the punchbowls to your room to wash out, I'll take care of the rest." Bella disappeared into her apartment and returned with a large garbage bag. She waved her fingers and all the paper cups and plates flew into the garbage bag. Within a minute, everything was cleaned up. Harold collapsed the card table and returned it to Bailey's apartment.

"It's time to go for takeout," Bailey announced. "Viola was supposed to join us, but since she's out of it, Jason can help." She dangled a key. "We have a way to get in. It'll be a piece of cake."

"This will be cool."

Harold had misgivings, but he had already told Bailey that Jason could come. He had visions of his grandson being arrested for breaking and entering. "I don't want Jason to run into any problems."

"What could happen?"

"Around this group, anything."

"We'll be helping Bailey and Viola get nourishment. I'm supposed to do a service project for credit at school. This will be perfect."

"I don't think this is what your teachers have in mind. It won't be something you can write up."

Jason shrugged. "Maybe I'll pick up an idea I can use for my creative writing class. I'll turn it into an action adventure story. You don't want to deprive me of that experience, do you, Grandpa?"

Harold gave an eye roll.

Bailey pushed Harold toward the hallway exit. "Now that's all decided, let's get cracking."

The four of them took the elevator to the ground floor and headed to the blood bank. Intermittent clouds sailed slowly from the mountains out over the plains, momentarily covering the gibbous moon.

Bella took Harold's hand and squeezed it and leaned toward him to whisper, "Thanks for letting Jason come. This will be an educational expedition for him."

"As long as nothing unforetold happens."

As they approached the door, strains of music wafted through the air.

"Sounds like a party going on inside," Jason said.

Bailey tilted her head to the side. "You're right. This place should be deserted at this hour. Something's wrong." She unlocked the door and led the others inside. They tiptoed through the reception area and came to the bay where blood was drawn. A strobe light flashed, and a group of college-aged kids in black capes danced to the beat of Kings of Leon's *Closer* vibrating from a boom box in the corner of the room.

Bailey gave a snort. "Those wannabe vampires have it all wrong. We never wear black capes. I prefer colorful clothing."

Harold spotted the security guard in his brown uniform sitting on a chair with a beer can in his hand, snapping his fingers. "Apparently the building security is sponsoring this party rather than preventing it."

"We'll see about that." Bella snapped her fingers. The music cut off, and the strobe flickered out. The dancers came to a stop and looked around.

A lanky kid swirled his cape. "Hey, what happened to the music?"

"The zombies are taking over," Bella announced. She flicked her wrist, and the kids flew against the walls and stuck there.

A girl screamed. "It's the zombie apocalypse."

The security guard stood and approached Bella. "You don't belong here."

"And you don't belong letting these kids in." She wiggled her nose and the guard flew upward and stuck to the ceiling like a fly caught in a spider web. He flailed his arms wildly.

Jason's eyes grew wide. "Cool. You really know how to disrupt a party, Bella."

"Everyone out!" Bella shouted. She flicked her fingers, and the kids all unstuck from the walls. They raced out as fast as their cape-covered bodies allowed, leaving only the security guard clinging to the ceiling.

"What were you trying to do?" she called up to the guard.

A weak voice from above answered. "It was only a harmless group of kids called Vampires-Are-Us who wanted to have a gathering here."

"For a little money in your pocket?"

The guard gulped. "The pay's not so hot."

"Let's get to work," Bella said. "Bailey, show us what you need."

Bailey led them into the refrigerated storage area and explained, "I only take the least useful blood types and check for whole blood that is approaching the thirty-five day shelf life. I can spot things quickly and will hand each of you two bags. That will keep Viola and me going for almost a month."

"Aren't you concerned you're taking blood that can save people?" Jason asked.

Bailey reached up and took a bag of blood. "That's why I check the expiration dates. This bank sometimes has to throw out some old blood. We should be able to find some that expires today or tomorrow, so it will never be sent to a hospital. I personally like aged blood — like good wine. Besides, I know your grandfather and his friends will be donating blood to help replace what we take. When you turn sixteen, get your parents' permission, and you can donate." She proceeded to select more bags and hand them out.

"Guess this beats biting people on the throat," Jason said.

"You got it, kid. Particularly since I developed my skin allergy. Also, I only wish they labeled the blood to distinguish spicy and mild. But I do a taste test when we get back. Any hot-blooded types, I give to Viola. Her stomach isn't as sensitive as mine. " Bailey looked around. "Now that everyone has two bags let's *vamonose*."

"What are you going to do with the security guard?" Jason asked.

"I'm going to leave him stuck to the ceiling."

"But won't he blab that we were here?"

"Nope." Bella wiggled her fingers. "He won't remember a thing."

They left the building, and Bailey danced a little jig. "There. No sign that we've been here tonight."

The sound of a siren pierced the air.

"Uh-oh," Bailey said. "The fuzz. Let's get into the bushes."

They ducked behind a hedge as a police car pulled up to the curb.

"And I thought we weren't going to get Jason in trouble," Harold whispered.

"Shh."

A police officer exited his car, came up to the building, tried the door handle and pushed the door open.

"Oops," Bailey whispered. "I should have locked it."

"Too late for that," Bella said.

The policeman took a flashlight from his belt, turned it on and disappeared inside the building.

"Okay," Bailey said. "Let's get going.

They scampered out of their hiding place and dashed toward the retirement home.

"Whew." Bailey wiped her forehead. "That was close."

Bella smiled. "And the best part—the security guard will have some interesting 'splaining to do."

# CHAPTER TWENTY-FOUR 🦇

On Saturday morning, Harold popped up at seven thirty, ready and raring to go. He shook Jason who lay sprawled out on the hide-a-bed couch in the living room.

"Up and at 'em."

Jason rubbed his eyes. "It's the middle of the night."

Harold drew the curtains. "Nope. Look at that sun streaming in. There's a beautiful day beckoning us."

Jason shielded his eyes. "This is Saturday. I always sleep until noon."

"Not around here. We have to grab some breakfast and go hiking. Remember, we need to check out some of the suspects in the senior hiking club."

Jason put the pillow over his head. "Later."

Harold picked up the pillow and whacked his grandson. "Not later. We have time to eat breakfast before meeting at the trailhead."

"Can't you go without me?"

"No. You're an important part of the investigating team."

Jason literally rolled out of bed, pulling the blanket with him, and curled into a fetal position on the carpet.

Harold grabbed the blanket. "Last warning before I have Bella cast a spell on you and stick you to the ceiling like the security guard last night."

"No way." Jason slowly stood. "Anything but that."

"Go get dressed."

Jason grabbed some clothes and slumped off into the bathroom.

While he waited, Harold pounded on the wall. Shortly, a disheveled and sleepy Bella stuck her head through the wall. "What's all the racket?"

"Hiking alert. Jason and I are going down for breakfast. We'll meet you and Bailey back here at 9:15. We need to be at the trailhead by ten."

"I forgot this excursion was so early."

"You sound like Jason. I had to threaten him that you'd stick him to the ceiling if he didn't get ready."

"Maybe I should stick you to the ceiling and go back to sleep."

Their conversation was interrupted by Jason stumbling back into the living room. "Hi, Bella. I didn't know you got up so early."

"I don't. Your grandfather is an evil taskmaster."

"Yeah. But now that I'm up, I'm hungry."

Harold pushed him toward the door before he changed his mind. "See you back here, Bella. Don't forget Bailey."

By the time they reached the dining room after the slow elevator ride, Jason was wide awake. "So what will I do to help investigate on the hike?"

"We're going to divide up the names on the waiting list. I don't know how many of them will be on the hike, but a good number of them should be. We'll strike up conversations and see what we can learn."

"I can handle that."

They found Ned Fister and joined his table.

"Ah, the only people who will sit with me. Good morning gentlemen."

Jason waved. "Hi, Mr. Fister. Grandpa wouldn't let me sleep in."

"You can call me Ned. Mr. Fister makes me sound like an old fogy." Ned chuckled. "And I haven't slept in for twenty years. When you get older, you'll wake up early as well."

"That's the problem. Research shows teenagers need lots of sleep."

Harold pointed his fork at his grandson. "You can go to bed early if you want more sleep."

"No way. There's too much that happens at night in the Back Wing. I don't want to miss anything."

They ate their pancakes, and Ned excused himself to continue his winterizing project.

Jason leaned toward his grandfather and whispered, "There's that crazy lady who had a tizzy fit while waiting to play shuffleboard."

Harold looked over to see Betty Buchanan scowling in their direction. He waved, and she turned her back on him. "Ignore the peons."

Back upstairs, they found Bella and Bailey waiting in Harold's apartment.

He shook his head. "My room is back to being a meeting place again."

"Sure. Staging area for the great hiking expedition."

"I'm ready." Bailey held up a Thermos. "I have fresh takeout for my snack."

Harold went and retrieved the waiting list. "Okay. Here are the names and assignments. I can't guarantee all these people will show up, but we'll be prepared if they do. We have six names. I'll take the president of the club, Edgar Fontaine. He tells dumb jokes, so I won't make anyone else put up with that. Jason, you've got Frederick Jorgenson."

Jason saluted. "Special investigator accepts his assignment."

"Next, Bella has Celia Barns, retired actress. We'll have to double up on some, so I'll take Duncan Haverson, retired engineer."

"Don't forget me," Bailey said.

"I haven't. Your assignment is Phoebe Mellencourt, a very cheery retired secretary."

"I'll grill her good," Bailey replied.

"And finally. Gertrude Ash. She worked for a non-profit organization. Bella, would you take her as well?"

"Got it."

"During the course of the hike, introduce yourselves to your contacts and start a friendly conversation with them. See what you can learn. If you have an opportunity without being too obvious, find out if they know the two dead women, Alice Jones and Henrietta Yates. We'll debrief afterwards."

"And if our victim... er... assignment doesn't show up?" Bailey asked.

"Enjoy the hike and observe the others."

Harold regarded his watch. "Now we better get hustling. We have to walk a ways to reach the trailhead."

"You mean you didn't line up transportation for us?" Bailey asked.

"No. It's not that far."

Bailey put the back of her hand to her forehead. "But I'll be pooped before we even start the hike."

"I'll provide transportation," Bella said.

"You have some brooms for us?" Jason chuckled.

"Better than that. Hiking poles. Harold, grab your pair, and I'll get mine." Bella disappeared through the wall and came back through the door holding her walking sticks.

"How is this going to help?" Jason asked.

"You'll see. Let's go downstairs."

Harold locked up, and they took the pokey elevator to the ground level.

Outside, Bella handed one of her poles to Bailey. "Harold, give one of yours to Jason."

Harold did as requested.

Jason grabbed the handle and held the pole out like a sword and swished it through the air. "How are these going to help?"

Bella wiggled her fingers. "Put your hand through the strap and place the tip on the ground and start walking."

"You *are* going to make me take a forced march," Bailey said in a whiny voice. "This is not what I signed up for."

"No more complaints. Do as I say."

Harold shrugged and followed the orders. All of a sudden he was propelled forward. "Whoa. I'm moving."

The others followed suit, and everyone began sailing along the top of the sidewalk.

"This easy enough for you, Bailey?"

"Oh, Bella. You're the best. This won't take any energy at all." Bailey flew into a small park and made a swooping circle back to rejoin the others.

Harold shot ahead half a block. "Follow me."

Within thirty minutes and with no exertion, they reached the trailhead where a group of seniors stood chatting. Bella deactivated the poles before they got too close and became targets of suspicion due to their strange mode of transportation.

Harold recognized Edgar Fontaine and stepped forward. "I'm Harold McCaffrey. I met you at the open house and spoke with you on the phone."

Edgar shook hands. "That's right, and you said you might bring some others. Welcome."

A sour looking woman crinkled up her nose. "This is a senior hiking group, not for kids."

A woman who Harold recognized as Phoebe Mellencourt said, "Oh, Gertrude, don't be a stick in the mud. It's nice to have young people along."

"Jason, here, is my grandson. He's visiting for the weekend so I invited him to join the hike. Hope it doesn't cause a problem."

"None whatsoever." Edgar glared at Gertrude. Then he faced Jason, "I hope you can keep up with us, young man."

Jason gave an exaggerated teenage eye roll, and Gertrude turned her back and crossed her arms.

"I think everyone is here who's coming today," Edgar said. "I'd like to welcome all of you to the first hike of October for the Senior Sneakers. We have a number of hikes planned. Today will be an easy climb to the top of South Table Mountain. If you find it too steep, you may have to table your conversation for a while."

Several of the people groaned.

Edgar bowed, obviously feeding off negative reactions. "For those of you who haven't been on this trail before, after the uphill, we'll reach a plateau for level walking and a terrific view of the mountains. I want to warn you to be careful along the trail. There are sometimes rattlesnakes in this area."

"Eek." Bailey waved her hand. "I'd hate to be bitten."

Edgar held up his hand. "Not to worry. No one has ever been bitten by a rattlesnake on a Senior Sneakers hike, because we're careful. I merely want everyone to be alert. Forward."

Harold sidled up to Edgar. "How long have you been in this group?"

"My third year. I find it invigorating to get outdoors any chance I get."

"And when did you become president of the Senior Sneakers?"

"Last year. The previous president moved to Arizona to be near his grandkids, so I offered to take over."

They reached a steep section of trail, and Harold concentrated on breathing rather than talking.

When Edgar paused to wait for the rest of the hikers, Harold looked back and saw that Jason, Bella and Bailey had each teamed up with one other person. He also spotted Duncan Haverson. Good. He'd be able to talk to both people he'd assigned himself.

They started up again, and once the trail leveled out and Harold caught his breath, he asked, "Seems like a number of people in Senior Sneakers are interested in becoming residents of Mountain Splendor."

"Yep. Frederick Jorgenson was the first who brought it up, and a number of us decided to check out the place. Once we get in we'll have a good portion of our group living together. Maybe we can get the retirement home administration to provide a van for our outings."

"It's possible. Peter Lemieux who spoke at the open house is amenable to suggestions like that."

"Good. I hope they work through the waiting list quickly."

"There is one opening in the Front Wing. A woman named Alice Jones is no longer going to be in residence. Have you ever met her?"

Edgar looked skyward for a moment. "Doesn't ring a bell. I'm not too far down the list. I hope I can move in within the next six months. I'm not in any rush to leave my condo, but I'll be ready when the opportunity presents itself."

Harold watched Edgar carefully. He didn't flinch at Alice's name being mentioned and didn't make any comments that would indicate he knew of her death. He decided to try another tact. "With Alice's apartment opening up, the first person on the waiting list would have taken her place. But that person won't be coming to Mountain Splendor." He paused to wait to see if Edgar had any reaction.

They continued on for several steps before Edgar asked, "Why's that? She decide to go live somewhere else?"

"She died. Maybe you met her at the open house. Woman named Henrietta Yates."

Edgar came to a stop. "Hmm. That name's familiar." He snapped his fingers. "That's it. She contacted me and indicated she might be interested in Senior Sneakers. If she died, that explains why she didn't show up today for this hike." He moved forward again.

Harold analyzed Edgar's reaction. Might be something there.

They reached the plateau and rested. Several people took out cameras and snapped pictures. Harold used the opportunity to mosey over to Duncan Haverson. "I met you briefly at the Mountain Splendor open house. I was manning the table when you signed up for the waiting list."

Duncan scrutinized him. "That's right. Now I remember."

"You asked a question at the meeting about the storage area."

"Yeah. I have some valuable furniture that won't all fit in an apartment. I'll want to store it."

"I didn't bring anything extra along when I came to Mountain Splendor." Harold had bad memories of that storage area from the summer, so he changed the subject. "Are you a long time hiker?"

Duncan patted his chest. "Been hiking since I was in college. Great exercise. During my working days, it kept me in shape and was a good break from designing circuit boards. And you?"

"Similar. I enjoy hiking and bought walking poles. They help the old body get up and down steep trails. Do you know any current residents at Mountain Splendor?"

"Why'd you ask?"

*Oops.* He'd have to be careful. "Just curious. Sometimes people move in because they have friends there. We have one open apartment— used to be the residence for Alice Jones. Ever meet her?"

"Common name, but not one I recognize."

"With Alice's apartment available, someone from the waiting list will have a chance to move in. Originally I thought it would be Henrietta Yates, but she's not coming after all. You might have met her."

Duncan shook his head. "I don't think so. I'm really good on technical matters but not much on names. If you'll excuse me I need to get a picture of the group. I'm the unofficial photographer for Senior Sneakers."

Harold took the opportunity to make the rounds. He leaned toward Bailey. "How's it going?"

She curved her thumb and index finger together. "AOK. Had a nice chat with Phoebe Mellencourt. Only problem was she said she forgot her water bottle and asked if she could have a sip from mine. I had to say that I had a cold and didn't want to risk anyone else drinking from my thermos." Bailey winked. "Otherwise, she would have been in for a big surprise."

Harold joined Bella and heard that she had made the acquaintance of both Celia Barns and Gertrude Ash.

Jason came bouncing over to see them. "Secret agent reporting in. Mission accomplished. I talked with Frederick Jorgenson. I'm glad he doesn't tell sucky jokes like the leader of the hike."

Harold patted him on the back. "Hang in there. We'll catch up on details after the hike.

# CHAPTER TWENTY-FIVE 🦇

The Back Wing foursome completed the hike with no rattlesnake sightings, wrong people drinking from Bailey's Thermos or other mishaps. As they strolled back to Mountain Splendor, Bailey complained, "This is entirely too much walking for one day. Can't you turn on the power for the walking poles, Bella?"

"I don't want to risk people seeing us do something unnatural. We needed it to get to the hike on time, but we can have a leisurely promenade home."

Bailey groaned. "Promenade, my sweet patootie. This is a forced slave march."

"It's not bad," Jason said. "That was a pretty short hike. I could have gone for twice as long."

"Maybe for you. My legs are older."

"Jason is right," Harold said. "That was an easy hike. You need to get out for more exercise, Bailey. You'll build up your endurance."

"In my next life."

They came to a small park and Bailey plopped down on the grass under a cottonwood tree. "I need a break."

Harold dropped onto the grass beside her. "This is as good a spot as any to debrief. What did all of you learn?"

Bella sat and carefully smoothed out her black dress. "I'll start with Celia Barns. She's somewhat of a dichotomy."

Harold smiled. "Like you, Bella? A beautiful, helpful witch who can also freeze people or stick them to the ceiling."

Bella glared at him. "No. Different. She comes across as ditzy. She blabbered on and on about her acting career and how she had been in movies with Cary Grant and Rock Hudson. She kept patting her

112

bleached blond wig—"

"That's a wig?" Harold interrupted.

"You don't really think that's natural hair at her age, do you?"

"I guess not."

"Anyway, you wouldn't think she had a brain in her head as she made inane comments regarding the weather, the sky being so bright, the changing leaves, and on and on. Then she would make an astute comment about some of the people in the hiking group. She told me that Edgar Fontaine prides himself on being a good president of the Senior Sneakers, but forgets to attend planning meetings."

"Interesting. I didn't pick up that aspect of him when I chatted with him."

Bella smiled. "You men aren't as observant as we women. She also mentioned that Duncan Haverson, who comes across as this precise engineer is always ogling her."

Harold waggled his eyebrows at Bella. "Nothing wrong with a little ogling."

She gave him her patented witch's evil eye. "Pay attention. My assessment of Celia is this. She's a shrewd operator who plays the role of a bimbo."

Harold swatted at a pesky fly but missed. "Any connection to Alice Jones or Henrietta Yates?"

"As you suggested, I surreptitiously brought up both names. She didn't register a spark of recognition."

"Do you think she's capable of committing a murder?" Bailey asked.

"Good question. I didn't pick up any indication of a violent nature, but she is an actor so could be playing a role. We'll have to keep our eyes on her."

Jason, who stood beside the other three, waved his hand in the air. "Ooh, ooh. I want to share next."

Harold said, "Go ahead."

"My target was Frederick Jorgenson. At first he didn't want to be bothered by a kid. But I found out he was interested in computers. He opened up when we discussed favorite web sites. He's not into music but likes to research genealogy. He's found relatives going back into the seventeenth century. He even mentioned that one famous ancestor had been poisoned. That gave me an opening. I asked him if he knew anything about poison."

"How'd he react to that?" Bella asked.

"He said he had researched arsenic, cyanide and strychnine. Later in the conversation I asked if he knew Alice Jones or Henrietta Yates. He scrunched up his nose as if he had smelled a skunk but said he didn't. That's my report."

"I'll go next," Bailey said. "Phoebe Mellencourt described her career of being a secretary. She worked for a small business in Denver that grew into a large, multi-national company. She eventually became secretary to the president. When companies started using more politically correct titles she became an administrative assistant. But she likes the word secretary. She did share a story regarding a coworker who tried to kill her husband by switching his pills. That ring a bell?"

"Hmm," Bella said. "Could be significant. What else did you learn about her?"

"Overly cheerful type. She'd be hard to be around for more than an hour."

"Any indication of being involved in killing Alice Jones or Henrietta Yates?" Harold asked.

"When I brought up Alice's name, she twitched, but clamed to not know her. Henrietta's name only drew a stare. She did say she was very anxious to move into Mountain Splendor. The landlord of her apartment plans to raise the rent by thirty percent starting in January. She wants to find a new home by then. That's it for my report. Do you think that's enough motivation to kill someone in order to open a space at Mountain Splendor?"

"Hard to tell." Harold proceeded to report on Edgar Fontaine and Duncan Haverson, concluding, "I didn't get much out of Duncan. Edgar professed to not know Alice, although he acted twitchy when I mentioned her name. He also admitted that Henrietta had contacted him about joining the Senior Sneakers. He's the most suspicious one so far, so I have him at the top of my list. Bella, you have the final word."

"Okay. On to Gertrude Ash. She's a piece of work. I never saw her smile the whole time we walked together. I had to keep after her to maintain a conversation. She isn't the complaining type. . ." Bella winked at Bailey, "... but she certainly didn't have anything positive to say about anyone in the group. She fits the image of the jilted spinster. No kind words for any of the men in the group and not much better for the women."

"Why did she join Senior Sneakers?" Harold asked.

"She likes to hike, but she's afraid to walk alone—doesn't want to be attacked."

"Concerned about vicious animals?" Jason asked.

"I think more of the human variety. She claimed not to know Alice Jones or Henrietta Yates. I watched her carefully and couldn't pick up any tells. I tried to poke some more at her reaction to the open house at Mountain Splendor and her desire to move in, but she clammed up."

Harold stood and dusted his hiking shorts. "So nothing specific from anyone yet. Of all of them, I think Edgar Fontaine bears the most future scrutiny."

"No reason to eliminate any of them from what I heard," Bailey said.

"I agree." Bella flicked a dried leaf off her dress. "What's strange is that I don't get a sense that any of these are very nice people."

Bailey also stood. "They'll fit right in with the Front Wing."

# CHAPTER TWENTY-SIX 🦇

Within two blocks of Mountain Splendor, Bailey began limping. "I think I have blisters all over my feet."

"Suck it up," Bella said. "We're almost home."

Bailey placed the back of her hand to her forehead and moaned. "I may have pulled a muscle. Can't you activate the magic walking poles?"

"If you insist." Bella wiggled her nose.

A hiking pole shot out of Harold's grasp and started whapping Bailey on the behind. She shrieked and started running.

"Looks like the cure worked," Harold said.

As they followed Bailey, Bella called out, "When we get up to my room, I have an ointment that will make your blisters go away and another for sore muscles."

Harold retrieved the hiking pole that had chased Bailey, and they took the elevator up to the fourth floor of the Back Wing. Bella tended to Bailey, and Harold and Jason returned to Harold's apartment.

Harold put his walking sticks in the closet and closed the door. "There. They won't fly away now."

"Not unless Bella wants them to. You sure have a cool girlfriend."

Hot was the word that Harold would use, but he nodded his agreement.

\*\*\*\*\*

After lunch, Harold realized the hike had enervated him. On a normal day, he would have considered taking a nap, but he wouldn't succumb to that while Jason visited. He had another idea. "If you want to get some more exercise, I bet Tomas would be up for a game of Frisbee. Let's see if he's around, and I'll come watch."

They knocked on Tomas' door, and he eagerly agreed to join them.

Outside on the lawn, Harold admonished Jason, "Remember to stay away from the windows."

"I'll only throw toward the open space." Jason readied his arm and let the Frisbee sail.

Tomas ran after it and disappeared into tall grass. As the Frisbee descended, a mangy mutt leaped up and grabbed it out of the air. The dog trotted back and deposited the Frisbee at Jason's feet.

"Good catch."

The dog panted.

"Here goes again." This time the Frisbee arced in the wind toward the shuffleboard court. The dog dashed in that direction and ran in front of two women holding their sticks as he leaped to catch the Frisbee.

Harold recognized one of the women as Betty Buchanan.

"Get that beast out of here," Betty shouted.

The dog lifted his leg on the side of the shuffleboard court.

Betty swatted at the dog with her stick, and the dog ran into the grass again.

"I'm calling the Humane Society," Betty bellowed.

In moments, Tomas came trotting out of the grass holding the Frisbee and rejoined Harold and Jason. "Man, that woman has a nasty temper."

Harold looked over and saw Betty waving her arms at the other woman. "Maybe you shouldn't have desecrated the shuffleboard court."

"I couldn't hold it any longer. When you gotta go, you gotta go."

"You better find a place farther away," Harold said. "We don't need to make relations any worse with the Front Wing."

Jason and Tomas followed the suggestion and disappeared along a trail that skirted the foothills. Harold sat down on a bench to contemplate the morning's excursion. He had learned one other thing from Edgar Fontaine. Given that good weather was predicted for the following week, Senior Sneakers planned a mushroom hike on Monday and a regular trail hike on Wednesday. Harold would definitely join those to observe the waiting list suspects. Also, his knowledge of mushrooms rested between miniscule and zippo, so he would have a chance to learn something new.

*****

Half an hour later, Tomas and Jason emerged from the brush. Tomas wiped his brow. "Whew. The kid wore me out."

"We saw a couple of rabbits. Tomas chased them but couldn't catch them."

"I must be getting old. There was a time when I could snag those bunnies. I think I better go take a nap."

Tomas headed toward the building, and no sooner had Jason taken a seat next to Harold than Pamela Quint appeared.

Pamela waved. "I need to experiment with my new hearing aids. Do either of you want to come with me into the trees to watch me test my sonar?"

Jason leapt up. "Sure."

"I'll wait here," Harold said. "Have at it."

*****

After dinner, the fourth floor of the Back Wing came alive as usual. Jason cruised the hallway talking to the friends he had made. Bella joined Harold and they sat on his couch discussing what they had learned on the morning outing. Harold mentioned the two upcoming hikes.

"I'll consider the mushroom hike, since that's something I have a modicum of knowledge about, as long as it isn't too early."

"Edgar indicated it would be an afternoon expedition. The trailhead isn't too far, so we can walk there."

"It's nice having trails so near Mountain Splendor."

Jason raced into the room. "Kendall invited me to go howl with him. You want to come listen?"

Harold squeezed Bella's hand. "We wouldn't want to miss it."

"Okay, meet you downstairs." Jason dashed out of the room.

Bella stood. "He certainly fits in well here."

"Yep. Shape shifters, vampires, werewolves, witches, warlocks and teenagers. Quite a combination."

Outside, Harold and Bella sat on a bench and snuggled together as a mild breeze ruffled a nearby pine tree. They gazed up at the nearly full moon.

"I could stay here all night," Bella said.

"Up to a point. It will get colder later."

"Cold doesn't bother me."

"I better take advantage of your warmth." He held her tighter.

A hacking howl pierced the silence.

"Ah, the sounds of the night." Harold squeezed Bella's shoulder.

"Kendall needs to clear his throat."

A loud, vibrating howl followed, and the hacking howl repeated, ending with a coughing fit.

"What we do for entertainment," Harold said.

The baying resumed with Kendall eventually getting past the phlegm to issue a deep and resonant howl.

Harold and Bella applauded.

The next round of loud barking and howls was answered by yips from a different direction.

"Sounds like the local wildlife is getting in the act," Harold said.

"I think Kendall and Jason have attracted some new fans besides us. The deer population will have scattered for higher ground."

After twenty minutes, Jason and Kendall emerged from the open space. Kendall pushed his walker up to them. "The kid's voice is improving."

Bella reached over and patted Kendall's hand. "Yours wasn't so bad either, once you got going."

"Yeah. Takes a while for the old engine to clear out the soot. I'm pooped. Think I'll head up for some sleep."

Harold regarded his watch. "It's only ten."

"I don't have the endurance I used to." He shuffled toward the building.

"Can I howl on my own for a while?" Jason asked.

"No. Without Kendall, there might be some other creatures that you wouldn't want to encounter in the open space. I promised your parents that I wouldn't let you get chewed or gnawed while staying with me."

# CHAPTER TWENTY-SEVEN 🦇

On Sunday morning, Harold let Jason sleep until nearly the end of the breakfast service period and then rousted him. "Up and at it. We have to get a move on or no food."

Jason rubbed his eyes and rolled over.

"Belgian waffles with maple syrup. Yum. You wouldn't want to have to wait until lunch for something to eat."

Hunger eventually won out, and Jason lurched out of bed. "Okay. Okay."

Jason dressed, and they took the stairs not wanting to risk the slow elevator. They entered the dining room with five minutes to spare and took a two-person table in the corner.

"We must have missed Ned this morning," Harold said.

"I'll eat for him." Jason proceeded to demonstrate his point by having two waffles, six pieces of bacon, a cup of fruit, a bowl of cereal and two glasses of orange juice.

Harold set his fork down after eating only one waffle. "I'm glad I'm not being charged by the pound, or you'd drive me into bankruptcy."

Jason burped. "Good snack. That should do for an hour or so."

"Right."

They left the dining room but before reaching the elevator were accosted by Peter Lemieux. "I'm glad I caught you, Harold."

"What are you doing charging around on a Sunday morning?"

Peter gritted his teeth. "This job is twenty-four, three-sixty-five."

"So you only get a day off every leap year?" Jason said.

Peter gave Jason a playful tap to the shoulder. "Good one, but I don't even get that day off. Harold, I have a favor to ask."

"As long as it doesn't involve anything illegal."

120

Peter rolled his eyes. "Like grandson, like grandfather. No, this is very simple and won't get you in trouble. We have another new resident for the Back Wing arriving this afternoon. Given that you're the only morning person from the Back Wing I can ever find during the day, I thought you might welcome him and tell him about the other Back Wing residents."

"Does he like to play catch with a Frisbee?" Jason asked.

"I don't know. You can ask him."

"If he does, I'd be happy to entertain him after Grandpa talks to him."

Peter nodded. "You can check with him. His name is Bartholomew Sampson. He'll be in the lobby at two thirty."

"I didn't think we had any openings in the Back Wing."

"Not until yesterday. Mil Manawydan on the third floor gave sudden notice. He received a job offer to be an extra in a werewolf film in Hollywood and left immediately. He said he didn't have many possessions and liked traveling light anyway. The apartment is in immaculate condition, and Bartholomew is anxious to move in. He's been staying in a motel."

"And his special power?" Harold asked.

"I'll let him explain that to you. A hint is that he should meet Alexandra Hooper as soon as possible."

"Okay. I'll show him around and make the introduction. Of anyone in the Back Wing, Alexandra should be up and around sometime in the afternoon."

"One other thing. We're hosting a dinner Monday night for the people on the Front Wing waiting list."

This caught Harold's attention. "Do say."

"We'll have a special table set in the dining room. Since you've met these people signing them up, I thought you'd like to join the function."

"You bet."

"Good. I appreciate your help." Peter saluted and charged off.

*****

That afternoon at 2:15, Harold knocked on Alexandra's door.

"Who's there?"

"Harold and Jason. We have some news for you."

Alexandra opened the door a crack. "Yes?"

"Jason and I are welcoming a new Back Wing resident in a few minutes. Peter thought you might also enjoy meeting him. I'll bring him up on the elevator if you want to join us there in twenty minutes or so."

"I'll be glad to. It'll give me time to pick out the right cushion type and texture. See you by the elevator."

Harold and Jason proceeded to the lobby.

"Let's see if we can guess this guy's special power," Jason said. "Like a contest. The closest one will get an afternoon snack fixed by the loser."

"You're on. The power of elder wisdom versus the impetuousness of youth."

They spotted Peter and a tall, skinny man with a pale complexion by the reception desk.

"Definitely a vampire," Jason said. "Slam dunk."

"Hmm." Harold regarded the man more closely. "I think a shapeshifter of some type. We'll see."

They approached and after introductions, Harold said, "Let's go up to the fourth floor. I have someone for you to meet."

"Good show. I'm looking forward to finding some kindred spirits here. I've heard excellent reports regarding this residence. Very different from the typical retirement communities in the greater Denver area."

"You'll meet all kinds of interesting people," Jason said.

Bartholomew raised an eyebrow. "You seem too young to be living here. Did you transform into a younger presence?"

"Nope. I'm visiting my grandpa for the weekend." Jason frowned. "I have to go home tonight and back to school tomorrow. Do you like playing catch with a Frisbee?"

"I'm not into athletics, I'm afraid. I don't like breaking into a sweat. I'm more of a down-to-earth person or should I say down-to-floor."

After the elevator ride to the fourth floor, they exited to find a Kubus sofa resting against the wall.

Bartholomew's eyes lit up. "Excellent material." He ran his hand over the arm of the couch.

A sigh emerged.

Bartholomew patted a cushion. "This seems to be more than an ordinary sofa. What a lovely specimen."

Alexandra transformed.

Bartholomew took her hand and looked into her eyes. "As I said, what a beautiful specimen."

Alexandra's face turned pink and then red. "You're not so bad yourself."

Neither of them released the other's hand.

Harold cleared his throat. "Um… Bartholomew? My grandson and I were speculating earlier on what your special power might be."

He gave Alexandra's hand a squeeze and then released it. "I'll be happy to demonstrate." He snapped his fingers and transformed into a patchwork throw rug.

Alexandra bent over and ran her hand over the rug. "What wonderful texture. So soft yet durable."

Harold winked at Jason. "I'll be looking forward to a tuna sandwich with all the trimmings that you fix for an afternoon snack. Never bet with an oldster."

"You won fair and square, Grandpa. And besides, I know you won't even eat a whole sandwich, so I'll have plenty."

In the meantime, Bartholomew had transformed back to his human shape, and he and Alexandra were engaged in a conversation about chenille, wool and cotton.

Harold waited to say something but realized he would have no chance of gaining their attention. "Bartholomew, it was a pleasure meeting you," he said. "Alexandra, would you mind showing him around the Back Wing?"

"I'd love to."

"My grandson and I are going back to my apartment to fill up his stomach again."

# CHAPTER TWENTY-EIGHT 🦇

Sunday afternoon, Jason packed his duffle in preparation for his parents picking him up after returning from their Glenwood Springs weekend. He folded up the bed, stopped and slapped his forehead. "Oops. I forgot to do my biology paper."

"What biology paper?"

He held up a spiral notebook. "I need to write three pages for Monday that describe how plants can help human health. I promised my folks I'd get that done before they came to get me. That was a condition for letting me stay here."

"You better get cracking."

Jason gulped. "I don't have a clue what to write."

"Hmm. I don't have any useful books, but I know how you can do some research." Harold pounded on the wall.

"What good is that going to do?" Jason asked.

"Bear with me a moment." He banged on the wall again.

Bella stuck her head through. "You called?"

"Yes. Jason needs to pick your brain on herbology. He has to write a school paper on how plants can help human health. I thought that would be right up your alley."

"I won't write anything for him, but I can show him a few concoctions that he can describe." Bella stepped all the way through the wall, grabbed Jason's hand and pulled him back toward the wall.

Jason dug in his heels. "Whoa. I'm not going to fall for that. I'll get my head smacked if I try to follow you through the wall."

"He remembered," Bella said. "Trying that again only works with people like Viola. I guess we'll have to use the doors. Harold, you want to come watch?"

124

"Sure."

Jason picked up the notebook and pen. Then the three of them went into Bella's apartment the conventional way, and Bella pointed to a plant sitting on her kitchenette countertop. "Here's a simple one—mint. Rub the leaves and smell."

Jason stroked a leaf and sniffed. "Cool. It smells great."

"Also, it can be used in mint juleps." Harold patted his stomach. "We should make some refreshments."

"Later. Right now I need to help Jason with his research."

Jason nodded. "Okay, but what are the health benefits of mint?"

"Several. It helps with indigestion and diarrhea. It's a simple way of treating bad breath, so you can chew a leaf the next time you want to kiss a girl."

Jason's cheeks reddened. "Whatever."

"It could come in handy," Harold said. "Jason has a girlfriend."

Bella tore off several leaves. "In that case I'm giving you some mint. It's much better than breath spray."

Jason tapped his pen on the notebook. "You've made your point. What else can mint do that I can describe?"

"It can help with cirrhosis of the liver, but a better cure is to not drink too much alcohol." Bella wagged a finger at Jason.

"Yeah. Yeah."

"I can also grind up the flowering tops to make a good headache cure. It's also excellent for backaches."

Jason scribbled like mad on his notepad and looked up. "Anything else?"

"Sure. It can be gargled for a sore throat treatment and can be used to reduce the pain of kidney stones and gallstones. Finally, it helps with anti-flatulence."

"That would help with all the old farts around here," Harold said.

Bella swatted him. "Stay out of the learning process. Now, Jason, here's another very useful plant—ginger." She held up a gnarled root.

"It looks like a wrinkled hand," Jason said. "What's it used for?"

"It provides another good remedy for stomach disorders. It's also an anti-inflammatory so it relieves symptoms of arthritis. You don't have to worry about that yet, but many people at Mountain Splendor suffer from achy joints."

"Do you make brews with these plants in big cauldrons?" Jason asked.

"I've been known to put together a few concoctions from time to time. Mine are healthy, not like what Warty does with his steaming punch."

Bella pointed to a succulent plant. "Here's one of my favorites. Aloe Vera. You can break off a leaf and dab it on cuts and burns to soothe the skin. If taken internally, it serves as a laxative."

"Cool. I have enough to write my three pages."

Jason thanked Bella, and he and Harold returned to Harold's apartment so he could write up his research.

Later, Harold answered a knock on the door to find Kendall standing there with his walker.

"I'm surprised to see you up at this hour," Harold said.

"I quit early last night, and there was a lot of noise this afternoon. Alexandra brought a new guy, Bartholomew Sampson, around and knocked on all the doors."

"I heard he replaced Mil Manawydan. Did you and Mil ever howl together?"

"Only once. He wanted to be the Alpha, so I quit going with him. Anyway, two reasons for my visit. First, I want to invite you to a party tonight to welcome Bartholomew."

Jason dashed up to join Harold. "A party. This place has parties almost every night. I want to come."

"You're going back with your parents."

"Aw. Things will be boring at home. The parties around here are great. Explosions and all kinds of cool stuff."

"That will have to wait until the next time you come to visit."

"Maybe I can convince Mom and Dad to take another trip soon."

"You're welcome to stay any time," Harold said.

"And you can join me howling whenever you're here." Kendall edged his walker to the side. "I like the kid. He doesn't try to act like an Alpha. Second reason for being here, I have a present for Jason." He pulled a book out of the pouch on his walker. "This is for you, kid. I thought you'd enjoy it."

Jason took it. "What's it about?"

"It's called *Wolf Gift* by Anne Rice. I understand you used to read vampire books. This is something with a different flavor for you. Much more interesting than vampires."

"Cool."

Kendall gave a salute. "It's a little R rated but that will be an incentive for you to read it. Got to go notify the others about the party. See you on your next visit, Jason."

Harold shut the door. "Your folks should be here soon."

"Too bad. I wish I could stick around to help with the investigation. You need to keep checking out those hiking people."

"I appreciated your help yesterday on the hike. I plan to go on their next hike tomorrow."

"Can I come?"

"No. You have school. It's an early afternoon expedition so won't fit into your schedule."

"Darn. You have to let me know what happens. Are you going to pass information on to Detective Deavers?"

"I left him a message, and I'm hoping to see him tomorrow morning. He's not completely convinced of my theory that the waiting list is key to the crimes, but I think he's coming around."

"I have an idea. Maybe my folks can invite you and Bella over for dinner this week. My dad could pick you up after work. Then you can give me an update on the investigation."

"I like seeing you and your folks, and Bella would also enjoy it. I'll check with her."

Jason rubbed his hands together. "I'll see if I can convince my parents."

"I'm sure you're good at that."

"Of course. I took lessons from my grandpa."

# CHAPTER TWENTY-NINE 🦇

Jason finished writing his report from the notes he had taken. An hour later Jason's parents arrived to take him home.

"How was Glenwood Springs?" Harold asked.

Sly grins were exchanged by Nelson and Emily. "We had a good time, Dad. Did you keep Jason entertained?"

"That, and he kept me entertained."

"How was your boring weekend with old people?" Nelson asked.

"I saw a bunch of my friends and made some new ones. There are two new residents of the Back Wing. Pretty interesting people."

Emily arched an eyebrow. "You don't usually find our older friends that interesting."

Jason shrugged. "I hate to say it, but your friends are kinda boring. This is a special place."

Nelson crinkled his brow. "That's quite a statement. Even your grandfather wasn't that enthusiastic when he first moved here."

Harold jumped in. "This place grows on you." He briefly had the image of kudzu crawling up the walls and had to contain a smile. "Besides, Jason fits right in. And Bella helped him with his biology report."

"I meant to ask if you finished it," Emily said.

Jason pumped his fist in the air. "All written and ready to hand in tomorrow. And speaking of Bella, to thank her can we invite Grandpa and Bella to come to dinner sometime this week?"

Emily's eyes widened. "You've never asked us to invite older people over before."

"Nothing like a first time. What do you say?"

Emily looked at Nelson. "We don't have any plans Tuesday night."

Nelson shrugged. "Works for me."

"Super. We're on." Jason gave Harold a high five and turned toward his father. "Can you give them a ride?"

"Yeah," Nelson said. "After work, Dad, do you need to confirm with Bella that she's available?"

"I'm sure she can make it. I'll call if there's any problem."

Nelson checked his watch. "We better hit the road and get out of your hair."

Harold ran his hand through his thinning locks. "No rush."

"Do I have to leave already?" Jason winked at Harold.

"We're tired from our drive," Emily said. "We need to get home."

"I guess you don't have the stamina of the people who live around here," Jason said. "They seem to get their second wind in the evening. And they have cool parties."

Emily grabbed Jason's arm. "Enough parties for you, young man. Time to go."

They headed out the door, and Jason waved. "See you Tuesday, Grandpa. Fun weekend."

After he shut the door, Harold tapped on the wall and Bella came through. "We have a dinner invitation for Tuesday night."

"I heard. I was listening through the wall."

"Pretty snoopy, aren't you?"

"I happened to put my ear against the wall and heard my name mentioned. No sense ignoring what was said."

"I hope you're available."

"Let me think. I could stay around here and avoid Warty and his misguided magic or I could come spend the evening with you and Jason, two of my favorite people. Which should I choose?"

Harold grinned. "Good. It's a date."

They discussed the hike they had taken. Harold said, "A reminder. We're have the mushroom hike tomorrow afternoon."

"Usually one hike in a week is enough for me, but I guess I'll join you so I can learn more about mushrooms and stay in shape as much as you do."

"As you know, I enjoy walking. I used to play golf three times a week and walked the course instead of using a cart."

"I've never played golf."

"Really? You'd be a natural. Why don't we try it sometime?"

Bella put an index finger to her cheek. "Hmm. I might enjoy that."

"When we go to Nelson's house for dinner, I'll have to pick up my golf clubs. When I gave up the sport, I stashed my clubs in his garage."

\*\*\*\*\*

After dinner and a healthy discussion with Ned Fister about the tradeoffs between grass lawns and xeriscaping, Harold returned to the fourth floor of the Back Wing to find a gathering in progress.

Bailey, who stood next to Viola, waved Harold over. "Have you met our new resident, Bartholomew Sampson?"

"Who's that?" Viola asked.

"He's the man with Alexandra."

Viola squinted and returned her gaze to Harold. "And who's this yahoo?"

Bailey let out a loud burst of air. "Viola, you keep forgetting. This is Harold who lives in the room between you and Bella."

"We don't allow any intruders there. That's our meeting room."

"Not any longer. Harold has been here for over three months."

Viola squinted at him. "Hmm. Don't recognize the throat. Have you seen my choppers?"

"They're probably in the pocket of your vest."

Viola patted her vest, pulled out her false teeth and popped them in her mouth. "That's better."

At that moment, Warty came stomping into the hallway. "What's going on?" How come I wasn't invited?"

"Because you disrupt parties with your inane and misguided attempts at magic," Bella said.

"I should turn you all into toads."

"Last time you tried that, you ended up with a rash," Bailey said. "As long as you're here, have a cookie, something to drink, and don't cause any problems."

"I could contribute some punch."

"No!" came a loud chorus.

"Better cut your losses, Warty," Bella said. "Grab a snack and leave it at that."

He harrumphed loudly and went over to a card table standing along the wall between Harold's and Viola's apartments to snag a brownie and a cup of juice.

Harold stepped over to the snack table, not to eat anything because he had had a large dinner with apple pie for dessert, but to speak with Warty. "I've learned something since I moved into the Back Wing."

Warty burped. "What's that?"

"I don't have any special powers, but I enjoy talking to people at these parties. Everyone has interesting stories. You might try mingling to chat without feeling you need to impress people with your attempts at magic."

Warty puffed up. "But I used to be able to do the most amazing tricks. I'm quite world-renowned."

"That may be the case, but for whatever reason, things have misfired for you lately. Don't keep trying so hard."

"I know it's only a bad spell I'm going through, so to speak." He shook his wand. "I'm ready to get back to my old form. Look at that spider on the wall. I'm going to zap it." He pointed his wand. "Zappa, zappa, dingo."

There was a bright flash, a loud report, and Warty fell to the floor with soot covering his face.

Harold bent over to examine Warty and determined he was out cold. He waved to Tomas. "Can you give me a hand? Let's take Warty back to his room. I think he's had enough partying for this evening."

Between the two of them, they lugged him to the elevator to return him to his room. The door was unlocked, so they staggered inside and deposited Warty on his bed.

"You think we can leave him alone?" Tomas asked.

"Let's see if we can revive him first." Harold stepped into the bathroom, found a plastic cup and filled it with water. He returned and splashed some water on Warty's face.

The warlock spluttered, wiped his face and opened his eyes. "What happened?"

"You tried to zap a spider on the hallway wall, but your wand backfired. I tried to suggest earlier that you enjoy a conversation with the others but not try your magic. I think that's a good suggestion."

Tomas nodded. "Good advice. You should listen to Harold, Warty."

"I'm not up to any conversation. I think I'll take a nap." Warty shut his eyes.

"Excellent idea." Harold led Tomas out of the room. He only wished whoever was involved in the recent deaths was as easy to deal with as a misguided warlock.

# CHAPTER THIRTY 🦇

Monday morning met Harold's glance out the window with the sight of drizzle and low clouds. Nothing like a dreary fall morning. Harold's knee ached from the cold, humid weather. So far it hadn't turned to snow. That would be reserved for Halloween. Harold remembered the many times he had taken his son, Nelson, trick-or-treating as a kid in a snowstorm, bundled up in coat, hat and gloves so no one could tell if the outerwear hid the costume of a cowboy, vampire or Superman.

After breakfast, the equally dreary figure of Detective Deavers appeared, knocking on Harold's apartment door.

"I've been looking forward to your visit, Detective."

Deavers raised an eyebrow. "Not the usual way people greet me."

"Come take a load off your feet, and we can chat."

After declining the offer for any liquid refreshment, Deavers took a seat. "You left me a cryptic message over the weekend."

Harold settled into his easy chair. "That I did. I went on a hike on Saturday with a group called the Senior Sneakers. It's very interesting that all the people on the waiting list for the Front Wing here at Mountain Splendor showed up. I thought you should be aware of that."

Deavers stared at Harold for a moment. "I know you feel strongly that this waiting list is connected with the deaths —"

"You said deaths and not crimes. Does that mean that Alice Jones died of natural causes?"

"We're still waiting. The initial tox results didn't give us a clear picture. We'll see when the whole report is completed."

"Have you ruled out suicide?"

"It remains an open issue. I shouldn't get into details with you, but you've helped me in the past and have a track record of being discrete, so I can tell you this much — we're still treating it as a suspicious death until we know more."

Harold's mind swirled. This posed all kinds of questions. Did someone know of Alice's penchant for medicine? Did a killer get his or her hands on her pills and manage to switch the medicine? Or did she accidently take the wrong medicine or purposely kill herself? Or was it a heart attack not related to her medication? Finally finding his voice, he said, "Anything show up in the background checks for the people waiting to come to Mountain Splendor?"

"Nothing unusual for all but one of the names you gave me."

Harold flinched at the sight of Bella sticking her head through the wall behind Deavers. She noticed the detective and disappeared. Harold realized what a mistake that would have been if Bella had dashed right through without looking.

Deavers looked over his shoulder. "You look like you saw a ghost?"

"Sorry. The light was casting a funny shadow. You might want to take a look at Edgar Fontaine. During the Saturday hike, he admitted knowing Henrietta Yates."

Deavers took out his notepad and jotted on it. "That's interesting. I'll have to follow up. But the only person with a questionable background was..." He leafed through his notes. "Cassandra Lemieux."

"Really?"

"She had a run in with the law twenty years ago." Deavers returned his notepad to his coat pocket.

There was a knock. "Excuse me a moment, Detective." Harold answered the door, and Bella came in.

"Hello, Detective Deavers." She ambled over and took his hand, while brushing close against him. "It's good to see you again."

Deavers stood and regarded his watch. "I need to see Mr. Lemieux. Let me know if you come across anything else useful, Mr. McCaffrey." He quickly left the room.

"I hope I didn't interrupt any male bonding." Bella said.

"When I saw your face through the wall, I thought I'd have a heart attack. I'm glad you noticed Deavers before you came through."

"I received a warning that he was here. Hold on a second." Bella opened the door and signaled. In a moment Cassandra dashed in.

"That was close." Cassandra put her hand to her chest to catch her breath.

Harold looked back and forth between Bella and Cassandra. "What gives, you two?"

Cassandra took a deep breath. "Detective Deavers caught me in the hallway and mentioned he had information on a past... uh... indiscretion of mine. I changed time back and asked Bella to... uh... borrow his notebook."

Bella held up Deavers's notepad. "Voila."

Harold groaned. "You and your sticky finger magic. He's not going to be pleased when he discovers it's missing."

"Hey, he accidently dropped it on your rug. Nothing more. Let's take a look at what he's written." Bella licked her finger and paged through. "Ah ha. Here are his notes on Cassandra. My, my. You were accused of shoplifting."

Cassandra gritted her teeth. "That's my one little past mistake. I was helping at a shelter and met this homeless woman who wore tatters. I didn't have any money myself at the time. I took some clothes from a discount store to give to the woman but got caught."

"Why didn't you go back in time to rectify the situation?" Harold asked.

"I was outside of my one hour window when I realized I had been noticed by a store security officer. He followed me and caught me with the goods. I paid the store back when I earned some money, but it went on my record."

"As long as I have this notebook, let's see if there is anything interesting on the investigation." Bella leafed through more pages. "I'll be darned. They found some similar fiber samples in Alice Jones's purse and on Henrietta Yates. One more thing that might link the two crimes."

"We better return this to Deavers," Harold said. "He's been open with me, and I don't want him to start stonewalling us."

"Okay. Let's go down to Peter's office and take care of it."

"I'm going to beg off," Cassandra said. "I need to maintain a low profile until this all blows over."

*****

Harold knocked on Peter's door, and the retirement home director opened and waved them in. "Harold and Bella. What brings you here?"

"We have something to return to Detective Deavers." Harold stepped over to where Deavers sat and handed him the notepad.

Deavers patted his jacket. "I put it away. How did you get it?"

"It must have fallen out," Bella said. "We found it on Harold's rug."

"It couldn't have fallen. It was secure in my jacket."

Bella wiggled her fingers. "Are you sure there isn't a hole in your pocket?"

Deavers put his hand in his jacket pocket, and a strange expression came across his face. "There's a hole there now."

Bella smiled. "That explains it."

Deavers glared at her. "I didn't have a hole there this morning when I first put my notepad there. And I would have felt it falling out if there was a torn pocket."

"Things wear out. Bye, Detective." Bella grabbed Harold's arm and led him through the doorway. Once out of hearing range, she whispered to Harold, "He's such an intense fellow that he needs a diversion once in a while."

# CHAPTER THIRTY-ONE

That afternoon, Harold and Bella joined the Senior Sneakers at the designated trailhead in the foothills. The morning clouds had cleared and the temperature had gone up into the high sixties, making it a pleasant autumn afternoon.

Harold adjusted his hat, wanting to keep the bright sunshine off his face as much as possible. No sense risking skin cancer.

While waiting to start, Harold engaged Celia Barns in conversation. "I understand you used to be an actor."

Her eyes lit up. "Yes. Did you see any of my movies?"

"I think so. Did you live in Hollywood?"

"For a while." She put the back of her hand to her forehead. "Then it became so frantic."

"And what brought you to Colorado?"

"The crisp mountain air. My doctor thought it would be good for my asthma." She took a deep breath. "Now I can walk for hours without gasping."

Edgar clapped his hands together. "Let's get started, people. How many of you have hunted for mushrooms before?"

All the hands except Harold's went into the air.

"Good. I consider myself a mycological, that is, fungi expert. As they say, there's a fungus among us." Edgar chortled.

Several of the group members groaned.

"I know a bit about local mushrooms, but anyone else can jump in as well. The purpose this afternoon is to have some exercise but also to see how many different types of mushrooms we can identify. Any questions?"

Harold raised his hand.

"Yes?"

"Since I seem to be the only neophyte, how do you distinguish edible from poisonous varieties?"

"Good question. Most of it comes from experience. So don't have a bad experience by eating anything you find." Edgar yukked, but no one else even smiled. He cleared his throat. "Best bet is to have an expert show you. There are some good books, so I'd recommend buying a guidebook to take along when you go on mushroom hunts."

Phoebe Mellencourt waved a book in the air. "I brought *Mushrooms of Colorado*. I always bring it along. It's the ideal reference."

"Yes, that's one of many sourcebooks that will give you information of what to pick and what to avoid. Also, you'll discover there are some edible varieties that are too fibrous or bad tasting. What you want to find are types like morels that are both safe and tasty. But you have to be careful because there are false morels that are toxic. It takes a practiced and distinguishing eye. Other questions?"

No one else raised a hand. Harold looked around for a moment and slowly lifted his hand in the air. "Are there any laws restricting us taking mushrooms?"

Edgar squinted at Harold. "Another good question. I should pay you to come along on all my mushroom hikes. You could be my mushroom plant." He slapped his thigh and guffawed.

Again, no one else laughed.

Edgar looked crestfallen for an instant and then regained his composure. "On Forest Service land you can pick mushrooms for your own personal one-night use or get a free permit to harvest up to three gallons per day for ten days per calendar year. There are some places like in Boulder County where you aren't allowed to take mushrooms. We'll be on land today where we can pick, so no one will end up in the slammer. Unless you try to poison someone."

Harold rolled his eyes. Great. That's all he needed—the leader of this group of suspects planting the idea to poison someone. He declined to ask any further questions.

They started up a narrow trail with Bella and Harold at the end of the single file line. Bella periodically pointed out some of her favorite herbs.

Harold leaned toward Bella and whispered in her ear. "Are you familiar with Colorado mushrooms?"

"I've studied the medicinal types."

"Hopefully not the hallucinogenic ones."

"No. I stay away from those. They cause too many problems."

Up ahead, Edgar came to a clearing and held up his hand. "Gather around, people. Here is a good morel at the base of this pine tree. Notice its full shape."

"I thought this was too late in the year to find morels," Frederick Jorgenson said. "The season is usually through September."

"Correct. But we've had such warm weather this fall that our little friends are still in the woods. The moisture this morning also helps. One of you can add this to your collecting bag."

Celia Barns bent over and removed the mushroom and dropped it in a plastic bag she carried.

"I didn't think to bring anything for actually collecting," Harold said to Bella. "And since I get all my meals at Mountain Splendor, I won't be preparing any mushroom meals anyway."

"Besides, you better go on a few more expeditions before you try picking your own mushrooms."

As they continued on a wider trail, Harold sidled up to Gertrude Ash. "You go on mushroom hikes often?"

"Once or twice a year. Why do you ask?"

"Only trying to be friendly."

She glared at him and strode ahead.

Harold shook his head. Not the loquacious type. She was definitely a candidate for the Oscar the Grouch award.

They continued along the trail, and Harold learned about puffballs and chanterelles. The forest grew denser and at one point, Edgar stopped the group again. "Pay close attention here. This is a death cap. A young one can be confused for a puffball. These babies are deadly. Scientific name is *Amanita phalloides*. They're sticky to the touch."

Yep. Looked like the toadstools Harold had removed from his lawn after rainy weather when he lived in Denver. He'd picked some that were six inches in diameter with a stem five inches high. They gave him the creeps.

139

As they continued walking, Harold took the opportunity to speak with Frederick Jorgenson. He remembered that Jason had said Frederick professed a knowledge of poison. "What do you think of these poison mushrooms?"

Frederick looked askance. "They're okay to look at. I enjoy seeing all the different kinds of mushrooms."

"I'd feel uncomfortable selecting the edible ones. From what Edgar said, there are too many resemblances between poisonous and edible mushrooms."

Frederick shrugged. "You can make the distinction with a little practice. In some of the southern parts of the United States, I've seen destroying angels. You want to avoid that killer. In their button stage, they can be mistaken for button, horse or meadow mushrooms. Also look like puffballs."

"I'll keep that in mind." Harold couldn't tell a puffball from a cheese ball.

They trudged on until Edgar shouted for everyone to gather around. "Here's a *Russula emetica*, also known as the sickener. Notice the bright red cap. Another one to avoid."

Harold craned his neck over the crowd and caught a glimpse. That's a mushroom he could remember—remember to stay away from.

All this talk of mushrooms had made him thirsty. He removed his water bottle from his daypack and took a swig. By the time he finished and returned his bottle to his pack, the group had moved forward. He looked at the spot where he had seen the *Russula emetica*. It had disappeared.

# CHAPTER THIRTY-TWO

Harold remained silent as he and Bella returned from the hike. He had much to think over in regards to these people who were hikers, mushroom enthusiasts and on the waiting list for Mountain Splendor. At the end of the hike, Edgar Fontaine had invited everyone to join another hike on Wednesday afternoon, stating that because of the continued good weather, they should get out as much as possible.

"Why so pensive?" Bella asked.

Harold let out a heartfelt sigh. "I don't know. This whole situation with the two deaths. Something is going on, but I can't piece it together. I guess I'm frustrated. I know I should leave it to Detective Deavers, but I keep thinking I can figure out what's happening."

"Your inherent sense of curiosity."

"I guess. Or maybe I don't know when to leave things alone. This keeps gnawing at me, or me on it. I'm like a dog with an old bone—I can't give it up."

"I picked up one tidbit for you," Bella said.

Harold barely had the energy to lift an eyebrow. "Yeah?"

"Phoebe Mellencourt said she and a number of the other Senior Sneakers would be at Mountain Splendor this evening for dinner."

Harold smacked his forehead. "Dang. I forgot to tell you. Peter mentioned that to me yesterday and asked me to attend."

"You're going to have your fill of these people today."

"I guess so. I'll have to see if I can learn anything useful this evening, as I certainly didn't pick up anything during the hike. I think I'll also go on the Wednesday hike. You want to join me?"

"Since it's in the afternoon, I should be able to."

Harold smiled. "We'll see if we can learn more than we did on the mushroom hike."

*****

Harold headed down to dinner at six and found a large circular table with a reserved sign. Peter sat there next to Edgar Fontaine with Frederick Jorgenson two chairs away from Peter on the other side.

Peter waved. "Come join us, Harold. The others should be here shortly."

Harold scooted in a chair allowing some open seats on either side of him for other people when they arrived.

"Harold came on one of our hikes today," Edgar said. "How'd you enjoy it?"

"Very informative."

Celia Barns was the next to arrive as she sashayed up to the table, patting her hair. "Good to see you gentlemen."

Edgar stood and held a chair for her.

She smiled. "You *are* a gentleman."

In short order Gertrude Ash and Phoebe Mellencourt came in together. Phoebe was waving her hands and talking rapidly, while Gertrude had a glum expression on her face as if she had lost her best friend in the world.

To Harold's surprise, Betty Buchanan entered the dining room and joined them, taking a seat next to Frederick Jorgenson.

Peter waved a greeting. "Betty volunteered to attend this evening. She offered to answer any questions about living in the Front Wing."

"Here's one," Edgar boomed out. "When will there be an apartment available for me?"

Betty gave a snort. "It all depends on when there are vacancies."

"I guess that's the key, isn't it," Edgar said.

And last, Duncan Haverson marched into the dining room with the determination of someone returning from a quest. He nodded and took the remaining seat between Frederick Jorgenson and Peter.

Peter signaled to a member of the wait staff, and in moments large bowls of crisp lettuce garnished with tomatoes, carrots and avocado were served. "We have three choices of dressing." Peter pointed to white tureens on the table. "Ranch, oil and vinegar, or thousand island."

Harold tried to strike up a conversation with Gertrude Ash, but she only responded with one word answers, so he turned to Phoebe Mellencourt, who cheerfully went on and on about the beautiful fall weather. Harold didn't know which was worse.

The main course arrived — large breasts of chicken covered in a rich Marsala sauce with large pieces of mushrooms and a side of mashed potatoes and peas.

Harold could enjoy some good food, even if the conversation wasn't up to snuff. He scanned the faces of the people at the table. Peter conversed intently with Edgar.

Frederick Jorgenson dropped his napkin on the table and announced that he needed to stand for a moment to stretch his legs after the hike today. Betty Buchanan and Duncan Haverson exchanged glances and leaned toward each other to converse. A loud clatter caused Harold to divert his attention toward the other side of the room where a member of the wait staff bent over to help pick up a fallen plate. When Harold looked back to the immediate vicinity, he saw Frederick sit and resume eating his meal.

Once everyone had finished, Peter clinked his glass with a knife, and the conversations came to a halt. "I'd like to welcome you back to Mountain Splendor."

"This has become our home away from home," Edgar said. "You going to pitch tents for us until rooms open up?"

Peter smiled. "That's why I thought it would be good to have all of you here for dinner. I want to give you an update on the room availability situation."

"I hope we can move in soon," Celia said.

Peter took a sheet of paper out of his jacket pocket and studied it for a moment. "We have one room opening. The first person on the waiting list is Frederick Jorgenson."

Frederick pumped his fist in the air. "Yes!"

Harold watched the performance. Given how enthusiastic Frederick acted, could he have tampered with Alice Jones's pills and bludgeoned Henrietta Yates? Through the process of elimination, he now had an opportunity to move into Mountain Splendor.

"There is one problem," Peter continued. "The room is a single bedroom. Mr. Jorgenson, you had requested a two-bedroom apartment."

Frederick looked crestfallen. "I wanted the second bedroom for my historical book collection." He brightened. "On second thought, I can fit into one bedroom. I'll take it. How soon can I move in?"

"We need to repaint and replace the worn carpet. "Within a week."

"And the others of us who want to move in?" Edgar Fontaine asked.

"We'll be working through the waiting list as soon as more openings arise. I want to make sure the rest of you are still interested in joining our community." Peter paused and looked around the table.

All the heads nodded.

"Good. I will keep you apprised of openings." He snapped his fingers toward a waiter. "Now on to dessert."

Large pieces of blueberry and peach pie with vanilla ice cream were served.

Harold resisted the urge to pat his stomach after the delicious meal. The food was consistently good at Mountain Splendor, but Peter had made sure that it was excellent this evening.

Edgar Fontaine raised a glass of water. "I'd like to propose a toast to Peter Lemieux and the wait staff at Mountain Splendor for this fine meal."

The others except for Gertrude Ash raised their glasses. Celia elbowed Gertrude. "Don't be a stick in the mud."

Gertrude raised her glass halfway.

"I hope to see all of you here on a permanent basis over time." Peter clinked glasses with Edgar. "Thank you for joining us this evening."

A glass crashed to the table. Frederick Jorgenson toppled over and rolled onto the floor, holding his stomach.

Peter shot upright, knocking over his chair. "Are you all right?"

"My stomach. I feel awful."

"Call 9-1-1!" Celia shrieked.

Harold took out his cell and made the call.

"Is there a nurse here?" Edgar asked.

"No, she's off duty at five," Peter replied.

Edgar pursed his lips. "There should be medical assistance at Mountain Splendor at all times."

"This is an independent living facility not an assisted living or a nursing home," Peter said.

"Since I was a dentist, I guess I'm the closest to the medical profession." Edgar bent over and placed a hand on Frederick's forehead. "Do you have cramps?"

Frederick groaned. "Yes." He began to shiver.

"Can someone get a blanket?" Edgar asked.

Harold pulled a tablecloth off an empty table. "Here's something you can use to cover him.

Within minutes a siren wailed and two EMTs dashed into the room with a stretcher. Everyone stood and watched as Frederick was carted away.

Phoebe put her hand to her cheek. "What a way for our dinner to end."

Gertrude gave a derisive snort. "It better be only Frederick's problem and not the food we all ate."

Phoebe put her hand on her belly. "Oh dear. I hope I don't get sick."

Peter frowned. "Is anyone else having stomach problems?"

Harold decided to minimize any hypochondriac reactions. "I feel fine. I'm sure it was some problem unique to Frederick." He truly wished that was the case.

# CHAPTER THIRTY-THREE 🦇

Harold slept fitfully that night, waking up once wondering if his churning stomach was a symptom of more than nerves. A fuzzy dream had imprinted images in his brain of giant red mushrooms flying above him and oozing sticky white liquid onto his head.

By morning, he dragged himself out of bed and checked in the bathroom mirror. A haggard face stared back. He pushed on his stomach and let out a belch. Nothing wrong there. A spike of hunger surged through his gut. All systems AOK. Time to replenish.

Downstairs, he found Ned Fister attacking a stack of pancakes and he joined him. Ned popped a piece of sausage in his mouth, chewed and looked at Harold. "I understand the kitchen tried to poison someone last night."

"Where'd you hear that?"

"One of the biddies this morning." He waved his fork toward the bridge foursome at the nearby table. "She yammered that some visitor had keeled over in the dining room last night."

Harold took a large bite of the pancakes the waiter had given him. "I was there."

"No kidding? What's the scoop?"

Harold dabbed at the corner of his mouth with his napkin and returned it to his lap. "A man named Frederick Jorgenson who is on the waiting list to come here was at a dinner for prospective residents. He had some kind of stomach disorder, fell to the floor and was carted out by the EMTs."

"Our food do him in?"

Harold paused for a beat. "It's possible but not likely. I ate the same things Frederick did, and I'm fit as a fiddle this morning."

146

Ned grinned. "Maybe a fiddle with a missing string. You look a little gaunt this morning."

Harold ran his hand through his thinning hair. "I didn't sleep well last night. I woke up, worrying over all the recent events."

"Yeah. We can't have people flopping over in the dining hall. Not good for business for Peter. Speaking of Peter, here he comes."

Peter Lemieux strode up to their table. "Harold, may I have a word with you?"

"Hey, I'm ready to leave anyway," Ned said. "You can take my place." He rose, saluted Harold and moseyed toward the exit.

Peter waited a moment and dropped into the vacated chair.

Harold regarded the retirement home director. He had dark circles under his eyes, and his suit jacket was crumpled as if he had slept in it. "You look like you didn't have any more sound sleep than I did."

"You got that right. I tossed and turned and finally came to work at four a.m. I spent most of the night convincing myself that I wasn't sick to my stomach."

"Same here. Any other reports of stomach problems?"

"I was concerned, so I called everyone on the waiting list. Not surprisingly, all the people were already up, probably having slept as well as we did. No problems, although Gertrude Ash said she would have to rethink coming here. She's at the bottom of the waiting list, so we'll see what she decides."

"She doesn't have the most pleasant disposition anyway." Harold didn't mention that she would fit right in with many of the Front Wingers who could have Surly as their middle names. "Any word how Frederick Jorgenson is doing?"

"I called the hospital and they put me through to his room. I spoke to his son who was there. Frederick is doing much better but will be kept in the hospital for another day for observation."

"Any indication of the cause of his stomach disorder?"

"Nothing yet. His son did mention one other item." Peter frowned. "He said Frederick is taking his name off the waiting list. After his experience here at dinner, he no longer wants to move into Mountain Splendor."

"That's too bad." Of all the prospects, Frederick was one of the more benign ones. And he didn't tell bad jokes.

"He was on the top of the waiting list. The next in line will get Alice Jones's room. That honor goes to Edgar Fontaine."

Interesting. The guy leading the mushroom hike and self-proclaimed mushroom expert had benefited from Frederick's illness. And the mushroom known as the sickener had disappeared. "Do you know if Detective Deavers will be here today?"

"He wanted to review the history of Alice Jones as a resident. Told me he'd be here at nine."

"When you see him, tell him I have some information to pass along."

Peter quirked an eyebrow. "You doing some investigating?"

"I went on a hike yesterday with a number of the people on the waiting list. I should share my observations with the detective."

Peter stood. "I'll let him know."

Harold watched Peter make the rounds to speak with people at other tables. In addition to being a competent administrator, Peter was friendly to everyone and had a genuine affection for his charges. His was a difficult job. He had to keep the place running, motivate the staff and deal with the vagaries of the eclectic set of people residing here. And handle all sorts of emergencies, such as someone getting sick in the dining room.

After observing a few more minutes of Peter's meet-and-greet, Harold slowly rose and ambled out of the dining room.

At the door, Betty Buchanan pushed past him. "Out of my way."

"Nice seeing you, too, Betty."

She harrumphed and thrust her walker ahead of her toward the green elevator.

Harold shook his head. There were pleasant people, and there were people like Betty. Oh, well. He had his friends in the Back Wing. A surge of warmth passed through his chest. And of all his friends, there was particularly Bella.

\*\*\*\*\*

After the red elevator deposited him on the fourth floor, Harold returned to his room. He opened the curtains and stared outside. A partially cloudy morning with rays of sunshine shooting through openings in the clouds. Kind of like his own existence. Clouds of problems with a few rays of friendship and companionship.

He read his book for a while, learning about witchcraft in the nineteenth and twentieth centuries, then tried the tube but couldn't find anything that appealed to him. He most wanted to see Bella but didn't think it would be fair to pound on the wall this early in the morning. He had awakened her early when Jason was visiting. She needed her beauty sleep, and it surely worked for her.

He stood and paced around the room before plunking back into his easy chair. It wasn't easing him this morning. Too much on his mind. He checked his watch. Hopefully, Deavers would contact him shortly.

Closing his eyes, he replayed scenes from the hike the day before. Too bad he hadn't been paying more attention and seen who had taken the poisonous mushroom. Then he reminded himself, he was only making a supposition. He couldn't prove that Frederick had received a dose of *Russula emetica*. And if so, how had the perp snuck it into Frederick's food but no one else's? A mystery.

Harold jumped up and resumed his pacing, to be interrupted by the doorbell jangling. He opened the door to find Deavers standing there. "I've been waiting for you."

"As I mentioned to you yesterday, you're one of the few people who acts glad to see me, Mr. McCaffrey."

"That's because I enjoy your smiling face, Detective."

Deavers scowled. "That's something I'm seldom accused of having."

"I have to test your sense of humor, or lack thereof. Come on in and take a seat."

He didn't ask where he should take it as someone with a warped sense of humor like Edgar Fontaine would have done.

"Mr. Lemieux told me you wanted to speak with me."

"That's right. It regards the incident last night with Frederick Jorgenson. I'm sure you're current on his suspicious stomach disorder."

"Yes. Mr. Lemieux and I discussed the event a few minutes ago."

"Here's the thing. I think it ties in again to the waiting list."

Deavers held up his hand. "I know you think the waiting list is the source of all problems around Mountain Splendor. Why this time?"

Harold sucked on his lip for a moment and then continued. "I went on a hike yesterday with a group called the Senior Sneakers, a group of old farts who like to hike. All the people on the Mountain Splendor waiting list attended. And the unique aspect of this hike — we searched for mushrooms. We learned about edible and poisonous mushrooms. During the hike we saw a *Russula emetica*, which is affectionately called the sickener. Everyone crowded around. Afterwards, I noticed that the mushroom had disappeared. Then last night Frederick gets sick. I would suggest that you and the medical authorities check to see if Frederick might have ingested some of that toxic mushroom."

Deavers took out his notepad and scribbled some notes. He regarded Harold. "Seems kind of farfetched, but I've learned not to ignore your *suggestions.*"

"Thanks, Detective. I don't know for sure, but it might be useful to your investigation."

# CHAPTER THIRTY-FOUR 🦇

Nelson stopped by Mountain Splendor early that evening to pick up Harold and Bella to transport them to Broomfield. Along the way, Bella said to Harold, who sat in the backseat, "Don't forget to get your clubs. You promised to teach me how to play golf."

"Thanks for the reminder. I had forgotten."

"Don't start losing your memory, Dad. I'm glad to hear you're going to take up golf again."

"Yep. This young lady expressed interest, so we'll get out to whack some golf balls one of these days. I'll have to see if I can still swing the clubs."

"And I'll have to learn from scratch," Bella added. "It will be my first time out."

*****

When they pulled into the garage and got out of the car, Nelson said, "First thing, while we're in the garage, let me retrieve your golf clubs, Dad." He removed the bag and push cart from the front of the garage and stashed them in the trunk of the car.

Jason came running into the garage. "Bella. You have to come see my room."

"Let me get into the house first."

He took her hand and let her inside. Harold tagged along as Jason took them up to his room, which was decorated with large posters. One had a picture of Howard Thurston holding a skull. Another of Harry Kellar levitating a woman. A third of Houdini in handcuffs.

"You could have been as good as Houdini," Jason said to Bella.

151

"He was a great magician and didn't have to resort to special powers. He did all of his magic through illusion and deceit."

Jason laughed. "And you never resort to deceit?"

"Mine is different."

"What are you going to be for Halloween, Grandpa?"

Harold scratched his head. "I hadn't considered it. Maybe I'll be a geezer."

Bella glared at him. "You need to come up with a costume. Halloween is a very special holiday in the Back Wing."

"I can imagine."

"I'm going to be a warlock," Jason said. "I'll do magic along the way, but not like Warty tries to do."

"Good thing," Bella said.

"I have an idea for you, Grandpa. I used it last year." Jason dashed into his closet and came out holding a box. "Don't show it to Bella ahead of time. You can surprise her on Halloween night."

"Some secret costume?"

Jason grinned. "You'll see."

"Dinner's almost ready," Emily called from downstairs.

Jason looked wildly around. "Oops. I promised Mom I'd help get things ready." He dashed out of the room.

Harold scanned Jason's desk. "He has his school books neatly stacked. Not the messy room of a typical teenager."

"He takes after his grandfather. Organized and efficient."

Harold groaned. "There's an idea for a tombstone, 'organized and efficient.'"

Bella patted his arm. "You have other redeeming qualities as well."

They headed downstairs and found Jason setting the dining room table. Banging sounds emerged from the kitchen.

Bella and Harold stepped into the kitchen. "Anything we can do to help?" Bella asked.

Emily held a container in her hand. "Darn it. I forgot to put butter on the shopping list. There's hardly any left for the baked potatoes and corn on the cob."

"Let me see." Bella took the container. "If you scrape the inside, I bet there will be enough. Give it a try."

Emily looked skeptical. "You think so?"

Harold watched and noticed Bella winking at him."I've learned to trust Bella's observations. I think we'll have enough butter."

Emily carried the container to the table, and they all sat down.

"We have ham, baked potatoes and corn on the cob," Emily said. "Unfortunately, we'll have to be sparing on the small amount of butter left." She passed the container to Jason.

He took his knife and scraped butter out and heaped it on his corn and potatoes."

"Don't take it all," Emily said.

"No sweat, Mom. There's plenty left." Jason passed it to his dad who also applied an ample amount of butter. Likewise with Bella and Harold. When the container reached Emily, she put her knife inside and came out with a large dollop of butter. Her eyes grew large. "Bella was right. We did have enough butter."

"Sometimes things have a way of working out," Bella said.

Harold noticed the twinkle in Bella's eyes and grinned. "You ever think of performing fish and loaves?"

"I don't know what you're talking about."

"I turned in my biology report today," Jason said. "Thanks for the help you gave me over the weekend, Bella."

"My pleasure. Any time you want to discuss plants and herbs come visit or give a call. I'll be happy to help again."

"How are you at geometry?"

"That's not my strong suit. I bet your grandfather could help with that."

"I bisected a few angles in my day," Harold said. He certainly wouldn't tackle the plants and herbs. He couldn't even distinguish the edible from poisonous mushrooms he'd tried to learn about on the recent hike.

*****

For dessert Emily served chocolate pudding. Harold was thankful there were no Jell-O shots like at the Back Wing parties.

Since it was a warm autumn evening, they adjourned to the back patio and sat around a glass-covered table that held battery-operated fake candles.

"I can't believe this weather we're having," Nelson said. "Who would expect that we could be sitting outside in comfort at this time of year?"

"There's been some snow in the high country," Jason replied. "I can't wait to start snowboarding."

Harold remembered the years he had taken Nelson skiing. A great father and son activity. He had retired the skis five years ago. That and the golf clubs. But, hey, he'd be trying golf again. He didn't think he'd hit the slopes, though. He didn't think his creaky bones were up to the risk of falling on hard-packed snow.

"What's that?" Jason pointed. "It looks like someone is going through the Hendersons' yard."

Nelson hurried over to the fence. "You're right. They're out at the Optimists Club meeting tonight. Someone is trying to break in through their back door."

"I'll take care of this," Bella said. "Harold, call 9-1-1."

Harold took out his phone and punched in the digits as Bella stepped over to the fence. She wiggled her fingers.

Emily wrung her hands. "Did he get into the house?"

"He seems to have run into a little problem." Bella returned and dusted her hands together.

Within five minutes a siren wailed, and a police cruiser pulled up to the curb.

Nelson went out to meet the officer and explain the situation.

Everyone waited by the fence as the policeman entered the Hendersons' yard, directing the beam of a flashlight toward the back door. "Don't move. Broomfield police."

A scuffling sound wafted through the air followed by the sound of handcuffs being snapped into place.

Bella wiggled her fingers again.

"I couldn't see clearly," Nelson said, "but it looks like the officer is taking the suspect out to his patrol car. Let's go check."

They trooped out to the curb, where the police officer was on his phone. When he completed his call he stepped over to them.

"Looks like you caught the burglar," Nelson said.

The policeman had a perplexed look on his face. "It was the darnest thing. I shone the light on the guy. He stood with the door open. He was as rigid as a statue. He didn't move an inch. He already had his hands behind his back. All I had to do was snap cuffs on him. At first I couldn't budge him. Then all of a sudden, he came free as if he had been frozen to the ground, and I was able to lead him to the patrol car."

Bella smiled. "Imagine that."

The officer scratched his head. "Never had a burglar be so easy to catch."

"All the result of good police work," Bella said.

# CHAPTER THIRTY-FIVE 🦇

On Wednesday afternoon, Harold and Bella took a pre-hike walk to the North Table Mountain trailhead. Since it was only the two of them and they had plenty of time, Bella did not provide any extra assist to Harold's walking poles.

"Any specific objectives in ferreting out the criminal within this hiking group?" Bella asked.

"Right now, Edgar Fontaine is at the top of my persons of interest list. I want to chat with him along the trail. If we work down the waiting list, Celia Barns and Duncan Haverson are the next ones in line."

"I'll chat both of them up along the way."

"Just don't freeze anyone, today."

"I save that for special occasions."

*****

They met the group at the trailhead. Harold looked around and noticed one person missing. "Where's Gertrude Ash?"

"She had a doctor's appointment," Phoebe Mellencourt replied. "We'll miss her, but the hike must go on."

"Right. Let's move out. Time's a' wasting." Edgar Fontaine signaled and started along the trail.

Harold and Bella brought up the rear as the others charged forward.

Bella leaned toward Harold. "You'd think this was an army training march."

"Edgar runs a tight ship. He obviously doesn't want anyone delaying his hike. Do you think he could have used his planning skills to kill Alice Jones and eliminate the top two people on the waiting list?"

"It's possible. He doesn't strike me as a killer, but none of the others do either."

"Monday night we had Frederick Jorgenson celebrating that he'd be coming to Mountain Splendor, which was short-lived. Now Edgar benefits as the one who will move into Alice's room."

After half an hour, Edgar brought his troops to a halt, and everyone took out their water bottles for a sip. Harold used the opportunity to step close to Edgar. "I understand you may be joining us at Mountain Splendor soon."

Edgar's eyes lit up. "Yeah. Peter Lemieux called yesterday afternoon telling me that Frederick had withdrawn his name and I was next. Imagine that."

Harold regarded him carefully. Entirely too chipper after what had happened to Frederick. "Aren't you concerned that your friend Frederick Jorgenson won't be living at Mountain Splendor?"

"I'm sorry to hear that he withdrew his name from consideration, but life goes on." He put his water bottle back in his daypack. "Let's move out, people."

Several of the others pushed past Harold, so he struck up a conversation with Phoebe Mellencourt who oohed and aahed over the wonderful weather.

During the next rest stop, Bella signaled to Harold, and they stepped aside from the others.

"Pick up anything?" Harold asked.

"Other than dust? I had a chance to speak briefly with Celia. She's aware that she'll be on the top of the waiting list after Edgar moves in. She went on and on about how she wants to put together an acting group at Mountain Splendor. She says she organized a group of seniors to put on plays in Denver when she lived there."

"Maybe we could suggest some Back Wingers who could participate. That would give Celia an experience."

"I don't think she's ready for that yet."

"And Duncan Haverson?" Harold asked.

"I couldn't get him to open up at all. He only wanted to lecture me on the different types of cloud formations he could identify."

"Onward," Edgar shouted.

Harold and Bella were the last to get going. They reached a steep section of trail, and Harold grabbed Bella's arm. "Hold on a second. I need to retie my shoelace." He bent down and took care of it.

The others had disappeared around a bend. As they moved forward to catch up, there was a loud cry followed by a crashing sound.

Harold and Bella scrambled forward to reach the others.

"What happened?" Bella asked.

Phoebe had turned pale. "Edgar slid off the trail and hit his head."

Harold peered over the edge. Edgar lay all akimbo in a pile of rocks.

No one moved, so Harold slid down the side to where Edgar lay. He examined him and didn't notice any protruding broken bones. He looked back up to the trail. "Someone call 9-1-1."

Edgar moaned.

"Can you hear me?" Harold asked.

Edgar moved his hand to the side of his head. "Headache."

"Any other pain?"

"My hip."

"What happened?"

"I don't know. I was walking along the trail, and all of a sudden I was tumbling down the hillside."

"Did someone push you?"

"I'm not sure. We were close together. I don't feel so good." Edgar leaned to the side and retched.

"Take it easy. Help will be on the way." Harold removed the water bottle from Edgar's pack and held it for him to take a sip.

"Thanks."

"Do you think you can sit up?"

Edgar shook his head and winced. "My hip really hurts."

"Are you warm enough?"

"Yeah." Edgar closed his eyes.

Harold took off his daypack and pulled out his light jacket. He bunched it up and tucked it under Edgar's head to provide a pillow.

"The call has been placed," Duncan Haverson shouted. "I'll head back down the trail to meet the emergency responders."

*****

158

It took half an hour before two EMTs carrying a stretcher appeared. They slid down the rocks to where Harold sat next to Edgar. After some maneuvering they lifted Edgar onto the stretcher, strapped him in and transported him to the trail before returning to the ambulance.

"I guess this is the end of the hike for today," Phoebe said.

Everyone headed down the trail.

Harold and Bella again were the last to leave.

"Did you find out from anyone what happened?" Harold asked.

"I spoke with each of them. No one saw exactly what occurred. They were clumped together along the trail. Then Edgar lost his balance."

Harold had a bad feeling in his gut. "Did someone push him?"

"It's possible, but if so, I don't know which one did it."

Harold leaned over to inspect the trail where Edgar had fallen. He saw loose gravel and a skid mark. Nothing that would indicate exactly what had transpired. "It could have been Celia, Duncan or Phoebe. The only person on the waiting list we can eliminate is the no-show, Gertrude Ash."

"There you go with the waiting list again."

Harold looked off toward the foothills. "All of this *has* to be connected to the waiting list."

"You obviously don't think this was an accident."

"No, do you?"

Bella shook her head.

Harold gritted his teeth. "Edgar is eliminated. We're down to three suspects.

*****

At dinner that evening, Peter Lemieux came up to Harold who was eating alone and sat down opposite him. "I received a phone call a short while ago. Edgar Fontaine had an accident today."

"Yeah. I was there. He fell while hiking. The EMTs had to come rescue him. How's he doing?"

Peter tilted his wrist back and forth. "Nothing life-threatening, but he suffered a concussion and a broken hip. He'll be having surgery tomorrow and will have to go through a stint at a rehab facility. His daughter informed me that he would be withdrawing his application to come to Mountain Splendor until after his recuperation. And I received another piece of bad news. An hour ago Gertrude Ash called to say she was no longer interested in becoming a resident."

"We're losing people right and left from the waiting list."

Peter bit his lip. "It's very disturbing."

"Now Celia Barns will be next in line to get Alice Jones's old room."

Peter looked over his shoulder. "I hope nothing happens to her."

# CHAPTER THIRTY-SIX 🦇

On Thursday afternoon, Harold called a taxi and with Bella following him wheeled his push cart with attached golf bag through the Mountain Splendor lobby.

"Going for a little exercise?" the receptionist, Andrea, called out.

"That we are. I'm going to teach Bella to play golf today."

"Maybe you can teach me sometime as well," Andrea said. "I've never tried it."

Bella patted Harold's arm. "Here's a whole new career for you. Teaching women how to play golf."

"We'll see how it goes today, before making any long term commitments that would change my retirement status."

"I'm sure you're a good teacher."

"I don't know. I imagine you will be able to make the golf ball do whatever you want."

"Posh. You'll have to show me everything. Besides, I would never use my powers to help myself. And thank you. I'm glad you scheduled this expedition for the afternoon and not the morning."

"I've learned that mornings aren't best when including someone from the Back Wing."

The taxi arrived, and they took the short ride to the Fossil Trace Golf Club.

Harold rented clubs and a push cart for Bella and bought a medium-sized bucket of practice balls for seven dollars. He showed her how to hold a club and had her practice swings with a seven iron.

"Good. Take the club back slowly and then swing forward with a nice smooth motion."

After a half dozen more swings, Harold lined up a ball on the one-inch thick mat. He helped her position her feet. "Now give it a shot."

Bella swung and struck the ball, which traveled a hundred yards.

Harold whistled. "Not bad." He placed another ball.

After a dozen balls, he had her try a driver, three wood, five iron and nine iron. She finished off the bucket, and Harold gave her a round of applause.

"I have no idea when to use these different clubs," Bella said.

"I'll suggest which one when we're on the course. Let's go to the putting green."

Bella learned the basics of putting after fifteen minutes.

"You're a quick study."

Bella smiled. "Good teacher."

Harold checked his watch. "Time to check in for our tee time."

"Is this an English sport and we're going to have a spot of tea?"

"Funny."

At the counter, Harold paid forty dollars, the rate for two seniors residing in Golden playing nine holes, a bargain compared to what Harold used to pay when he played golf.

The attendant said, "I've matched you with another twosome. You'll be up in ten minutes, playing the back nine."

A worried expression crossed Bella's face. "I have to play with other people?"

"Don't worry. Most golfers are understanding."

"You said 'most.' That implies that some aren't."

"I'll be there to protect you."

Bella gave Harold's hand a pat. "My hero."

The attendant returned Harold's credit card. "You'll be joining the Haverson party."

Harold flinched. "Would that be Duncan Haverson?"

"Let me check the first name." He searched through a clipboard. "Yes. That's the name. And his partner is Phoebe Mellencourt."

"I'll be darned. See, Bella, you won't be playing with strangers. We'll be joining two members of the Senior Sneakers." He leaned close to her ear and whispered, "And we can schmooze with two of our suspects."

"We'll be able to kill two birds with one golf ball today. As long as one of them doesn't try to dispatch the other with a golf club to the head."

"I hope we can avoid any violence today."

They wheeled their clubs toward the tenth tee staging area and found the other two waiting. Phoebe grinned when Harold and Bella informed them they'd be making a foursome.

Duncan scrunched up his face. "I had hoped we could play as a twosome."

Harold wondered if Duncan had some romantic interest in Phoebe and wanted time with her alone.

"Do you play often?" Phoebe asked.

"I used to play a lot, but haven't for several years. Bella is new to the game."

Duncan groaned. "I hope you won't slow us down."

Anger flared in Bella's eyes. "I don't think I'll be the problem."

*Uh-oh.* Harold realized Duncan was in for some special treatment today.

They agreed to tee off from the white markers. Harold checked the scorecard and saw they had 270 yards to go. When their turn came, Duncan wasted no time in placing his tee in the turf, taking one practice swing and whacking his ball straight down the fairway.

"Nice shot," Harold said.

"That's how they always go," Duncan said.

Harold figured that would not be the case for the whole afternoon. Duncan was in for a rude awakening.

Phoebe followed with a shorter drive that sliced slightly.

"You need to keep your wrist firm," Duncan said.

Phoebe glared at Duncan. "I don't need your advice."

Harold reconsidered his earlier thought. He certainly didn't pick up any warm feelings between the two of them. He wondered why they were here together. Hopefully not something sinister.

Bella took her turn and hit a respectable drive, shorter than Phoebe's, and Harold drove twenty yards past Bella.

Duncan and Phoebe took off with their push carts, and Harold walked with Bella to her ball.

"Now what?" she asked.

He pulled the three wood out of her bag. "Here you go. This will be a little harder than when you practiced because you don't have the benefit of a smooth mat. Take a practice swing and have at it."

Bella did as directed and hit a shot that sailed over a hundred yards down the fairway.

"Not bad."

Farther along, Bella had trouble with a seven iron shot that dribbled only twenty yards, but her next shot landed on the green.

Duncan was waiting as they approached the green. "About time."

Harold, Bella and Phoebe all sank their putts. Duncan who was twelve feet away picked up his marker and lined up his putt. He struck the ball and it sailed ten feet past the hole. He snarled. "That never happens to me." He stomped over and lined up the next putt. This one came to an abrupt halt three feet from the hole. He clenched his putter and proceeded to line up the gimme which circled the cup and popped out. He finally sank his ball from three inches away.

Bella gave Duncan her most pleasant smile. "About time."

Duncan put down everyone's scores and announced that he had a four. He grabbed Phoebe's arm and propelled her toward the next tee.

Bella leaned toward Harold and whispered, "He's cheating. He really took five shots."

Harold whispered back. "I know."

As they approached the eleventh tee, Harold stopped to sip from his water bottle and then caught up to Duncan, Phoebe and Bella. "It's a shame that Frederick Jorgenson got sick and decided not to move into Mountain Splendor."

Duncan took a cloth from his bag and wiped his driver. "Yeah, I'm not sure I want to move in either after Frederick went to the hospital from eating a meal there."

Harold wondered if another name might be dropped from the waiting list, but he decided to press on. "And then Edgar Fontaine had an accident while hiking."

Phoebe sucked on her lip for a moment. "His fall was horrible."

"Did you see what happened?" Harold asked.

She shook her head. "We were all bunched together. One moment he was there, and the next he was tumbling down the side of the hill."

"Duncan, did you see it?" Bella asked.

"Nope. I was looking at the hawk circling above us. I missed everything until Edgar screamed."

On this hole, which was only 126 yards, Bella asked Harold, "What club should I use?"

"If you're asking, you shouldn't be playing," Duncan said.

Bella glared at him. "I wasn't speaking to you."

Duncan gave a dismissive wave of his hand.

Harold pulled a seven iron out of Bella's bag and handed it to her. "Try this."

"You should be using a nine iron." Duncan said.

"Bella will be fine with a seven."

And she was. Her drive rolled onto the green. Duncan ended up overshooting the hole into the rough. His next shot went straight up and landed two feet away.

"Good altitude," Bella said.

As they approached the tee box for the twelfth, Duncan said, "Here's the longest one on the back nine." He didn't make any further comment on Bella's play.

When they reached the green, Phoebe showed Bella and Harold Triceratops footprints and other fossils nearby. She pointed to the ridge. "You can also see old mining equipment up there. This is my favorite golf course with all the unique scenery."

They continued through the course, and Duncan only had one ball stuck in a tree, one stolen by a hawk and one that exploded. He did end up in sand traps on two occasions.

When they completed the eighteenth, Harold told Duncan and Phoebe he had enjoyed the game. Duncan only scowled and headed toward his car.

Phoebe said, "Good seeing the two of you," and traipsed after Duncan.

Once they were out of hearing range, Harold said, "At first I thought those two might have some type of romantic relationship, but it became clear that they had no such feelings for each other. Do you think there's any chance that one of them wanted to injure the other to get that person off the waiting list?"

"That's a possibility. But it would have to be Phoebe trying to eliminate Duncan since she's lower on the waiting list."

"If that was the case, the little... uh... incidents that Duncan suffered kept them far enough apart that nothing bad could happen." Harold put his arm around Bella's shoulder. "In any case, it was great to be out playing golf. I didn't think I'd ever play again. I needed a little incentive. You. What did you think of the game?"

"An interesting sport. Very unpredictable. Duncan had a very inconsistent game. He could be good but had some very poor shots." Bella gave a Cheshire Cat smile.

"I don't think Duncan had much fun today," Harold said.

"Couldn't happen to a nicer guy."

# CHAPTER THIRTY-SEVEN 🦇

Harold called a taxi to take them back to Mountain Splendor. The warm day had suddenly turned chilly with cold gusts of wind shaking the nearly bare maple and ash trees. Bella huddled against Harold in the back seat. "I think we're in for some true autumn weather. Just in time for Halloween."

Harold smacked his forehead. "I forgot all about Halloween with everything going on. Then again, it isn't such a big day as when I took Nelson trick-or-treating. I used to enjoy those outings with him all bundled up, dashing from door to door."

"With Halloween being a major holiday for the Back Wing, you'll find everyone gets in the act. You'll see some truly unique costumes, and everyone goes around to collect goodies, so you better stock up. You don't want tricks played on you."

"And I've seen what Warty can do."

"You don't have to worry about him because his tricks misfire. Some of the others won't be so careless. One year Viola forgot to get treats. Someone left her a bottle, which she thought was blood. It was cheap wine. She took one sip and conked out."

"How does trick-or-treating work if everyone lives by themselves in their own room?"

"We do it by floor. Second floor at seven, third at seven-thirty, fourth at eight, fifth at eight-thirty and sixth at nine. That way everyone can roam the halls, knocking on doors, but we also have half an hour to give out treats on our own floor. Then we congregate in the Back Wing lounge for a party."

"Sounds like a good system. You Back Wingers are certainly party animals."

"Why not? We enjoy our celebrations. Whenever someone arrives or leaves or a holiday or whenever the mood moves us."

"Do you go trick-or-treating in the Front Wing?"

"We tried that once a few years ago but scared the bejabbers out of all the prissy Front Wingers. One woman nearly had a heart attack and another got sick to her stomach. We decided to maintain the peace thereafter by sticking to the Back Wing."

"At least you aren't terrorizing kids in the nearby neighborhoods."

Bella laughed. "That isn't the problem. We did go out in the community once, but Viola freaked out when she saw the bloody costumes worn by a bunch of the kids and she fainted. We had to carry her home and decided not to risk it again."

"I know what you mean," the cabbie shouted over his shoulder. "My kids want to dress up like those zombies. My wife and I told them no way. They're going to go as werewolves and vampires instead."

"That's much more reasonable." Bella winked at Harold.

Harold leaned toward Bella and whispered. "Speaking of zombies. I've never seen one in the Back Wing."

"That's because they don't exist. They're only in books and movies."

"That's a relief."

*****

Back at Mountain Splendor, Harold paid the taxi driver and wished him and his kids a happy upcoming Halloween. Ned Fister stood near the parking lot, trimming a bush. Harold and Bella strolled over.

"You never seem to run out of gardening projects," Harold said.

Ned wiped dirt from his forehead. "I'm finishing my final winterizing before the weather turns bad. You can feel it coming. Snow flurries are forecast for tomorrow."

"Good thing we played golf today," Bella said.

"While you two were off frolicking in the sunshine, I slaved away with my clippers and shears."

Bella put her hands on her hips. "Don't give me that. You can't fool me, Ned Fister. You love working outside."

Ned grinned. "I know. But I have to complain once in a while. How else do I stay in the running for curmudgeon of the year?"

"You're not even close," Bella said. "You're too nice a guy."

"Don't tell the aphids that. They think I'm the terminator."

They left Ned to continue his pruning, and Harold wheeled his clubs into the lobby. At the clacking sound, Andrea looked up from the reception counter. "Harold, Detective Deavers was looking for you earlier. I told him you were playing golf."

"Is he still here?"

"He had something to do in the Front Wing. When he comes by I'll tell him you're back."

"I'll be upstairs if he wants to see me."

They took the red elevator to the fourth floor.

"Why don't you stash your clubs and come to my room," Bella said. "I'll fix you a snack."

"That would be great. I'm starving."

Harold quickly deposited his push cart and clubs in his closet and dashed to Bella's room. Several candles sent wisps of smoke into the air. Harold sniffed. "Ah. An aroma of cranberries."

"Very good sense of smell. I make my own candles, and these do have cranberries in the wax. I also use vanilla, sage and peppermint. Food choices include a sandwich, soup, salad or a cheese plate."

"Whatever you have on hand."

"I don't actually have much on hand, but I can materialize whatever you'd like. Your wish is my command."

Harold frowned. "You have all these unique powers, Bella, but I'd prefer you only use them when absolutely necessary."

"Now's a good time. You're hungry."

Harold pounded his fist on the kitchenette counter. "I don't want special treatment. I think you should reserve your special powers for emergencies only."

Bella's eyes flared. "Oh, yeah. Are you trying to tell me what to do?"

Their mutual glares were interrupted by a pounding on Bella's door. "Now what." Bella stomped over and angrily thrust open the door.

Cassandra stood there wringing her hands. "I heard shouting. Do

I need to change time back an hour so you two won't fight?"

Bella looked over her shoulder toward Harold, and her angry face softened.

Harold let out a loud sigh. "I'm sorry, Bella. I got carried away."

Bella gave a wan smile. "I also overreacted." She turned back to Cassandra. "I think we can work things out without going back in time. Thanks for the offer, though."

Cassandra nodded. "Good. I hate to hear people fight. I hope you don't mind that I butted in."

"That's okay," Harold said. "It gave me a moment to reconsider my overreaction."

Cassandra waggled her fingers. "I'll be on my way. You two be nice to each other. You don't deserve discontent." She spun on her heels and disappeared along the hallway.

Bella closed the door. "That woman is interesting. She seems to sense our arguments. She did the same thing yesterday when Viola and Bailey disagreed over the most nutritious type of blood. They became quite heated, and Cassandra intervened. Said the same thing, that she'd change time back so they could avoid the argument. It worked. They decided their friendship was more important than who was right."

Harold put his arms around Bella's waist. "I feel the same way."

"You're right on one point. I should reserve my powers for emergencies, not for mundane situations."

"And I won't try to run your life. Friends again?"

Bella gave him a kiss. "More than friends."

# CHAPTER THIRTY-EIGHT 🦇

Glad that he and Bella had resolved their little spat, Harold returned to his room to take a shower before dinner. As he scrubbed, he whistled his rendition of "Catch a Falling Star." He smiled to himself. He couldn't carry a tune worth darn, but he tried. The one cautionary note, he made sure to never whistle or sing too loudly. That only led to complaints.

After drying, he put on clean slacks and a long-sleeved blue shirt. He was ready for the evening. Checking his watch, he determined he had half an hour before dinner started and sank into his easy chair to read a chapter on witchcraft in the twenty-first century. He knew something about that subject.

He had only finished two pages when his doorbell jangled. Although absorbed in the chapter, Harold rose and opened the door to find Deavers standing there. "Detective, I heard you were looking for me earlier."

"That I was. May I come in?"

"Sure. Make yourself at home."

Deavers sank into the couch, and Harold returned to his easy chair. "What hot topic is on your mind?"

Deavers tapped the armrest of the couch. "I don't usually go into details with someone outside of law enforcement, but you've provided a great deal of information on this case, and I thought you might have some useful insights into what's happening. I want you to be aware of an arrest we've made."

Harold ran through the list of people on the waiting list and tried to predict which one Deavers had arrested. Could be any of them, since he didn't have anything specific on which one it would be. He didn't think there had been enough time after the golf game to arrest either Duncan Haverson or Phoebe Mellencourt. Could it be Celia Barns? He would let Deavers divulge the information as he saw fit. "Sounds like you're making some progress."

The detective wiggled his wrist back and forth. "One step backward, two steps forward. Let me review the history with you. You stayed in Alice Jones's apartment for two nights and said you had found a list there with the names of people waiting to get into Mountain Splendor."

Harold's heart beat faster, and he leaned forward. He resisted the urge to pump his fist in the air. "And that list has helped you?"

"Not directly. But you told me that someone had been inside and took that list. We went back and checked for fingerprints in the apartment. Besides yours and Alice's, we found one other set. Those of another Mountain Splendor resident named Betty Buchanan."

Harold pursed his lips. This wasn't what he expected to hear. "I've met her. Not a very pleasant woman."

A sparkle shone in Deavers's eyes. "I'm not going to comment on her personality. Ms. Buchanan is being held currently at the Jefferson County Detention Center."

"How do you know Betty's fingerprints weren't from an earlier visit to Alice's place?"

"A good question. The kitchenette countertop where we found Betty's fingerprints had been cleaned by housekeeping the afternoon of the open house because the room was being used for a tour."

All kinds of thoughts swirled through Harold's mind. Why Betty? How did she tie in to the waiting list? He voiced the most important one. "Is Betty being held on murder charges?"

"I don't have evidence of that... yet. I did have enough proof to book her for breaking and entering into the apartment of Alice Jones, which she admitted upon questioning. She has a lawyer and will probably be released on bond tomorrow."

"So if I understand this correctly, she broke into Alice's apartment and left the waiting list there, which I found. Then she came in again and took it. Why would she do all of that?"

"That's where I thought you might be of assistance. She admitted 'borrowing' a master key from one of the cleaning staff and duplicating it. Then she clammed up. I thought you might have a little chat with her when she returns to Mountain Splendor, and see if you can pick up any useful information."

"She isn't the most friendly person."

"Maybe not, but you have a way of finding pertinent information. I thought you might be willing to help."

Harold shrugged. "I can try." He puzzled through this new twist. Betty Buchanan hadn't been on his radar one iota. "How does this relate to Alice's death?"

"We think Betty went into Alice's apartment several times, even before the night you stayed there. She may have tampered with some of Alice's medication when she was in the apartment. We found a partial fingerprint on one of the bottles in Alice's medicine cabinet, but it's not good enough a print to definitively match to Betty."

"So one possibility is Betty switched some medication of Alice's that led to her death."

"You catch on fast. The coroner ruled that Alice died of heart failure, but we're waiting for the full toxicology report on chemicals in her blood. Then we can see how that matches what was in Alice's purse since she had so many bottles of pills."

"Why would Betty want Alice dead, and why did she have the waiting list?"

"Yet to be determined. Since you've been so concerned with the waiting list, I want you to know this and see if you can learn anything more from Betty."

Harold saluted. "Undercover operative, Harold McCaffrey, at your service." Another thought occurred to him. "If you matched Betty's fingerprints, they must have been in your database. How come?"

"Another good question. It seems Betty had a little problem when she was younger. She was arrested and convicted for stealing medication from a pharmacy. See the pattern?"

"Hmm. She apparently has some knowledge and experience with pharmaceuticals. Fits that she could have been switching Alice's medicine."

"That's what we're working on."

Harold stood and began pacing around the room. "I understand the connection between Betty and Alice. Could she also have been responsible for the bludgeoning death of Henrietta Yates?"

Deavers shook his head. "Nope. She has a clear alibi for the evening Henrietta Yates was bludgeoned. She was at a dinner party at a restaurant. A number of party-goers and wait staff have verified her presence in Denver. She never would have been able to get to the murder spot to cause Henrietta's death."

"Then we have the case of Frederick Jorgenson being possibly poisoned by toxic mushrooms. Could Betty be linked to that in any way?"

Deavers gave Harold his cold, steely stare. "She was in the dining room that evening, but that's the only connection. I know you've been very insistent that the waiting list is key to a number of deaths and accidents related to Mountain Splendor. I think the only link is that Betty took it and left it in Alice's apartment."

"It doesn't explain why she had the list and why she left it in Alice's apartment. I'm not giving up on my list theory."

"I won't try to convince you otherwise."

Harold clenched his fist. "Also, there was the accident when Edgar Fontaine fell off a trail. Too many people on the waiting list have had accidents. I think one of the other people on the list has been causing all the havoc."

Deavers held up a hand. "Let's take it one step at a time. First, we need to deal with Betty Buchanan. She's the one definitive lead we have."

"I'll find out what I can, but hear me out on the waiting list again." Harold held up his right index finger. "The top person on the list, Henrietta Yates is bludgeoned." He added a second finger. "The next person, Frederick Jorgenson gets sick, most likely from a poison mushroom and that mushroom could have come from a hike that same day attended by other people on the waiting list." He held up three fingers like a Cub Scout salute. "Edgar Fontaine gets pushed off a trail while surrounded by people on the waiting list and ends up in the hospital. One other person has taken herself off the waiting list — Gertrude Ash. That leaves three people who want to get into Mountain Splendor — Celia Barns, Duncan Haverson and Phoebe

Mellencourt. I'll make a deal with you, Detective. I'll find out what I can from Betty Buchanan when she gets out of jail, but I expect in return that you give serious consideration to these three as suspects. I want them looked into. Agreed?"

Deavers took out his notepad and jotted in it. He looked up and met Harold's gaze. "Agreed."

# CHAPTER THIRTY-NINE 🦇

The next morning after breakfast, Harold stopped by the reception desk and found Andrea on duty.

She greeted him with a huge smile. "Good morning, Mr. McCaffrey. Lots of sunshine this morning."

"For the moment, but it's supposed to turn cold this afternoon. We always seem to get a touch of winter on Halloween. You going trick-or-treating?"

"I'm going to take my niece and nephew so my sister and her husband can give out candy to neighborhood kids. I love Halloween."

"This will be my first experience with it at Mountain Splendor, but I understand it gets kind of crazy in the Back Wing on Halloween night."

Andrea looked toward the ceiling as if inspecting the tile. "That it does. I had duty last year and the noise—you wouldn't believe the howling and shouting. Most of the Front Wing people went up to their rooms and locked their doors."

"I guess I'll be in for a treat... or a trick."

"What are you going to dress up as tonight?" Andrea asked.

"My grandson gave me a mask to wear. I'll put it on this evening. On another subject, I have a favor to ask."

"Sure. What is it?"

"Betty Buchanan should be returning today. I'd like to speak with her when she gets here. Could you give me a call?"

"Be happy to."

Harold left the lobby and took a walk. He welcomed the chance to stretch his legs, and he had one errand to run. No time like the present.

*****

That afternoon, Harold's phone rang, and he answered to find Andrea on the line. "Betty Buchanan just came through the lobby. Boy, does she look tired."

"I'm sure she has had a difficult time over the last day. Thanks for letting me know she arrived."

Harold grabbed his purchase from the morning and took the red elevator down and then the green elevator up to the fifth floor of the Front Wing and knocked on Betty Buchanan's door.

There was a pause followed by the clanking sound of a walker. The door opened a crack, and Betty peered through the opening. "Yeah?"

Harold noticed her tone was much more subdued than on their previous encounters. "We've met before. I'm Harold McCaffrey. I want to welcome you back and have a present for you."

She opened the door wider and squinted at Harold as if inspecting a loaf of bread. "Oh, yeah. Alice's cousin."

Harold winced but kept his smile. "I brought you a box of dark chocolate truffles."

Betty's eyes lit up. "I love dark chocolate. And truffles. Yum."

Harold was glad that he had paid attention when he had first met Betty. "May I come in for a moment?"

The lure of dark chocolate truffles overcame her usual gruff demeanor. "Sure. Take a seat."

Harold handed her the box of candy and sat on a worn gray couch. He looked around the apartment. A few pictures of ocean scenes on the wall and the curtain closed, so no light entered the stark surroundings. Two cat miniatures rested on an end table.

"Do you collect ceramic cats?" Harold asked.

"No, those were given to me by my niece. She's the cat fanatic." Betty pushed her walker over to a chair and maneuvered into it. She opened the box and popped a piece in her mouth. She closed her eyes, chewed and then licked her lips. "Delicious. I needed that."

"I'm sorry to hear that you had a little problem yesterday."

"Crummy detective. Arrested me over nothing."

"I'm sure he was overzealous."

"You can say that again. That whole jail thing gave me the creeps." She took another chocolate without offering any to Harold.

He didn't care. Fortunately, she didn't ask how he knew she'd had a problem. And one other accomplishment—he had broken through her thorny façade enough to be invited in. Next, he had to figure out a way to get her to open up to him. He had one thought. "I know you enjoy playing shuffleboard. Any time you want a game, let me know."

She glanced up from her chocolate. "I'm looking for someone new to clobber. My regular partner is too easy to beat. I'm too tired today. Maybe another day."

"When you get rested up, let me know." So far so good. Now to ease into the difficult part. "When I was staying in Alice's apartment, I found a list. It had names of people who wanted to become residents at Mountain Splendor. I thought you might have left it there."

Betty finished chewing another piece of chocolate, let out a burp and pounded herself on the chest. "Good chocolate. That detective knows I left the waiting list in Alice's apartment so no skin off my back telling you. I saw it lying on the desk in the director's office when I passed by and thought I'd give it to my friend Celia Barns. She wants to move in here."

Harold took a deep breath to control his excitement at learning this. "I know Celia. She belongs to the Senior Sneakers hiking group."

"That's the one. I'm not up to walking anymore, but she gets a kick out of going on those treks."

"I've been on a few of their hikes. I've met several other people. Do you know Duncan Haverson or Phoebe Mellencourt?"

Her eyes grew wide. "I... uh... met them at the dinner for prospective residents that Peter Lemieux held."

Harold watched her carefully. He had a touchy question. "Why did you go into Alice's apartment?"

Alice gave a snort. "That's what the detective nailed me for. I couldn't resist going into her apartment. I've done it a number of times. Don't get me wrong. I didn't steal anything. But I like looking through people's stuff."

"How'd you get into her apartment?"

"You're a nosy cuss. The detective knows. I… uh… got a master key. The detective took it away from me."

Harold wondered how many apartments Betty had entered. "One other thing. Why didn't you take the waiting list with you?"

A sheepish grin crossed her face. "You showed up. I heard a key in the door. I panicked, stuck the list in the bookshelf, went out the sliding door and hid on the balcony. Good thing it wasn't too cold. I was going to have to wait until you went to sleep, but I heard you leave the apartment. I waited for a few minutes and snuck out but was so frazzled I forgot to retrieve the list."

Harold thought back to the night he'd come to stay in Alice's apartment. Sure enough. He'd parted the curtains but hadn't bothered to open the sliding door to inspect the balcony. "But the next morning the list disappeared again." Harold snapped his fingers. "You went down the elevator with me that morning, but you said you'd forgotten your comb. You went back up to get the list."

"Yeah. Now I need to get some rest."

Harold decided he'd try one more delicate subject before leaving. "Alice sure had a lot of medication. Did you ever help her with her pills?"

Betty stared down at the box of chocolate. Harold followed her gaze and saw the box was half empty. She looked up at Harold. "What's that supposed to mean?"

"You made a comment once before when we spoke in the hallway concerning all the pills Alice took."

"Out. I don't want to talk any more about Alice."

Harold let himself out the door and stood in the hallway thinking. He had learned one interesting piece of information.

\*\*\*\*\*

Back in his apartment, Harold called Detective Deavers. He got voicemail and left a message to call back as soon as possible.

As soon as possible ended up being an hour and a half. When they connected Harold said, "I had a chance to speak with Betty Buchanan."

179

"Pick up anything useful?"

"One item. She told me why she had the waiting list."

"Don't keep me in suspense."

Harold laughed. "I want to make sure you're listening. Betty took the list from the retirement home director's office because she wanted to give it to her friend, Celia Barns. She's one of the three people on the waiting list that I think could be responsible for the deaths and accidents."

There was a pause on the line. "I'll look into it. Anything else?"

"I tried to poke more at the medication issue, but that seemed to be a sore subject. She wouldn't say anything further."

"Too bad. Let me know if you find out anything else." The line disconnected.

Harold stared at the phone. As the detective had said, one step backward, two steps forward.

# CHAPTER FORTY 🦇

Harold's stomach rumbled. He checked his watch. He had half an hour before dinner. How he had become a slave of the meal schedule at Mountain Splendor. He used to eat when he felt like it. Now he had his three square meals a day, right on schedule. Then he remembered how he had fallen into the habit of eating too much junk food. Since coming to Mountain Splendor, he had been eating much more healthy food — lots of fruit and vegetables.

There wasn't enough time to take a nap, and he didn't want to watch television. He picked up his book and stared at the cover for a moment. He'd rather see his favorite witch than only read about witchcraft, but he guessed this would have to do. He heard loud thumping and rattling sounds from the hallway. Unusual. Typically no one made any sounds until the evening around here. He moseyed to the door and peeked out.

Bella stood on a chair taping a streamer to the hallway wall. He squinted. He thought it was Bella. He had never seen her dressed this way before. She looked like a cloth swatch from one of Alexandra's couch experiments.

"What's going on?" he asked.

Bailey, standing near the patchwork apparition, waved to him. "Come lend a hand. We need to get all the decorations ready before trick-or-treating tonight."

Harold did a double-take. Bailey had fur on her neck and the back of her hands. She growled at him.

"What the heck are you?"

Bailey reached down into a large cardboard box and handed Bella a paper pumpkin, which she attached to the wall. "I'm a werewolf."

Bella looked over her shoulder. "Harold. You can start taping black cats to the other side of the hall. They're in the other box next to your door."

Harold padded out, opened the box and pulled out a black paper silhouette of a cat.

Bailey handed him a roll of masking tape. "You can go wild. Fill up the walls. We can't have too many decorations."

"Is this your regular preparation for Halloween?" he asked.

Bailey pulled out another pumpkin cutout. "Yep. We need to get the whole floor decorated."

Tomas came out of his room. "Oh, good. I want to help, too."

"Come lend a hand." Bailey waved him over.

Tomas wore a black cape. He stepped up to Harold and opened his mouth to reveal long fangs.

Harold retreated. "What's with the vampire outfit, Tomas?"

"It's what I wear on Halloween. We always cross-dress. I go as a vampire, Bella is a shape-shifter, Bailey as a werewolf. What are you going to be, Harold?"

"It's a surprise. I'll put on my costume after dinner."

Tomas reached in a box and pulled out a black bat, which he stuck to the wall. "You and your dinners. You still mingle with those snobs from the Front Wing?"

"There's one guy who I eat with, Ned Fister. He's very down to earth."

"That's Harold ongoing joke," Bella said. "Ned is a gardener."

Tomas swirled his cape. "I get it. Ha. Ha." He reached over and picked up another black bat cutout. "I hope the Front Wing doesn't rub off on you, Harold."

"Nah. I love all you guys. You're stuck with me."

Viola came out of her room wearing pink slippers and a silk robe. "What's all the hullaballoo?"

"We're getting ready for tonight," Bella said. "Go get your costume on."

"Costume? What's happening tonight?"

"You've forgotten, but it's Halloween."

"I'll be danged. I don't remember going through Thanksgiving yet."

182

"There you go getting your holidays out of sequence again. First, Halloween, then Thanksgiving."

"Oh, yeah. I'll go get ready." Viola disappeared into her apartment and slammed the door.

At that minute, Alexandra and Bartholomew appeared. "Yoo-hoo, wait for us." Alexandra wore a black dress and had a black pointed hat on. Bartholomew flourished a red cape.

"Good duds," Bailey said.

Pamela came out of her room, wearing a wispy gown.

"What are you?" Harold asked.

"I'm dressing like Cassandra. I'm a time-shifter."

"Did I hear my name mentioned?" Cassandra appeared flapping her arms that were covered in black cloth. She had black pointy ears on her head.

"It's bat woman." Pamela giggled. "Good job."

There was a loud thump, and Kendall came out of his room, thrusting his walker ahead of him. "Don't start all the festivities without me." He also wore a cape and opened his mouth to display large fangs.

"We're only decorating right now," Bailey said. "You're welcome to join in."

"I need a throat to get energy." Kendall bared his fangs.

"Don't overplay it," Bailey said.

Within twenty minutes, the hallway walls were covered with a collage of spider webs, jack-o-lanterns, bats, black cats and ghosts.

Bella stepped off the chair. "Good job. We're ready for visitors."

"Who has the trick-or-treat bags?"

"Warty was in charge of that," Bailey said. "Uh-oh."

"Uh-oh is right." Bella pointed down the hall. "Here he comes."

Warty wore pieces of rug on his arms, stomach and head.

"Not bad," Bartholomew said as he swooshed his red cape. "I'd go for more shag but it will do."

Bailey put her hands on her hips. "It's about time. You have the trick-or-treat bags, Warty?"

He cringed. "Oops. I forgot."

Bella let out a loud sigh. "Never mind. I have a whole roll of trash bags. That way you can collect as much as you want." She disappeared into her apartment and returned to distribute the bags.

Harold indicated he would go downstairs for dinner.

"Don't take too long," Bella called after him. "We start trick-or-treating on the second floor in forty minutes."

"I'll be back with my costume on with time to spare."

"I wonder what Harold will be?" Bailey said.

Bella pushed a box back toward her room. "Hard to predict. He's being very secretive. Jason gave him a costume."

"If it's from Jason, it's got to be good."

"Everybody be patient. You'll find out soon enough." Harold waved and headed to the elevator.

# CHAPTER FORTY-ONE 🦇

Harold returned from dinner with a full tummy and ready to join the Halloween festivities. His hallway was alive with creatures of every form and type, but not their usual form and type.

Bailey waved a furry arm. "Here comes Harold. Get your costume on. We're all anxious to see what you'll be. I bet he's going to be a warlock."

"No," Pamela said. "I think he'll appear as a shapeshifter to be like Bella tonight."

"Everyone be patient." Harold entered his apartment and retrieved the box Jason had given him. He changed into a torn sweatshirt, pulled the mask over his head and inspected himself in the mirror. He flinched at the gruesome face staring back at him—a bald head with an eaten away mouth and blood on his cheeks. A perfectly gruesome zombie. He was ready for trick-or-treating.

Harold quietly opened his door to find Viola and Bailey waving their hairy arms at each other in animated conversation. He snuck up on them and said, "Boo."

Bailey shrieked.

Viola gasped and fainted, sprawling out in a heap on the floor.

Bella came over. "Look what you did to Viola."

"What?" Harold said. "I thought we were supposed to scare people tonight."

Viola moaned and raised herself to a sitting position.

"I'm sorry I scared you," Harold said.

Viola took one look at Harold and passed out again.

Bella bent over and patted her cheeks. "It's okay, Viola."

Viola smacked her lips but kept her eyes scrunched closed. "There was this horrible creature. It was going to attack me."

"It was only Harold wearing a zombie mask."

"Who's Harold?"

Bella put her hands on her hips. "We keep going over this. He's our neighbor in the room between us."

"Oh, that yahoo." She opened her eyes and then scrunched them shut again. "I've never seen anything so frightening."

Bella signaled to Harold. "Cover your face for a moment so Viola won't faint again."

Harold did as instructed, peeking out between his fingers to watch what would happen.

Bella raised Viola to her feet. "Now, remember. Harold is wearing a mask."

"Who's Harold?"

"He's standing right there."

Viola regarded him. "The bald guy covering his face?"

"That's the one. He's going to lower his hands and has a scary face, so don't panic."

Harold did as instructed.

Viola swayed, but Bella held her up. "Don't conk out on me again, Viola."

"Who let that beast into our building?"

"He's not a beast, I am." Bailey let out a howl.

Viola turned away from Harold and regarded Bailey. "What are you doing?"

"You and I are werewolves tonight," Bailey said.

Viola looked at her arms. "Is that why I have all this fur?"

"Yep."

Tomas came sauntering along the hallway. He took one look at Harold and yelped.

"Not you, too?" Bella said.

"Uh-oh." Tomas turned red. "I think I need to go change my pants." He dashed back to his room.

Bella wagged her index finger at Harold. "You're certainly causing havoc tonight."

"I thought we were supposed to wear scary costumes."

"You have to be careful. Some of our residents are kind of

sensitive." Bella clapped her hands. "Okay, everybody, it's time to go trick-or-treat on the second floor."

"Where's my bag to collect candy?" Viola asked.

Bella handed out the trash bags, and everyone headed to the stairwell with Tomas catching up at the last minute.

"Where'd you get that horrible mask?" Tomas asked Harold.

"Jason lent it to me. He wore it last year."

"It scared the piss out of me."

"Sorry about that."

They came out of the stairwell on the second floor and found the place crawling with ghosts, goblins, witches, warlocks, shapeshifters, vampires, bats and werewolves.

"This is great," Pamela shouted. "The whole gang is here."

Every time someone passed Harold, he was greeted with a shriek.

Bella steered him toward an open door. "You're having quite an effect on the Back Wing."

"That's okay. It's had quite an effect on me."

The resident who greeted them at the door wore a sheet with eyeholes, gasped and dropped a bowl of candy.

Bella bent over to help pick it up and asked, "Do you have a large paper sack?"

The ghost nodded, disappeared for a moment and returned with the requested item.

Bella punched two holes in the brown paper and put it over Harold's head. "There. That will work better."

Harold adjusted the eyeholes.

As they proceeded along the hall, they encountered Tomas putting his false fangs up against the throat of an attractive witch.

She slapped him.

"Oh, no." Cassandra ran up, flapping her wings. "I'll change time so you won't get slapped, Tomas."

He grinned. "No need to do that. At least this time she noticed me." He blew a kiss at the witch, who turned her back and stomped down the hallway.

"Women," Tomas said. "Maybe she likes dogs better than vampires."

They collected candy on the second and third floors and returned to the fourth floor for their turn at handing out goodies.

Harold retrieved the bags of Butterfingers, Snickers and Baby Ruths he'd bought. The paper sack was making his face too hot, so he took it off. When the first group of trick-or-treaters arrived at his door, he greeted them, and they all screamed and ran away.

Harold shrugged. If he didn't give out the candy, he'd have it for snacks himself. Plus the large garbage bag full of treats he had already collected.

Bella stuck her head through the wall. "I heard a complaint that you were scaring people again. You better put the paper sack back on or take off the zombie mask."

"Wimps."

Harold gave in to the inevitable and removed his zombie mask. Maybe it would work for teenagers, but for the older Back Wingers, he didn't want to cause any heart attacks.

The next group appeared at his door.

"How come you're not wearing a costume?" a woman in a black cape asked.

He handed her a handful of candy bars. "This is my costume. I'm really a black cat."

"Oh. That makes sense." She departed and was replaced by Warty.

"Trick-or-treat," Warty said.

"I'm not going to risk a trick from you." Harold handed him a Snickers bar.

Warty tore it open and popped it into his mouth.

"Don't you want to save your candy?"

"Nope. I've been eating it as I get it." He burped and pounded his chest. "Uh-oh. I don't feel so hot. May I use your bathroom?"

Harold stepped aside, and Warty dashed past him.

Retching sounds emerged from the bathroom, the water ran and Warty reappeared wiping his mouth with the back of his hand.

"A sugar overdose?" Harold asked.

"Yeah. I guess my stomach isn't used to so many sweets."

"You better pace yourself for the rest of the evening."

Warty nodded and stumbled out the door.

# CHAPTER FORTY-TWO 🦇

After trick-or-treating on the fifth floor of the Back Wing and rather than continuing on to the sixth floor, Harold convinced Bella and Bailey to join him for a foray to the fifth floor of the Front Wing, his rationale being that he had lived there for two nights recently and it would be an opportunity to catch up with his temporary neighbors.

As they rode up the green elevator, Bailey complained, "We're probably going to get cooties from the Front Wingers."

Harold slipped the zombie mask onto his head. "No cooties, but some of them are kind of grouchy."

Bella grabbed Harold's arm. "I think you have an ulterior motive for this jaunt."

He forced a grin, which didn't show through his grotesque mask. "Could be. I need to check up on Betty Buchanan. What better way than trick-or-treating at her apartment."

"I hope someone has chocolate covered cherries." Bailey licked her lips. "That's the next best thing to the real deal."

They exited the elevator and knocked on the first door. A frazzled woman in a robe answered.

"Trick-or-treat," the threesome shouted.

The woman smiled. "Look at those cute costumes. I particularly like the zombie."

Harold snarled.

The woman giggled. "Don't you sound scary. Let me get some candy." She disappeared inside and returned with a bowl of wrapped mints. "Take as many as you want. I think everyone else is done around here."

At the next door, no one answered. They proceeded down the

hallway, and Harold pointed out the room he had stayed in. "No one there yet, so we can skip it."

They came to Betty Buchanan's room, and Harold rapped on the door. It took a few moments before he heard rattling sounds, and the door opened a crack.

"Trick-or-treat!"

"I don't have any treats, since I didn't have a chance to get to the store today."

"We're going to have to play a trick," Harold said. "You want a card trick or a disappearing trick?"

Betty glared at Harold. "I really don't need any tricks since I've had a tough couple of days."

"I'm not leaving until I get a treat," Bailey said.

Betty gave a disgusted sigh. "Let me see what I can find in my kitchenette." She disappeared for a minute and returned with something in her fist. She thrust her hand in each bag and dropped something in.

Harold gave a growl and said, "Thanks."

"Aren't you scared of him?" Bailey asked.

"Are you kidding? He doesn't look any worse than some of the people I saw in lockup yesterday. Now you can do that disappearing trick since I need some sleep."

They called it quits on the Front Wing and headed back to the party in the Back Wing lounge.

Harold removed his mask and tucked it under his arm. "I know. The party capital of the universe—the Back Wing."

Tomas was dashing around the lounge swirling his cape and trying to bite people on the throat. Viola swatted him with her hairy arm. "Get away from me, you letch."

"Aw, come on Viola," Tomas said. "It's Halloween."

Two punch bowls rested on a card table. One had apple cider, and the other contained a bubbling red liquid. Harold knew which one he'd stick with. He filled a glass and guzzled it down, realizing how thirsty he had become from the night's activities. He suddenly felt very weary, but with all the commotion in the Back Wing, he realized it would be too noisy to get to sleep. He decided to tough it out for a while longer.

Warty appeared in the lounge. "How come no one told me a party was going on?"

"Looks like you found it anyway," Bella said.

"It's my warlock special sense. I can sniff out parties." He took in a deep breath and started coughing.

"Have some punch," Bailey said.

Warty turned up his nose. "I should have brought my own concoction."

"That's all right. Take what's here."

He helped himself to a glass of cider and smacked his lips. "Not bad, but maybe I'll cast a spell to give it more kick." He pulled his wand out of his pocket.

As he pointed it at the cider bowl, Bella wiggled her fingers and Warty froze.

Viola pulled off the false fur covering her arms. "These are getting itchy." She placed the fur on Warty's outstretched wand. "I'll leave 'em here on the statue."

Everyone continue to help themselves to liquid refreshments.

"You're quite adept at freezing people," Harold said. "I hope you don't ever try that on me."

"Just don't be a jerk like Warty."

Harold went over and jabbed a finger in Warty's side, which felt as solid as marble. "Are you going to leave him frozen all night?"

"I think it's time to unfreeze." Bella wiggled her fingers.

Warty's arm dropped, and Viola's fur fell to the floor. He rubbed his head. "What happened?"

"You had a little seizure," Bella said. "Nothing to worry about, but you should probably go back to your apartment to sleep it off."

"Good idea." Warty wobbled toward the elevator.

"I think I'll take a break from the festivities." Harold gave Bella a peck on the cheek and went up to his apartment. He spotted the garbage bag full of candy sitting on the floor where he had left it.

What would he do with all the candy? He could ration it out a little at a time and save the rest for the next time Jason came to visit. He certainly didn't need all the sugar he had collected. He turned the bag upside down to empty the contents onto his kitchenette counter. There were all kinds of wrapped candy bars, a popcorn ball, candy corn and even a box of raisins. He picked this up and put it on his pantry shelf. Something healthy. He rummaged through the morass and separated a blob of gumdrops stuck together. One unusual item caught his eye — a piece of mushroom.

# CHAPTER FORTY-THREE 🦇

Harold peered at the Halloween treats he had collected. Was someone messing with him? He didn't recognize the type of mushroom he had found, but then again, he wasn't much of an expert, only what he had learned on that one hike.

Was this something he should save for Detective Deavers? He couldn't be sure that this connected in any way with the suspicious activities, but he put the mushroom piece in a baggie and set it aside on the corner of his kitchenette counter.

He separated the rest of the candy. Nothing else other than what one would have expected. The events of the last few weeks pulsed through his tired brain. The death of Alice Jones had started everything. Then the bludgeoning of the first person on the waiting list, Henrietta Yates, followed by the poisoning of Frederick Jorgenson and the injury to Edgar Fontaine. To this was added Betty Buchanan being arrested and released. She certainly had seemed more subdued since her return from a stint in jail. And a mushroom showing up in his candy stash. He couldn't put the pieces together. *Think.* There had to be a thread that tied this together.

He heard a thumping sound and looked up to see Bella had jumped through the wall. He winced, being surprised at this means of visitation.

"Couldn't you knock on the door?"

"I like surprising you. Besides, I was missing you. Come back to the party for a while."

"I guess."

Harold followed Bella to the door, grateful that she didn't try to pull him through the wall as she had once tried unsuccessfully to do.

Downstairs, Harold had another cup of cider and started to feel more awake again. He exchanged some wilderness stories with Kendall and watched as Viola accidently dropped her false fangs into the bubbling punch. She reached in and retrieved them before wiping the liquid off on her sleeve.

"I'm going to go trick-or-treating around our neighborhood," Tomas shouted. "Who wants to join me?"

"I'd come, but the old legs aren't up to any exercise," Kendall said.

Pamela swished her gown. "I wouldn't want you to try to bite me on the throat."

"I can't guarantee that when my vampire blood gets boiling." Tomas let out a piercing howl.

"That's a good one," Bella said. "A howling vampire."

"I'm looking for volunteers," Tomas said.

Harold turned to Bella. "What say we join him? We don't want him getting in trouble."

Bella nodded.

"Okay, Tomas. You have two volunteers."

The three of them headed outside.

"Let's not go for too long," Bella said. "My feet are getting sore."

Tomas hopped from one foot to the other. "Don't wimp out on us. We'll go to a few houses."

They passed a group of teenagers dressed as zombies. "Cool mask," one of them shouted to Harold.

He waved in passing. "I guess I fit right in everywhere except the Back Wing."

"We've always thought you were kind of different," Tomas said.

Harold suddenly had a strange feeling that someone was watching them. He whirled around but only saw a group of teenagers coming back from a house where they had collected candy.

He thought of mentioning his concern to Bella, but by then Tomas was dashing toward another door.

Harold and Bella followed and climbed to a lit porch where Tomas shouted, "Trick-or-treat!"

A man opened the door and handed each of them a paper sack. He smiled at Harold. "Good mask."

As they walked away, Tomas kicked a pebble off the walkway. "I don't get it. How come everyone likes your horrible mask?"

"That's the way people without special powers act, I guess."

After two more houses, Bella convinced Tomas to call it a night. As they headed back to Mountain Splendor, Harold came to a stop, his heart pounding. Again, the feeling of being watched. He spun around three-hundred-sixty degrees. "Do either of you sense someone is watching us?"

"Nah," Tomas said. "You're only getting old. I'm full of energy. I'm going to run again and see if I can find anything interesting in the dumpster behind the Mountain Splendor loading dock." He took off.

"I'm not up to running," Bella said.

"Me neither. But we better follow Tomas. He can get into trouble when he starts raiding the trash."

They picked up their pace.

"It's good... that we're still agile... at our age," Harold said between gasps.

"I don't know about you, but I don't feel a day over sixty."

Harold paused to catch his breath. "And you don't look a day over forty."

"Save the compliments for later. We need to catch up to Tomas."

They went around to the back of the building to the loading dock.

Bella pointed. "We have a problem."

Tomas lay on the pavement next to a dumpster, convulsing. A gnawed steak bone lay next to him. Harold stared in disbelief. A shriveled mushroom also rested on top of the steak bone.

"Hold his head up!" Bella shouted.

Harold did as commanded.

Bella reached in a pocket and pulled out some leaves, which she crumpled up. She propped Tomas's mouth open and thrust the leaves in his mouth.

He coughed and sputtered.

She opened his mouth again. "A little bit more." She added more leaf particles.

Tomas shivered, and his spasmodic motion ceased.

"Do we need to call 9-1-1?" Harold asked.

"I've treated him before. This happens when he gets into rancid food he shouldn't eat. If we take him upstairs, he should be fine. Let's see if we can get him up on his feet."

Between Harold and Bella, they raised him upright. He was out cold.

"He's pretty skinny and light," Harold said, "but it will be difficult to carry him all the way to the elevator."

"Not a problem." Bella wiggled her fingers, and Tomas floated an inch off the pavement. "Now we can move him like pulling a balloon on a string." She gave a gentle push and Tomas floated toward the lobby. Between the two of them, they guided the unconscious man through the lobby. The security guard gawked and added a shake of his head.

Harold guessed that security staff around Mountain Splendor became inured to strange sights.

After the elevator ride, they floated Tomas to his room, tipped him horizontal and positioned him over his bed. Bella pulled back the covers and snapped her fingers. Tomas sank onto the mattress. She reached over and covered him with the blanket.

"Is it safe to leave him by himself?" Harold asked.

Bella adjusted the pillow. "We should take turns watching him for the next hour or so."

Although tired, Harold volunteered for the first watch.

"I'll come back in fifteen minutes," Bella said. "If he wakes up give him some water to drink. He's usually dehydrated after one of his fits."

Harold saluted and watched as Bella left the room.

"It's you and me, Tomas."

Tomas's mouth moved as if he were tasting something bitter, but he remained unconscious.

"I'll let you rest."

Harold sank into a chair in the bedroom and maintained his vigil. After a few minutes his head nodded, and he almost fell asleep when a rustling sound brought him to full alert.

Tomas thrashed around in the bed.

Harold stepped over and placed a hand on Tomas's forehead. Very warm.

The thrashing continued.

Harold wondered if he needed to call Bella, but at that moment Tomas opened his eyes. "What's going on?"

"Good, you're awake. Let me get you a drink of water." Harold dashed into the bathroom, filled a cup with water and brought it back to his patient. He placed it to Tomas's lips. "Here. Take a sip."

Tomas greedily gulped the water.

"Take it easy. I don't want you getting sick again."

Tomas took one more swallow and smacked his lips. "That's better."

Harold placed a hand behind Tomas's back and helped him sit up in bed. "How are you feeling?"

Tomas put his hand to his head. "Hurts."

"And your stomach?"

"A little rumbly but not too bad."

Harold scooted the chair closer to Tomas and sat down. "Do you remember what happened to you?"

"After our trick-or-treating through the neighborhood, I galloped to the dumpster. I couldn't resist. After all the candy, I wanted something to take away the sugar taste. I opened the lid and sniffed. There was one bag of leftovers that was too good to pass up. I took it out and opened the bag. After that, it's kind of fuzzy. The next thing I knew I woke up in bed."

"You must have eaten something bad from the bag."

"Could be. I don't remember."

Harold knew he had to go check. "You keep resting. Bella will be here in a few minutes to see how you're doing." He left Tomas's room and knocked on Bella's door.

"I was going to check on you and Tomas."

"Why don't you go keep an eye on him? I'm going back to the loading dock to see what he ate."

"Okay."

They went their separate directions, and Harold took the elevator this time, not wanting to charge down the stairs again. He passed the security guard who attempted a partial smile. Outside, he went around to the loading dock and approached the dumpster. One small bulb from the loading dock cast a sparse beam of light onto the pavement.

Harold looked around and spotted an empty paper sack. The steak bone and mushroom he had seen earlier had disappeared.

# CHAPTER FORTY-FOUR 🦇

Harold searched all around the dumpster. Tomas had gotten into some tainted meat. What had happened to the evidence that had been there earlier? He thought back to what he had seen briefly before his attention became focused on reviving Tomas. Could the mushroom have been like the poisonous one on the hike? The light had been too dim. He'd have to see if Detective Deavers could find anything in daylight. If so, Deavers should be able to have the police lab do some analysis. He bent over to check under the edge of the dumpster.

He had that sense again of someone watching him. He jerked his head up at hearing a scuffling sound. Something blocked the light as a hard object bashed into the center of his forehead. All went black.

*****

Harold awoke with a searing pain shooting through his skull. He tried to sit up, but couldn't muster enough energy to move. He opened his eyes.

Bailey knelt next to him.

"Thank goodness, you're awake."

Harold put his hand to his forehead and encountered a jagged wound. His hand came away with blood. "What happened?"

"You have a huge gash on your head," Bailey said. "Here, I'll take care of it." She bent over and licked his wound. "Yum."

Intense heat seared Harold's forehead, and then it tingled. He put his hand to his head again, and instead of sensing the gash, he found the wound had healed. "What did you do?"

"My saliva has a special effect on cuts." She licked her lips. "You have very tasty blood, Harold."

He patted his forehead again. "That was more than a cut."

"Maybe so, but it's fine now. Do you think you can move?"

Harold raised himself up to his elbows, then to his knees and finally stood.

Bailey steadied him. "Let's see if you can walk."

He took a tentative step, and the loading dock began to spin. "I don't think so." He sank to the pavement and sat, bracing his back against the dumpster.

"I'll get some help." Bailey pulled out her cell phone and punched in some digits. "Bella, get right down to the loading dock. We need your assistance. Harold has been hurt." She returned her phone to her pocket.

"How did you happen to find me?" Harold asked.

"Bella got worried when you didn't return. She was watching Tomas and asked me to go check."

"Good thing." A wave of nausea gripped him, and he took several deep breaths to contain it. "Oh, boy. I have a headache."

"I could call 9-1-1, but Bella will have a better cure than any hospital."

Harold remembered what he was doing before being knocked out. He could spot no sign of the steak bone and mushroom.

"Did you see some food remnants on the ground?" Harold asked.

"Nope. Only you sprawled out, looking like death warmed over."

"Don't remind me."

Bella appeared and bent over to inspect Harold. "Look in my eyes."

Harold tried to gaze in her direction. "I enjoy that, but I'm having trouble focusing."

"We need to get you up to your room," Bella said.

"I tried to get him to walk, but he couldn't handle it," Bailey said.

Bella wiggled her fingers, and Harold floated off the pavement. "We'll go with special transportation." Together Bella and Bailey pushed Harold around to the entrance and through the lobby. The security guard only stared, wide-eyed and open-mouthed.

After the elevator ride, they navigated him into his room.

"Watch him while I get some medicine," Bella instructed Bailey. "And Harold, keep your eyes open. No falling asleep yet."

Bella disappeared through the wall and returned in a few minutes with a vial in her hand. She placed it to Harold's lips, and he drank.

"That will help you. Now you can sleep."

Harold closed his eyes.

*****

When Harold awoke, he found Bella sitting next to the bed. He blinked. "What are you doing here?"

"I've been keeping a watch. How do you feel?"

Harold tapped his forehead. "Better. I'm hungry."

"That's a good sign. I'll fix you some broth." She disappeared, and Harold heard banging sounds coming from his kitchenette. He was too tired to get up, so he closed his eyes and rested. A little later he felt a touch on his arm and opened his eyes.

Bella put an arm behind his back and helped him sit up. She placed pillows behind his back and handed him a cup of steaming liquid. "Drink up."

He put the cup to his mouth and gulped the hot soup. When he finished he smacked his lips. "Delicious. What time is it?"

"Nine o'clock. You've been out since midnight."

"I don't usually sleep that long."

"You had a nasty bump, but you'll be all right. I've called Detective Deavers. He said he's very busy, but will come speak to you when he has a chance. Tell me everything that happened."

"Not much to recount. I went to look for the food that Tomas had got into—a steak bone and an old mushroom. The leftovers had disappeared. I bent over to look more carefully. Then someone whacked me in the head."

"Did you see the attacker?"

"No. All I saw was something coming toward my head. I didn't catch any glimpse of who did it." Harold put his hand to his forehead, amazed once again that he felt no wound. "And that mushroom. That's the strange part. I can understand Tomas getting hold of a steak bone, but what was a mushroom doing there? I wonder if he ate some of it as well as the meat. Tomas was unclear on what happened to him when I asked him last night."

"And he's still that way this morning. I checked on him earlier, and he couldn't remember what happened after he found the paper bag with leftovers. Hopefully Detective Deavers can check the scene."

"Won't do any good. The paper bag, steak bone and mushroom all disappeared. No evidence left."

"Cleared out?"

"Exactly. The perp must have removed it." He sucked on his lip for a moment and gazed at Bella. "Thanks for taking care of Tomas and me. You've been busy nursing all these old men."

"I have to keep all of you alive, otherwise it would be too boring with only old women on this floor." She kissed his forehead.

"Hmm. That feels even better than when Bailey cauterized my wound."

"I should hope so. Why don't you get some sleep until Detective Deavers arrives? We'll let him take it from here."

Harold decided not to argue. Bella had the situation under control. He only wished he knew who had attacked him. Had it been one of the three remaining people on his suspect list? If so, what had that person been doing at Mountain Splendor at night? Or had it been someone from Mountain Splendor? And if so, why? He was too tired to think clearly. Maybe the answers would come after he slept.

# CHAPTER FORTY-FIVE 🦇

Harold awoke two hours later with no new insights other than it wasn't wise to have your head get in the way of someone swinging a hard object. He lay in bed, grateful that he wasn't in a condition any worse than having a headache. He ran his hand over the lump, not feeling any torn skin. The wonders of vampire saliva.

He popped two aspirin, and his pain settled into a dull background roar. He could live with that. He would have to. After a hot shower, lunch and a chat with Ned Fister brought him farther back into the land of the living, he felt almost human again. Back in his apartment the sound of the doorbell interrupted his cogitation.

Shuffling over, he answered to find the grim face of Detective Deavers standing there in his crumpled suit. "I received a call to see you as soon as possible."

"Come in and we can share the latest events around Mountain Splendor, the crime center of Golden."

They sat, Harold in his easy chair and Deavers on the couch. Harold realized this had become a common scene over the last few weeks with the two of them having their little confabs. They would never be best buddies, but Harold respected Deavers, and the detective appeared to hold a mutual respect for him.

Deavers took out his ever-present notepad and pen and readied himself. "What do you have for me?"

No chitchat with Deavers. "It's like this. Some of us went trick-or-treating last night, collecting candy in garbage bags."

Deavers gave an eye roll. "That must have been quite a sight."

"If you could only imagine. Anyway, back in my apartment, I dumped out my loot. In addition to candy, I discovered one unusual object. Let me show it to you."

Harold strode into his kitchenette and retrieved the mushroom he had put in a baggie. "You can take this for your lab people to analyze. I think it might be poisonous."

Deavers jotted a note, accepted the offering and put it in his jacket pocket.

"There's more. On our way back from traipsing around the neighborhood, Tomas Greeley, one of the residents of the Back Wing, raced ahead. He… uh… found some food that had been left by the dumpster. He got a little sick, you might say. I looked at what was on the ground and found a steak bone and a mushroom. We have a common theme for the night—mushrooms. And they've played a part before."

"Yes. The poisoning of Frederick Jorgenson."

"I'm not an expert on mushrooms so I can't say for sure, but it also might have been a poisonous one with the steak bone. The suspicious part is two mushrooms showing up the same night. We got Tomas up to his room, and he started recovering. I decided to go back down to check on what I had seen. When I returned to the dumpster, the steak bone and mushroom had disappeared. I bent down to examine the pavement more closely and someone whacked me on the head." He pulled back his thinning hair to show the bump.

"Did you get a look at who did this?"

"No. I heard a sound and looked up but someone bashed me before I could discern anything useful."

Deavers stood. "Let's go take a look at where this happened."

Harold led the detective out to the loading dock and pointed to the dumpster. "Right in front of that green monster."

Deavers circled the dumpster, looking at the ground. He came to a stop, put on rubber gloves, bent over, picked up an object and dropped it in a paper sack. He continued to circle the dumpster, moving closer as he spiraled in toward it. Twice more he repeated the bend, lift and stash routine.

"Find anything useful?" Harold asked.

"Could be. I'll have the lab tech take a look."

Harold removed a piece of lint from his sleeve and gazed at Deavers. "Anything new on the case that you can share with me?"

"I'll mention one occurrence because you might have some insight. Betty Buchanan, who had been arrested for breaking into Alice Jones's apartment, has disappeared."

"What? When did that happen?"

"Sometime last night or early this morning. Two hours ago, Peter Lemieux went to check on her and found no one there. He contacted me immediately, and I put out word to try to locate her."

"She flew the coop." Then it struck Harold. "Wait a minute, here's something for you. I saw her last night."

"What time was that?"

Harold calculated. "Between eight thirty and nine. After traipsing through the Back Wing and handing out some candy myself, Bella Allred and Bailey Jorgenson and I went to the fifth floor of the Front Wing. Betty opened the door when we shouted trick-or-treat."

"Any sigh of agitation?"

"No. She appeared more subdued than usual."

Deavers wrote on his pad before regarding Harold with his intense gaze. "Could she have slipped a mushroom in your trick-or-treat bag?"

Harold recreated the scene in his mind. "It's possible. She didn't have any candy to hand out because she didn't have time to go shopping after being released from jail. She disappeared into her kitchenette for a moment and returned with something she put in my bag, but I never saw what it was."

"She was under court instructions not to leave the state. I called her family earlier, but they haven't heard from her. No sign of her yet."

Harold thought for a moment. How did Betty's disappearance, the mushrooms and the knot on his forehead tie together? He sensed he was close to figuring out something, but the solution continued to elude him. "The waiting list connects all of this somehow."

Deavers grimaced. "You and that waiting list. I fail to see how Ms. Buchanan's disappearance and your encounter by the dumpster are related to the waiting list."

"I can't prove it yet, but they tie together. The Senior Sneakers hiking club comprises many of the past and current names on the waiting list. One was poisoned, one fell, and one voluntarily took her name off the list. That leaves three people who I think could be involved—Celia Barns, Duncan Haverson and Phoebe Mellencourt. And Betty Buchanan took the waiting list to give to Celia Barns. Have you thoroughly checked those three, Detective?"

"They passed the background check with flying colors. I've interviewed each of them. Ms. Barns said she received the waiting list from Ms. Buchanan and gave it to Ms. Mellencourt."

Harold jumped up. "So either Celia Barns or Phoebe Mellencourt could have been responsible for trying to eliminate people on the waiting list."

Deavers held up his hand. "Slow down. So far there's nothing that directly links them to the crimes."

"Any alibis for when Henrietta Yates was killed?"

"Interesting you should ask. All three were at a party for this Senior Sneakers group that night. I've interviewed other group members who corroborate their being at the party. They all went their separate ways afterwards."

Harold smacked his right fist into his left hand. "So any of the three might have committed the crime after the party."

"Possible, but again no direct evidence to connect any of them to the crime scene. I haven't ruled out their involvement."

Harold smiled. "Hold that last thought."

"I need more than your suspicions to build a case." Devers snapped his notepad shut and put it in his pocket. "If you come up with any new insights, be sure to tell me."

"You'll be the first to know."

# CHAPTER FORTY-SIX 🦇

After Detective Deavers let himself out the door, Harold sat in his easy chair contemplating what the detective had said or, more importantly, not said. No indication if there was a real suspect in the murder of Henrietta Yates. He needed to do some more of his own investigating to see if he could determine which of the three people left on the waiting list might be the culprit. He remembered something.

He got up and checked his calendar. He had noted a hike the next day with the Senior Sneakers. Yes. That would give him a chance to check on his three persons of interest. He could also inquire about their whereabouts on Halloween night. Maybe one of them would let something slip. The hike would begin at the trailhead of the Lubahn Trail at two in the afternoon. He'd ask Bella to join him. Between the two of them they'd have a chance to pick up some new information.

His ruminations were interrupted by Bella sticking her head through the wall and clearing her throat.

Harold jumped. "There you go again, startling me."

Bella came the rest of the way through the wall. "I couldn't sleep. I heard you and Detective Deavers talking."

"Are the walls that thin?"

Bella gave a bashful smile. "I did happen to have my ear against the wall."

Harold clenched his fists, feeling heat rising through his body. "You can't be spying on me all the time, Bella. That's completely unacceptable!"

"What! I'm not spying. I'm merely interested in the case we're *both* trying to solve. We're a team on this."

"But being on a team doesn't mean invading my space unannounced. Kindly knock on the door, and you're welcome to join the conversation. And this jumping through the wall and scaring the daylights out of me. It has to stop!"

Bella's eyes flared. "I'll stop when I want to, not under your orders."

"Now you're accusing me of ordering you around. That's rich. Who's the one always using her magic to manipulate others and casting spells when someone does something you don't like?"

"I've had enough of your sass." Bella pointed her right index finger at Harold and wiggled it.

Harold took a step toward her and froze. He couldn't move a muscle. Damn. She'd turned him into a statue like he'd seen her do to other people. He couldn't move his mouth to even complain.

Bella stomped up to him and put her face inches from his. "I'll have no more of these accusations. You need to think things over. I'll unfreeze you after you've had some time to reconsider your ranting at me." She sat down on the couch facing him with her chin jutted out, and crossed her arms.

Harold could see her but not so much as move his gaze or close his eyes. What a predicament. He couldn't argue back. All he could do was stare ahead and think. All right. She was being unreasonable and shouldn't have invaded his space. True, but he had overreacted. He didn't have to shout at her and make a scene. He had let his temper get the better of him. His outburst of the moment had interfered with their relationship. He'd lost sight of what was really important.

He wanted to apologize but couldn't open his mouth. Then he had another insight. This being frozen in place was like counting to ten when mad instead of blurting out a negative reaction. It was a cooling off period to think. Anger seeped from his system like water going down a drain.

He would have taken a deep breath and sighed, but couldn't move the muscles to perform those simple acts.

Instead, he remained in place taking in all in his field of view. What he saw was Bella. What was so bad about her coming through the wall? He wanted to see her, and then she appeared. Rather than being pleased, he had become angry. He should have welcomed the opportunity when she took interest in coming to see him. She could be ignoring him. That really would be painful.

He could live with her little idiosyncrasies. Rather than getting pissed off, he could appreciate her unique qualities and interest in him. How many old farts had a beautiful witch as a girlfriend?

He got it.

Bella stood. "Okay. I think you've had some time to review things." She wiggled her fingers, and Harold came unstuck.

He put his hand to his face. He was back.

"Do you have anything to say?" Bella asked.

"Yes. I learned my lesson. I shouted at you when I shouldn't have. Your timeout technique gave me a chance to review my actions. I apologize. I know that your intentions were good coming into my apartment, and since I like seeing you, there was no need for my overreaction." He stepped over and gave her a kiss.

She put her arms around his neck. "That's better. Making up is more fun than fighting."

"I agree, but I'd like to make one point."

She stepped back and quirked an eyebrow. "Oh?"

"I will do my best to avoid unreasonable accusations, but one thing is unfair. You have this ability to freeze me when I do something you dislike. I don't have any equal recourse if you were to get mad at me."

A sparkle showed in Bella's eyes. "You make a good point. Since we're going to be living next to each other and seeing a great deal of one another, I have a suggestion." She paused a beat. "I'll give you the ability to freeze me."

Harold stared. "Huh?"

"It's very simple. I can make it so you can freeze me if I need to have a timeout. Here's how it will work. I'll give you the power to wave your hand and say, 'freeze.' You can wave again and say 'unfreeze.'"

"You'd trust me doing that?"

"If we're in this relationship together, we need to trust each other." She waved her hand in a circle. "It's all set."

Harold paced around the room and came to a stop facing Bella. "I don't know if this is a good idea."

"Give it a try."

Harold took a deep breath, waved his hand and mumbled, "freeze."

Bella turned rigid with her arm half lifted.

Harold went over and gave her a gentle shove. She didn't budge. He tried to pick her up. Dead weight as if glued to the floor. He kissed her on the lips. No reaction. "I'll be damned. I like kissing you much more when there's a response. Oops, I better undo this spell." He waved and said "unfreeze."

Bella's arm came down. She smiled and gave Harold a kiss. "Is this better?"

He came up for air. "Much."

"So things are even. We can freeze each other. But the freezing will only work on me. You won't be able to go around freezing anyone else."

Harold grinned. "Are you going to let me float you around as well?"

"Don't press your luck."

# CHAPTER FORTY-SEVEN 🦇

The next day, Harold prepared for the hike with the Senior Sneakers. Bella had agreed to go with him. In his living room as he laced his hiking boots, Bella hopped through the wall to join him.

This time rather than getting mad at Bella, he smiled. "Good to see you."

"We have one other Back Winger who wants to hike today," Bella said.

Harold gave a firm tug on his shoelace and looked up. "Bailey going to come along again?"

"No. Cassandra mentioned that she likes to hike. I invited her, and she's down in the lobby waiting for us."

Harold grabbed his walking poles, and after the usual long wait, they entered the red elevator. Harold checked the dinner menu. Beef stroganoff. He wondered what kind of mushrooms would be in the dish.

In the lobby, Harold winced when he saw Cassandra sitting in the same chair where Alice Jones had died. That had been the start of this whole sequence of suspicious events including the bludgeoning of Henrietta Yates, the poisoning of Frederick Jorgenson and Edgar Fontaine's accident on the trail, to say nothing of the attack he had suffered near the dumpster on Halloween night.

Maybe this hike would provide an opportunity to learn more about his three suspects — Celia Barns, Duncan Haverson and Phoebe Mellencourt.

Cassandra popped out of the chair holding her walking poles, and as they headed outside, she asked, "How are we getting to the trailhead? I don't want to use up all my energy before the hike starts."

"Bella, are you going to give us your special power boost today?" Harold asked.

"That can be arranged. Besides, it isn't very far." She flicked her wrist, and Harold's body levitated an inch off the ground. "Use your walking poles, and you'll zip along with no effort."

Cassandra pushed off and sailed down the street. "This is like flying. Whoopee!"

"Be careful not to go out in the street in front of any cars."

Cassandra floated in a circle and returned in front of Bella. "How come you're not using walking poles?"

"No need. I have good balance and can boost myself along on steep sections of the trail."

Harold discovered a rhythm of pushing off with his walking poles, floating for ten yards or so and pushing off again. As the three of them floated along, Harold asked Cassandra, "What was your son, Peter, like as a boy?"

"Somewhat strange. He was always doing homework and didn't watch television or play video games. The one time he refused to take out the trash, I punished him by taking away his homework and making him watch television. After ten minutes of viewing *Seinfeld*, he promised never to neglect his chores again."

"He is a conscientious administrator of Mountain Splendor."

"But he still doesn't watch television. Claims he can get by fine without it. Can you imagine that?"

Harold could identify. He didn't particularly care for much television himself. A little news, a few programs on the History Channel and some comedy movies. That did it for him. He used to watch the Broncos, but even sports didn't appeal to him that much anymore. He preferred spending time with a certain neighbor of his.

As they floated along Nineteenth Street, Bella announced, "I'm turning off the power assist. We don't want to freak out the hikers if they see us traveling this way." She snapped her fingers, and Harold's feet thumped to the ground.

"That was pleasant," Cassandra said. "I should cause time to go back an hour so I can experience it again, but I do want to get some real exercise."

"How do I know you haven't taken time back numerous times already this afternoon?" Harold asked.

Cassandra grinned. "You don't."

They arrived at the trailhead, and found a group congregated. Cassandra went through the crowd introducing herself.

Bella whispered in Harold's ear, "She's quite the mixer."

Phoebe Mellencourt clapped her hands together. "It's time to begin. Since the head of our club, Edgar Fontaine, is indisposed, I've been selected as the hike leader. This is a short trail, but has some steep sections, so be careful. We'll have a terrific view over Golden when we get near the top. Everyone set?"

Heads nodded.

"Forward." Phoebe set off at a good clip.

They followed a dirt trail through tall, dried grass. Up ahead a cliff face dominated the view with the spire of Castle Rock off to the left.

Harold sidled up beside Celia Barns. Time to begin his careful interrogation. He wanted to understand her friendship with Betty Buchanan. This would also be a chance to find out if any of his three suspects might have attacked him on Halloween night. "I know Betty Buchanan who resides at Mountain Splendor. Before she disappeared, she mentioned she was a friend of yours."

"Poor Betty. She's had some recent trouble from the police."

"Yeah. There was some commotion concerning a resident's room. A woman named Alice Jones."

"She's never mentioned that name."

Harold watched Celia carefully. He couldn't pick up any indication that she might be involved in anything unscrupulous with Betty. He decided to move on to his other subject. "At our senior residence we had quite an evening of trick-or-treating on Halloween. How did you celebrate?"

"I had a gals' get-together at my condo." She pointed ahead. "Phoebe came. We dressed up in the most outrageous costumes."

"Did you go trick-or-treating?"

"We did. For an hour right after dark in my neighborhood. Then we came back and had a party like when we were kids. You know, bobbing for apples, pin the tail on a black cat, that sort of thing. The only difference was that we had a good supply of bubbly." She giggled. "I must say Phoebe and I consumed quite an amount. She ended up sleeping on my couch for the night."

"You didn't go out again?"

"Nope. We had… uh… imbibed too much for that."

*Interesting.* He'd have to verify that alibi with Phoebe.

"I understand Betty gave you a copy of the list of people waiting to get into Mountain Splendor."

"That's right. I took a look and passed it to Phoebe. I thought she'd like to see it."

Harold nodded. That coincided with what he had heard previously.

They came to a stop and everyone took out water bottles to have a drink. After Harold had a sip, he approached Phoebe. "I understand you had quite a Halloween celebration."

"That we did. Celia held a party late into the night."

"Do some trick-or-treating?"

"Only for a short while early in the evening. After that, we had some excellent champagne. I have to admit that I had more than I should have. But so did Celia."

"I understand Celia gave you a copy of the waiting list of people who want to move into Mountain Splendor."

"That's right. She bragged that she was closer to the top of the list than I was. Duncan heard I had it and asked me to give it to him, which I did."

"When did you do that?"

"Oh, it must have been a day or so after the open house. Definitely before we came back for the dinner."

Harold winced. All three of the suspects had seen the waiting list. Which one had acted to eliminate people ahead of them on the list?

Phoebe clapped her hands together. "Time to move out." She stepped onto the trail and headed uphill.

Harold walked along thinking. Okay, he had verified that Celia and Phoebe corroborated their alibis for Halloween night. All three had seen the waiting list. That left Duncan Haverson as his prime suspect. He wanted to speak with Duncan, but the trail was narrow, and too many people separated them. He'd have to wait until they came to a wider stopping point.

After another fifteen minutes, they came to a spot where a bench had been installed, looking out over town. They paused for another drink, and several people took out cameras and cell phones to snap pictures of the view west. The large M for School of Mines could be seen on the side of Mount Zion. Down below the bare trees cast a gray pall over the residential streets.

Phoebe cleared her throat loudly. "We're approaching the steepest part of the trail. We have to scramble through a slot to get up on the plateau above us. If any of you don't want to risk that, this can be a place to rest.

Bella came up and whispered in Harold's ear. "I had a chance to speak with Duncan Haverson. I mentioned mushrooms, and he acted a little twitchy."

Harold bent toward Bella and whispered back, "I've verified that neither Celia nor Phoebe could have been out on Halloween night to whack me over the head. That leaves Duncan."

Phoebe clapped her hands again. "Time for the final assault."

She took off with Duncan and Celia right behind her. No one else followed.

Harold motioned to Cassandra. "Come on. You, Bella and I need to complete the hike."

The three of them caught up with the others. They traversed a switchback and reached the base of the cliff. A small gap provided the space to move up to the plateau. Everyone scrambled up, and Harold was the last. He put his poles under one arm and grabbed onto a rock outcrop to pull himself up part way. Then his hiking shoe got stuck.

Bella peered down from above and wiggled her fingers.

Harold's foot came free, and he floated upward to join Bella. He dusted himself off. "Thanks."

Bella pointed to the southwest. "There's the golf course where we played."

Harold peered over the edge and spotted the swatches of green grass. He turned and saw the rest of the hikers moving on. "Let's go. We need to catch up to the others."

They proceeded to the north and rejoined the others who had come to a stop on the plateau.

"I'm going to take some pictures," Phoebe announced.

"Me too," Celia said.

Duncan began moving and shouted over his shoulder, "I'm going up to the top of Castle Rock."

"Let's join him." Harold waved Bella and Cassandra forward.

Cassandra grabbed Harold's sleeve and pointed ahead to Duncan. "There's something I don't like about that man."

"You're absolutely correct, Cassandra. There's something I don't like about him as well."

"And he cheats at golf," Bella said.

They reached a set of stone stairs, and Cassandra dashed upward. "Come on, Bella. Let's go check the view." This gave Harold a chance to get close to Duncan.

"Have you been up here before?" Harold asked.

"Several times."

They reached the top of the rock surface. Ahead, Bella stood by the edge. Cassandra came racing back and twirled in a circle. "What a view!"

Harold decided he had a chance here to catch Duncan by surprise. He grabbed the man's arm and brought him to a halt. "I understand you asked Phoebe to give you a copy of the waiting list for people wanting to become residents at Mountain Splendor."

Duncan put his hand on the left front pocket of his pants.

Harold smiled inwardly at the tell. Time to move in for the kill. "During the open house you saw the name of the first person on the list, Henrietta Yates, and killed her. Why did you hit me over the head on Halloween night?"

Duncan's eyes flared. "You interfering SOB. I should have hit you harder." Duncan lashed out, struck Harold in the chest and knocked him to the ground. "I'm going to get rid of all of you, starting with her." He pointed toward where Bella stood facing away at the edge of the cliff and took off running.

Harold realized Duncan intended to push Bella off the hundred foot high cliff.

"Cassandra, change time back an hour. Bella's in danger."

Cassandra wrung her hands. "I can't. I made that up. I don't have the power to change time."

# CHAPTER FORTY-EIGHT ༺

Fear gripped Harold's chest. He lay helpless on the rock surface as Duncan raced toward Bella who continued to look over the edge, unaware of the impending danger. Cassandra couldn't do anything to save Bella.

It was as if time had slowed down. Harold's tunnel vision focused on Duncan who was within feet of Bella.

Harold had no time to call out to warn her. Then he remembered. He waved toward Bella and shouted, "freeze!"

At that moment Duncan, with his arms outstretched, crashed into Bella to push her off the cliff. He bounced off her like a ping pong ball hitting a cement wall, stumbled and ricocheted toward the cliff. With arms flailing, he disappeared over the side.

A loud scream echoed, followed by a thud.

Harold raised himself to his knees and carefully stood. His hip hurt from where he had hit the rock when Duncan knocked him over. He stretched his leg, determined that nothing was broken, limped to where Bella remained frozen and looked over the side. More than a hundred feet below, lay the splayed figure of Duncan Haverson, motionless. Blood oozed from a crushed skull.

Cassandra came running up and grabbed Harold's shoulder. "This is terrible. What are we going to do?"

"I have two phone calls to make." He called 9-1-1 and then punched in the number for Detective Deavers who answered on the third ring. "You'll want to get to the Lubahn Trailhead as soon as possible."

"What for?"

"Duncan Haverson, who is on the Mountain Splendor waiting list and is responsible for a number of crimes, fell off Castle Rock and died. You'll want to check the scene." With no further explanation, Harold returned his phone to his pocket.

"What about Bella?" Cassandra asked.

Harold slapped his forehead. "I almost forgot." He pointed toward her and said, "unfreeze."

Bella rolled her shoulders and turned to face Harold. "That was a strange experience. I was looking over the side and suddenly couldn't move. Then something bashed into me, and I saw a person fly off the cliff. What happened?"

Harold wrapped his arms around Bella. "Duncan Haverson tried to push you off the cliff. Apparently, he figured it would open up one more room at Mountain Splendor and eliminate some of our interference. He obviously didn't make a distinction between residents of the Front Wing and Back Wing."

Bella shivered. "That was a close call."

"It's fortunate that what you taught me caused him to go over the cliff instead of you. We don't need to worry about him any longer. He's dead. He's the one who eliminated people on the waiting list. He even tried to divert our attention when we played golf with him by saying that he was considering taking his name off the waiting list."

"That's right," Bella said. "He tried to act disinterested when he really wanted to get in."

"Harold did something to save you, but I don't exactly know what." Cassandra stepped close and joined in a group hug.

Harold emerged from the scrum and took Bella's hand. "We need to hike down the trail quickly to direct the first responders to his body."

As they descended the stone steps to the plateau below the top of Castle Rock, Harold asked Cassandra, "What's with your statement that you can't change time?"

Cassandra bit her lip and then sighed. "I made that up. I had to have some special power to be accepted by people on the Back Wing and thought being a time-shifter would be very unique. No one could ever prove or disprove it."

Harold thought back to all the times Cassandra had claimed to shift time. Then he broke out in laughter. "Very good. No one caught on until you couldn't actually do it when we had a real emergency."

Cassandra gave him a sheepish smile. "Busted."

Harold looked off in the distance for a moment and said to Cassandra, "I've told you before that I don't have any special power but have been accepted by everyone in the Back Wing. You don't have to worry. And besides you have a very special power."

Cassandra came to a halt. "What's that?"

"Your intuitive ability. You may not be able to go back in time an hour, but you certainly can sense things in people. You picked up vibes about Bella and me right off the bat and understood when we had a conflict. You intuitively knew there was something wrong with Duncan Haverson."

"I agree entirely," Bella said. "Your intuition is as important as any of the other special powers in the Back Wing. It's a great ability and very useful. So you don't have to worry about being accepted."

They caught up with Phoebe and Celia on the plateau.

"Where's Duncan?" Phoebe asked.

"He had a little accident," Harold explained. "We need to get down to the trailhead as emergency personnel should be here shortly."

"I hope it isn't too serious," Phoebe said. "He was going to give me a golf lesson tomorrow."

"I think you'd better find another golf instructor," Harold said.

Phoebe put her hand to her cheek. "Oh, dear. And I was finally learning how to use a wood on the fairway."

They climbed down through the small rock corridor, rejoined the others who had waited at the bench and descended the rest of the trail. Down below an ambulance and a police car pulled to the curb on Belvedere Street. Harold waved to the two EMTs and the police officer. They would have some hiking to do to reach the body.

# CHAPTER FORTY-NINE 🦇

Members of the Senior Sneakers gave their names to the attending police officer at the trailhead and departed. The two EMTs returned from checking the dead man and left in the ambulance since there was nothing they could do. The contingent that included Detective Deavers, an assistant medical examiner, a police officer, a crime scene investigator, Harold, Bella and Cassandra, bushwhacked through the tall, dry grass to reach Duncan Haverson's body.

Harold sidled up to Deavers. "Detective, you'll want to check the left front pants pocket of Duncan Haverson. I suspect you'll find a copy of the waiting list you and I have discussed so often."

Deavers only grunted.

Once in sight of the splayed figure, the police officer put up a hand to hold the citizens at a distance while the professionals moved forward to inspect the remains.

Detective Deavers came back to where Harold, Bella and Cassandra stood. "I need to get a statement from each of you."

Cassandra waved her hand. "I'll go first."

Deavers signaled to her, and they moved out of earshot.

Harold continued to watch as the assistant medical examiner leaned over the body. He didn't think there would be much new that could be learned from that inspection.

Bella spoke next to Deavers, then it was Harold's turn. They stepped aside. "Now recount what happened from the time you arrived for the hike."

Harold summarized the trip up the trail, through the rock slot to the plateau and then the four of them going to the top of Castle Rock. "I suspected that Duncan Haverson had no alibi for the Halloween attack on me near the dumpster at Mountain Splendor. I confronted him, and he knocked me down. He threatened to kill the three of us and took off toward Bella who stood at the edge of the cliff with her back to the rest of us. Haverson intended to push her off." Harold paused. How to best describe what happened next? "When he reached Bella, the next thing I knew he stumbled and flew off the cliff."

Deavers crinkled his brow. "That's the part I don't understand. Ms. Alred says she didn't see Mr. Haverson approaching and only noticed when he went over the cliff. Ms. Lemieux corroborates your statement of being threatened by Mr. Haverson and indicated Mr. Haverson bumped into Ms. Alred before disappearing over the cliff. Would you clarify?"

Harold shrugged. "It's hard to explain. He must have tripped or something. Somehow his momentum carried him over the side. The important part is that he attempted to kill Bella. By his actions, he effectively admitted attacking me Halloween night. I think he is also responsible for the death of Henrietta Yates, the poisoning of Frederick Jorgenson and the injuries to Edgar Fontaine."

"Your waiting list theory?"

"Yes. Did you check his pocket like I suggested?"

"No. The coroner's assistant still has responsibility for the body."

"Also, I bet when you check Duncan Haverson's personal effects and his place of residence, you'll find more evidence."

Deavers snapped his notebook closed. "We'll see. The three of you are free to go. I'll want to speak with you again."

"We'll be at Mountain Splendor when you want us."

*****

As they walked back to the retirement home without any special assist from Bella, Harold remained deep in thought. Finally, he said, "I'm sure the crime spree is over, but Deavers doesn't have all the evidence to link Duncan to the various deaths and injuries. Duncan attacked me on Halloween night and tried to kill you, Bella. That much is clear."

"You're right," Bella said. "Nothing has been proven to link

Duncan to Alice Jones, Henrietta Yates, Frederick Jorgenson and Edgar Fontaine."

That was the darn problem. He thought back over all that had happened. Images of Alice Jones slumped in the chair in the lobby and all the mushrooms he had seen lately. Frederick Jorgenson keeling over at the dinner for prospective residents. He pictured that event and how people were positioned around the table. It clicked. Of course. He had a hunch to follow up on.

*****

Back at Mountain Splendor, Bella and Cassandra headed toward the red elevator, but Harold stopped at the front desk to speak with the receptionist, Andrea. She greeted him with her ever-present smile.

"It's nice to see your happy face," Harold said.

"People like you, Mr. McCaffrey, make me smile."

"You're probably going to be running this joint one of these days or starting your own public relations agency. I have a question for you. Have you seen Betty Buchanan recently?"

"Funny you should ask. She's been gone for a while, but returned earlier this afternoon."

"Did she mention where she'd been?"

"I asked her, and she said she'd taken a little vacation. She should be up in her room."

"Thanks." Harold headed to the green elevator and took it to the fifth floor. He marched down the hallway and knocked on Betty's door, which she opened a crack.

Harold didn't wait for any niceties. He pushed through, forcing Betty to stumble backward as he stormed into the room. "You and I need to talk."

"W — what's this all about?" Betty stammered.

Harold slammed the door behind him. "Duncan Haverson is dead. I think it's time you came clean on your involvement with accidents and deaths occurring because he wanted to move into Mountain Splendor."

Betty slumped onto the couch. "Dead?"

"Yes. He tried to kill someone today on a hike and ended up falling off a cliff."

She put her hands to her face. "That can't be."

Harold pointed his right index finger at her. "You told me before how you took the copy of the waiting list and gave it to Celia Barns. She passed it on to Phoebe Mellencourt, and Duncan got it from her. That was all a ruse. You intended for that waiting list to end up in Duncan's hands."

Betty looked up with large tear-filled eyes. "It was only to help Duncan."

"Did you or Duncan kill Henrietta Yates?"

"I had nothing to do with it. That was Duncan's idea." She broke into a crying jag.

"And at the dinner for prospective new residents, you and Duncan sat on either side of Frederick Jorgenson. Which of you put poison mushrooms in his food?"

"I wouldn't do something like that."

Harold watched Betty carefully. "The thing I don't understand is why Duncan went to all the trouble to kill and injure people to get into Mountain Splendor. Seems to me like a pretty extreme thing to do."

"He had this moneymaking scheme." Betty regarded her hands, not making eye contact with Harold. "He planned to get into the storage area and, over time, sell off things that residents had left there. He figured there would be things of significant value."

Harold thought back and remembered Duncan's interest in the storage area. "And you became an accessory to murder to help Duncan make money by selling furniture and belongings."

"I have nothing more to say." She began sobbing again.

Harold pulled out his cell phone and called Detective Deavers. "You need to come to Mountain Splendor right away. There's a final piece to this puzzle involving Duncan Haverson that you need to hear." He gave Deavers the room number.

Harold waited, not wanting to give Betty a chance to run away again. She stayed on the couch sobbing. He took the opportunity to look into Betty's kitchenette. On the sink rested several mushrooms.

*****

When Deavers arrived, Harold excused himself and told the detective he'd be waiting in his own room when the interview with Betty Buchanan was completed. He suggested getting Betty's permission to look at the mushrooms in her kitchenette. Then he took the green elevator down and the red elevator up to the fourth floor of the Back Wing.

In his room, he was too keyed up to read or watch TV. Instead, he paced around. To work off his nervous energy he should have taken a walk, but he didn't want to miss Deavers when the interrogation with Betty Buchanan finished.

An hour later, a robust knock on his door announced the arrival of the detective.

Harold ushered him in to the living room, and they sat.

Deavers took out his notepad. "Describe your conversation this afternoon with Ms. Buchanan."

"She admitted helping Duncan Haverson. He wanted to get into Mountain Splendor and apparently had no qualms about taking any step to eliminate people ahead of him on the waiting list."

"Once again, your waiting list theory."

"I think you can call it more than a theory."

Deavers gave a grim smile. "This time I agree with you."

Harold arched an eyebrow. "That's good to hear. What changed your mind?"

"I shouldn't mention this, but it will come out soon anyway. The assistant medical examiner checked Mr. Haverson's pockets and found that interesting piece of paper, which you suspected would be there. It was a copy of the Mountain Splendor waiting list. The very same one you've been harping on all this time."

Harold's pulse quickened. He wanted to pump his fist in the air but contained himself. "And?"

"There were lines drawn through the first three names on the list with the notation, 'taken care of.' There remained one name before his. If he hadn't fallen from the top of Castle Rock, I suspect there would have been one more accident or death."

"Betty Buchanan told me that Duncan wanted to get into Mountain Splendor because he intended to make money by selling off residents' belongings from the storage area. Did she confess her role in this sordid situation to you?"

"After I advised her of her rights, she volunteered a wealth of information. The shock of Mr. Haverson's death caused her to open up like a well-oiled gate. She was infatuated with Mr. Haverson and wanted him to move into the apartment vacated by Alice Jones. With him dead, she said she had nothing more to live for and readily confessed to her role in assisting him."

"Did you check the mushrooms in her kitchenette?"

"I collected them and will take them to the lab to be analyzed."

# CHAPTER FIFTY 🦇

The next day after Harold finished lunch, he felt the urge to stretch his legs so he headed to the lobby. Andrea at the reception counter wished him a good afternoon, which he heartily agreed with.

Before taking more than two steps outside the door, Detective Deavers accosted him. "Just the person I want to see."

Harold smiled. "Ah, my favorite detective. What can I do for you?"

"I want to thank you for your assistance in solving this case."

"Wow. I wasn't expecting that. Is it all signed, sealed and delivered?"

Deavers gave an exaggerated eye roll. "Not likely. I have days of paperwork to complete. You wouldn't believe what's involved with all the incidents including Alice Jones's death in the lobby of Mountain Splendor, the bludgeoning of Henrietta Yates, Frederick Jorgenson's poisoning, the injury to Edgar Fontaine, the attack on you and, finally, the demise of Duncan Haverson. It'll be as many pages as *War and Peace*."

"Can you tell me how it ended up?"

"There are parts I can't discuss yet, but I can say this much. The mushroom you found in your trick-or-treat bag matched the ones in Betty Buchanan's kitchenette. They're also the same type that poisoned Frederick Jorgenson. Ms. Buchanan admitted she and Mr. Haverson had become quite proficient at locating poisonous mushrooms. Between the two of them, the mushrooms ended up in a number of places around this facility."

Harold thought for a moment. "And since both Betty Buchanan and Duncan Haverson attended the dinner when Frederick Jorgenson ate some poison mushroom, either of them could have spiked his meal."

"Let's leave it that one of them confessed to this." Deavers winked.

"Another question. Did Alice Jones die as the result of Betty Buchanan tampering with her medication?"

"That's an interesting point. No. It turns out Alice really had a heart attack, and it wasn't due to improper medication. We went through all her pills, and determined there had been no tampering."

Harold shook his head. "So all of this started with her death. That's when I came up with the idea of the waiting list being involved."

Deavers clapped Harold on the back. "Ironic, isn't it? That set things in motion. The waiting list became the smoking gun. Duncan Haverson decided to eliminate the people ahead of him waiting to get into Mountain Splendor. I never would have thought this would be such a popular place."

"I guess it depends on the individual. With Haverson dead and Betty Buchanan locked up, we can get back to normal at Mountain Splendor.

"I don't think things will ever be normal here, but the crime wave is over."

*****

After Harold's walk, he stopped by Peter Lemieux's office.

Peter waved him in. "Mom says you had quite an exciting outing yesterday. I don't know if I should let you take her on hikes."

"She handled herself well."

"Mom's enjoying it here. Making lots of friends."

"With her outgoing personality, everyone likes her. On another subject, I understand we'll have another vacancy opening up in the Front Wing with Betty Buchanan going to jail."

Peter pursed his lips for a moment, and then his eyes lit up. "Fortunately, we have two people on the waiting list. With Alice's and Betty's apartments available, Celia Barns and Phoebe Mellencourt will be able to move in shortly."

"Perfect. That takes care of the waiting list. Are you going to have an open house again to build up a new waiting list?"

"Not for a while. From what Detective Deavers tells me, that waiting list caused a few problems."

"That it did."

"Oh, while you're here, I have one other piece of information. We do have a prospective resident interested in the Back Wing."

"I thought we were done with waiting lists for the time being," Harold said.

"We're filling vacancies one at a time. We had a Back Wing third-floor resident who flew off… I mean… departed yesterday. My mom has a friend who she said would be interested in coming here."

"Special abilities?"

"She shapeshifts into different ages from teenager to your age."

Harold grinned. "That sounds unique. She can get along with all of us old fogies and can also hang out with my grandson, Jason, when he comes to visit. How soon will she be moving in?"

"As soon as the room is repainted and aired out. There were a lot of scratches on the walls and ceiling."

*****

Right before dinner, Harold's phone rang and he heard his grandson, Jason, on the line.

"Good to hear your voice, kiddo."

"I want to check on you, Grandpa… and my other friends at Mountain Splendor. Did you solve the crimes?"

"Everything is resolved."

"Tell me what happened."

Harold recounted all the details, and Jason wouldn't let him summarize. He wanted all the specifics. Once he had satisfied Jason's curiosity, Harold said, "And there's a new resident who will be coming to the Back Wing soon. A shapeshifter who I think you will enjoy meeting."

"Cool. I'll see if I can get my folks to drop me off for a weekend visit. Maybe after Thanksgiving. You and Bella have to come to Thanksgiving dinner."

"We'd enjoy that."

*****

That evening after dinner when Harold returned to his room, Bella popped through the wall. "I've been waiting for you to get back."

"I've been waiting to see you, too. Detective Deavers stopped by earlier today, and the case is all wrapped up."

Bella rubbed her hands together. "Give me all the gory details."

Harold recounted his conversation. "I also spoke with Peter Lemieux, and he doesn't plan to keep another waiting list. Too risky."

"Strange how things work out. It has been crazy around here lately. With the murders, accidents, investigation and Halloween, we never got around to watching *Bell, Book and Candle*."

"That's right. You suggested it several weeks ago."

"So tonight is the night. I'm inviting you to my apartment. I'll make some popcorn, put in the DVD, and we can enjoy the movie together."

"Sounds interesting."

Bella winked at him. "You'll have to join me to discover how interesting."

"With an invitation like that, how can I resist?"

"I should hope not."

"As long as you don't try to drag me through the wall."

"We'll go through the door like normal people."

*****

At the conclusion of the movie as Harold and Bella snuggled on the couch, she asked, "What did you think of it?"

"Good plot. But I have a question. Do witches really lose their powers if they fall in love with a mortal man?"

"That's a myth like the one that vampires and werewolves don't age."

Harold gave Bella a kiss. *Good thing*. He was a very lucky mortal man.

# ABOUT THE AUTHOR

Mike Befeler is author of six novels in the Paul Jacobson Geezer-lit Mystery Series, two of which were finalists for The Lefty Award for best humorous mystery. He has eight other published mystery novels: *Death of a Scam Artist, The V V Agency, The Back Wing, The Mystery of the Dinner Playhouse, Murder on the Switzerland Trail* and *Court Trouble;* an international thriller, *The Tesla Legacy, Paradise Court, UnStuff Your Stuff;* and a nonfiction book, *For Liberty: A World War II Soldier's Inspiring Life Story of Courage, Sacrifice, Survival and Resilience .* Mike is past-president of the Rocky Mountain Chapter of Mystery Writers of America. He grew up in Honolulu, Hawaii, and now lives in Lakewood, California, with his wife, Wendy. If you are interested in having the author speak to your book club, contact Mike Befeler at mikebef@aol.com. His web site is http://www.mikebefeler. com.